HERE COMES A CANDLE

JANE AIKEN HODGE

HERE COMES A CANDLE

HODDER PAPERBACKS

Copyright © 1967 by Jane Aiken Hodge

First printed in Great Britain 1967

Hodder Paperback edition 1969
Second impression 1970

Printed in Great Britain for Hodder Paperbacks Ltd.,
St. Paul's House, Warwick Lane, London E.C.4, by
Hazell Watson & Viney Ltd, Aylesbury, Bucks

ISBN 0 340 10734 0

ONE

"FOR GOD, AND KING GEORGE!" The rifle dropped from the old woman's hands and she fell slowly, loose-jointed, to the ground, a puppet in a gray flannel nightgown. Hurrying forward to kneel beside her on the cold, half-thawed earth, Kate Croston felt the pulse in the thin wrist flicker and go out. The Americans' aim had been too true. There was nothing more she could do for her only friend in Canada—in the world. Except blame herself bitterly, uselessly, for those few moments of exhausted inattention that had let old Mrs. McGowan find the rifle and get out of the house. To her death. She found she was muttering to herself, a strange mixture of prayer and apology. Very gently, with a hand that shook, she closed the staring eyes and came back from the shadow of death to the facts of her own position.

Only a thin straggle of trees and bushes at the end of the garden screened Mrs. McGowan's house from the center of York, and part of her mind had been aware, all the time, of the sounds of marching feet, of command and countercommand, as the Americans took over the town. Now a small group of American militia burst through the trees and paused for a moment, in oddly unmilitary conference, staring at her.

At last one of them pushed forward, plump and furious in his gray uniform. "Who fired that shot? Who winged my sergeant?" And then, seeing the rifle that lay under the old woman's hand, "Her, was it? Don't you know York capitulated an hour ago? What do you mean by letting the old crone loose with a rifle? She'll be lucky if she ain't strung up here and now."

"She is lucky." Kate faced him across the limp body.

"She's dead. You've killed her, gallant soldiers that you are. An old woman, ill, a little mad, who didn't know what she was doing. She thought it was the other war, George Washington's war."

"Dead is she?" He confirmed it with a casual glance. "Well, so much the better, I guess. It don't much matter which war it is, '75 or 1812, when it comes to breach of truce. Maybe she was old and mad, but that don't help my sergeant. He won't be walking for weeks, will Sergeant Mackelford. I reckon you've got something to answer for, if you were in charge of her. What were you thinking of, letting a mad woman loose with a rifle?"

"I thought she was asleep." The long, anxious nights of nursing had left Kate too tired to think, too tired to care. Anyway, he was right. It was her fault. I'm a Jonah, she thought; I bring disaster wherever I go. I infect whatever I touch. She raised tired brown eyes to the militia captain's. "Shoot me, then," she said. "Why not? It's all of a piece with killing a woman old enough to be your mother."

"That's about enough out of you!" And then, the fatal comment she had been expecting. "You speak kind of queer. You're English?"

"Yes. And proud of it."

"Proud! A fine lot you've got to be proud of. Impressing our sailors, searching our ships, sinking them when it takes your fancy. The Canadians are one thing—they're our kin, misled maybe, but we'd as lief not fight them, if they'd just have the sense to join us, but you bloody English are another matter. I've hated you since I was knee-high to a grasshopper. What d'you say, boys? I reckon she put the old dame up to shooting Sergeant Mackelford. Just the kind of thing a dirty Britisher would do. Shall we string her up, and be done with it?"

There were shouts of "yes" from several of his men, but others demurred. "After all," said one, "she's only a girl. It was the old one did the damage. I don't reckon this one had much to do with it. Dearborn's orders was mighty strict, remember, about respecting civilians."

"That was before they blew up General Pike," said the captain. "I reckon that's a breach of the rules of war, and once they're broken, anything goes. Well, look what we're doing back there, firing the Assembly Buildings."

"Yes, and I guess old Dearborn will just about blow his top when he gets out of bed and hears about that." This was a man who had not spoken before, and Kate found herself thinking, with strange detachment, how oddly these American soldiers behaved. Imagine an English private speaking up to his captain like that.

"I tell you what, boys," said the captain now. "Let's do it the American way. Let's vote on it."

This precipitated a hot argument as to how the vote should be taken. Listening, Kate was amazed to care so little. In ten minutes, five perhaps, she would probably be dead. Well, and why not? It would only finish here what Charles Manningham had started and Fred Croston prevented in England. Poor Fred. It was she who ought to be dead, not he, not Mrs. McGowan. I should never have run away, she thought. It was waiting for me, all the time. And yet, oddly, now at this last moment when, she saw, her captors had agreed on a secret vote, she felt a sudden urge to go to them, to plead for her life, to try to escape . . . The spring sun was warm on her back; somewhere in the trees an unknown bird was singing; eighteen is young to die.

Hurrying toward his grandmother's house, Jonathan Penrose slowed his pace at sight of the little group of militiamen busy casting their votes in their captain's hat. Beside them, the girl looked so tiny that he thought her a child at first until, getting closer, he saw the widow's weeds and the thin, brown face so drawn into hopelessness that he stopped for a moment, despite the urgency of his errand.

"What's going on here?" He had recognized the militia captain as a fellow passenger on the crowded American transport that had brought them across Lake Ontario from their base at Sackett's Harbor.

"Oh, it's you, Mr. Penrose." The militia captain was delighted to see him. On board the *Madison* this tall, bronzed New Englander had been treated with the respect due to an old friend and fellow captain of Commodore Chauncey's. Now, meeting the piercing gaze of blue eyes under bristling brows that should have belonged to an older man, he thought he saw how to avoid a difficult decision. "You're a civilian, sir, and a friend of the Commodore's. Maybe you might know better than me what's best to do. It's a question of truce-breaking, see? That old hag down there got loose and shot my sergeant. He won't be walking for months. Well, we've disposed of her all right and tight, as you can see. But what's to do with the young one who let her do it? There's half of us says string her up, here and now, as an example. But the other half ain't so sure. And nor am I." Oddly, he found he had changed his opinion under the stare of those penetrating blue eyes. "We say she's just a young thing and mebbe it would be best to let her go with a caution. So if you'd just give us your casting vote, Mr. Penrose, I reckon we'd be almighty obliged to you . . ."

His voice trailed off. Jonathan Penrose had stopped listening and moved forward to stare with horror at the corpse. "Dear God," he said. "It's old Mac." And then, to the girl: "Liz! What happened?"

She raised dark-shadowed brown eyes to gaze at him dully. "I'm not Liz McGowan," she said. "I'm Kate Croston. Not that it matters . . . And you?"

"Jonathan Penrose. Mrs. McGowan's grandson. The American one."

"At last! But why didn't you get here sooner? She was so sure you would. She said she'd written ages ago. After Liz went, she looked for you all the time."

"Liz gone? I don't understand anything. I've had no letters. When I heard how things were on this front, I came as fast as I could. Too late. My dear old Mac." He brushed a hand across his eyes. "I was going to take her home. Her and Liz. To look after them. But what happened? The fighting's over. York surrendered an hour ago."

"That's just it." The American captain sounded anxious

now. "I'm mortal sorry, sir, if the old lady was kin of yours, but she still shot my sergeant in the leg one whole hour after the truce had been signed. I reckon the young lady's got some explaining to do."

"She was ill." Kate Croston said it wearily, as if nothing mattered any more. "She'd been ill all winter. Liz told me. She said she thought it was as much misery over this war between her two countries as anything. You should know about that." She turned almost accusingly to Jonathan Penrose. "Liz said that even though she'd lived in Canada ever since the other war, she still loved America, loved you particularly. Every time there was news of another raid across the St. Lawrence, Liz said, she'd be worse. And not hearing from you was the last straw."

"But I did write. Of course I wrote. I suppose she never got them. But where is Liz? What's she thinking of, to leave her grandmother alone with a stranger at a time like this?"

Something flashed in the tired brown eyes. "What else could she do? You didn't come. Nobody came. But, of course, you say you'd not heard." Doubt in her voice. Did she believe him?

"Heard what? Pull yourself together, girl. Explain!" Impossible not to speak impatiently to this wraith of a girl who stood and spoke like an automaton, without even a tear for old Mac's death.

She was beyond resenting his tone. One thin brown hand pushed the tumbling curls back from her forehead as she marshaled her thoughts to answer him. "About your cousin Mark," she said. "He was wounded on the Lacolle River last autumn. He's been in hospital at Montreal all winter, very ill. Mrs. McGowan only heard a few weeks ago. She sent Liz to him at once. She said it didn't matter about her. Besides, I was here to look after her."

"This is all very fine," the American captain broke in impatiently, "but what we want to know, miss, is how you came to let the old"—he remembered Jonathan Penrose—"the old lady loose with that rifle."

"I must have fallen asleep for a moment," Kate replied. "I'd been up all night, with Mrs. McGowan restless, and the panic in the town. The doctor said it would kill her to move her." She turned to Jonathan Penrose. "So there was nothing for it but to stay. Dr. Brown said he'd come this morning; let me know how things went. I suppose he's been too busy. It was horrible. When the firing started, she roused up and started talking about her husband, about Bunker Hill. I didn't understand at first. It was all I could do to keep her quiet. At last I managed to give her some of the drops the doctor left . . . the firing had slackened . . . I thought she'd fallen asleep . . . I sat down for a minute in the chair by the bed. The explosion woke me—only it woke her first."

"Yes, that explosion !" said the captain. "The mine that killed General Pike. We'll not forget that in a hurry." Behind him, the Assembly Buildings, burning fiercely now, gave grim point to his words. Through the trees, they could catch glimpses of American soldiers going about the sordid business of the sack. And yet it was oddly quiet now that the firing had stopped, since almost all the able-bodied inhabitants of York had taken to the woods when the Americans landed. "So you just went off to sleep !" The captain had not finished with Kate Croston. "And left her loose to fire on us ?"

"I've sat up with her seven nights running," said the girl. "And nursed my husband before that. But why should you care? Yes—I did drop off, just for a few moments. When I woke she'd got the rifle up from the cellar. I didn't even know it was there—still less loaded. Liz should have told me . . . She turned it on me. Said I was a rebel . . . Said all kinds of things . . . about Gage, and Prescott, and Putnam. I didn't understand for a while. I just thought she'd catch cold." Savage irony in her tone.

"Bunker Hill," said Jonathan. "Her husband—my grandfather was killed there. That's when she came to Canada. Poor darling, she was always homesick for Boston." And then, turning with sudden fury on the American captain :

"Don't you think you've done enough? You've killed a harmless old woman, who thought she was fighting another war, in another country. And now you talk about hanging a girl whose only crime seems to have been her willingness to stay and risk her life nursing a stranger. You make me ashamed to call myself American. Must we become barbarians because we are fighting a war that was not of our choosing? Look! Look there beyond the trees! It's not just the Assembly Buildings that are burning, though that's bad enough, the library's gone, the archives, everything. I tell you, the fires you've lit here today will be paid for sometime, in blood and tears." He and the captain had both turned, as he spoke, to look at the burning buildings. Now the sound of scuffling made him turn back in time to see two of the American soldiers manhandling the girl toward the open door of the house. One of them had his hand over her mouth. Above it, her eyes met his, without hope. "Stop it!" His voice was different now, commanding, the sea captain's voice, used to carry above wind and weather.

The two men stopped in the doorway, but still held the girl, not gently. "She tried to escape," said one of them, and winked broadly at his captain. "You all saw her try to run for it, didn't you? I reckon anything goes after that. But not hanging—that would be kind of a waste, I guess." His free hand, moving down over her shoulder, gave point to his words. She writhed against it, her eyes still fixed, with that gaze of mute despair, on Jonathan.

The captain looked frightened. "But General Dearborn said—" his tone as he began the protest warned Jonathan that he was a broken reed, a soldier for Sundays only.

One long stride and he had the two men by their collars, tearing them away from the girl. "I say you're to leave her alone." He stood there, unarmed, in his civilian black, staring them down.

There was an odd, ugly moment of silence. But this angry young man was a friend of Commodore Chauncey's and everyone knew that only the American Navy had distinguished itself so far in this war that no one wanted. Besides, he was clearly not to be trifled with. "If I were you," he went on more mildly, addressing himself to the captain as if he were still in command of his men, "I'd be inclined to get back to the assembly point. Dearborn doesn't much like stragglers. I'll take care of the young woman. And be answerable for her to the authorities, if necessary."

"Oh, in that case . . ." The captain reached for dignity, but achieved only the tones of heartfelt relief. "We'd better get back to work, boys, but you're responsible, sir, don't forget."

"I won't." He was furious with himself as he watched them go. Madness to have saddled himself with the responsibility for this poor little brown thing who was leaning now against the door of the house, shuddering as if she would never stop. "Its all right." He said it as kindly as he could manage. "They've gone."

"Yes." She raised dull eyes to his and he found himself wondering what in the world the Americans had seen in her. "I should thank you. You saved me—" she clenched her teeth on her lower lip to stop it trembling.

"Oh, as to that—" Impatiently. "I don't imagine you were in any real danger. We're not, in fact, barbarians, we Americans."

"No?" Disconcertingly, she left it at that.

He turned away from her with a spasm of irritation as much at himself as at her. "Get her bed ready, would you?" He bent and picked up his grandmother's body. "My dear old Mac." Holding the limp little corpse in one arm, as if it weighed nothing, he bent to brush straggling gray hair away from the forehead.

She watched dully for a moment, surprised at the strength he showed, then turned away to hurry indoors and smooth the sheets on the narrow bed. Now, at last, tears she had not shed for herself began to flow easily down her cheeks.

"I should be crying, not you." He drew the sheet up gently over the lined old face. "I could, too." She could see that this was true. "But there's no time. If I am to protect you, I must know more about it all. Who are you? How do you come here?" And then, angrily: "And what are you doing?"

She had been moving about the kitchen-living room, putting a few things into a shabby carpetbag. "I'm nobody," she said. "Nothing. I'm grateful, of course. I'll not trouble you further."

"Nonsense!" Once again, the anger was as much for himself as for her. He wanted to be rid of her, but could not let her go. "You can't go now. I'd not let a dog out there today. Besides, you heard what I said. I'm responsible for you. When I can, I will be happy to escort you to your friends."

"Friends? I have none. Or rather—she was my friend, and look what I did to her. It's not safe to be my friend."

"Ridiculous!" The anger warmed him. "You're tired out and talking nonsense. Sit down, pull yourself together and tell me what's been going on here."

The tone of command worked. She let herself fall limply into the old rocking chair by the stove, and he felt a quick pang, remembering it as sacred to his grandmother. "Well, I told you," she said. "Most of it. Mark, your cousin, was ill in Montreal. Liz didn't like to leave Mrs. McGowan alone. You see, she'd been ill all winter. They were almost frantic, the two of them. The letter about Mark came through when the trails were still open—before the thaw. He needed Liz —needed nursing. So when we were billeted here—and Fred died—she said I was a godsend. Liz did." And then, with a surprising, wry touch of humor. "She almost said it was. Fred's death. Poor Liz. So she left the same day. You couldn't blame her. And I had nothing else to do."

"Fred was your husband?" He regretted the dry question as he asked it, but she seemed beyond noticing.

"Yes. He was in the British Army. Sergeant Croston."

"I'm sorry."

"There's no need—" She was staring past him at memory, and speaking with the frankness of sheer exhaustion. "I didn't love him. There was no question of that between us. But he was wonderfully good to me. He saved me—' She

13

stopped. "He took me away. He was ill already then. He didn't tell me. Oh well, what's the difference . . ." The phrases came out disjointedly. "I didn't understand till we were on the troop transport, coming over. But I did the best I could for him . . . I nursed him as well as a real wife could have done."

"I'm sure you did." Her explanation, such as it was, left him more puzzled than ever. He had spent long enough in England to recognize the clipped accents of an English lady. What in the world had this child been doing married to a sergeant? But his next question was forestalled by a knock on the door. "Don't worry." He moved before she could open it. "I won't let them hurt you."

But instead of the angry group of soldiers he expected, one man stood outside, old and bent in his rusty professional black, a doctor's bag in his hand. There was a great smear of blood, of which he was quite unaware, on the side of his face. "I came as soon as I could," he began. And then, "Jon Penrose! Thank God!"

"Dr. Brown!" Jonathan shook his hand warmly and drew him into the house. "So you didn't run with the rest of them?"

"I? A doctor? What do you think? But how's your grandmother? I told Mrs Croston I wouldn't be answerable for the consequences if she had to spend the night in the woods. How is she, Mrs Croston?"

"Dead." The girl raised her head to stare at him with lackluster eyes. "I killed her, Dr. Brown."

"Nonsense." Quickly, Jonathan explained what had happened.

"Ah, poor old Mac." The doctor put down his bag. "So I'll not be needing this. Not your fault, Mrs. Croston. Mine, if you like. After all, I made you stay. Or rather, made her." And then, to Jonathan. "I thought Mrs Croston should run for it, like the rest of them, but she wouldn't. A young girl . . . I'm ashamed not to have been here sooner; I meant to; but, Jon, that explosion! It was horrible; more than the army doctors could deal with. I oughtn't to have

14

come away now; I mustn't stay. Thank God you're here to look after Mrs Croston. But, just the same, what are you doing here, Jon?"

Jonathan Penrose laughed savagely. "I came to rescue my grandmother," he said, "and my cousin Liz. Chauncey wouldn't let me land sooner." Raw feeling shook his voice.

"Don't blame yourself, Jon. There was nothing you could have done. It's over ten years since you've been here, isn't it? Your grandmother could no more have stood the journey to Boston than she could have jumped over the moon."

"So it's all for nothing." The despair in his voice made the old doctor look at him sharply.

Even the girl roused herself from where she sat huddled in the big chair. "Not nothing to me, Mr. Penrose," she said. "I find I'm glad to be alive. But why did you want your cousin Liz?"

He gave her a longer look than he had spared for her so far. She was no fool, this shrimp of a girl with the untidy hair and the huge brown eyes. "Quick of you," he said. "It's quite true. I did have a selfish reason for coming. Oh"— impatiently—"of course I wanted to get my grandmother and Liz away from the seat of the war. That was true enough. It was no place for them, two women alone. Well, so it has proved. But I did hope that Liz . . . Did Mac tell you about my Sarah?" He turned to the doctor to ask this, it seemed, almost reluctantly.

"She did say something. Is the poor child no better?"

"Worse. I'd hoped that Liz might help with her. God forgive me, I suppose that's mainly why I came. Arabella said it was a mad start. Well, she was right. My poor little Sarah."

"But what's the matter with her?" Jonathan's tone, as he spoke of his daughter, had caught Kate Croston's attention.

"Nobody knows." He turned to speak to her directly. "It began last year, when I was away in England. I had to go—" he seemed to be arguing with himself. "I've business interests there. My ships go there all the time. Went there, I should say. By last spring, what with Jefferson's embargo on trade, and the British Orders in Council, things were pretty well at a standstill. And then the threat of war—I thought it my duty to go. To settle things there. Besides, despite all the War Hawks' talk in Congress, we never believed, in Boston, that this crazy war would happen, that President Madison could be such a fool. Anyway, I went. I'd not left home before, not for five years—not since Sarah was born. I'm a sea captain," he explained to Kate. "Used to be. I settled on shore when I married, six years ago. I sailed as a passenger for England last spring. Everything went wrong: winds, tides, incompetence . . . We did not reach Plymouth till mid-June. Things looked bad by then. I pressed on with my business as fast as I could. No use. Before I was done, war was declared, my ship impounded. I spent a couple of nights in jail myself. That didn't matter. Getting home did. It took me till fall. And then—"

"Yes?" She could see how hard it was for him to go on.

"You have to understand about Sarah. Before I left, she was the brightest, quickest little thing. Early with everything: sitting . . . smiling at me . . . pulling herself up in the cot. Then walking . . . talking. You couldn't hold her back. She followed me everywhere, to the mill, even, if I didn't take care. Then—when I got home last fall, I couldn't believe my eyes. I'd had no letters, of course. Nobody had warned me. They hadn't realized at first how bad it was."

"But what?"

"It's like black magic." The flight of fancy came strangely from him. "She didn't even recognize me. She doesn't speak; she doesn't smile; she doesn't look at you. It's enough to break your heart."

"The poor lamb." He had her full attention and sympathy now, and Dr. Brown, watching, thought it was good for her to be taken out of herself. "But there must be some explanation," she went on. "What happened to her?"

"If I'd only been there!" He would never forgive himself. "She was on a visit with Arabella—with her mother—at Saratoga Springs. She used to play on the hotel porch there, good as gold—she was such a good child always, my Sarah.

One day, when her mother was out, she disappeared. They searched for her all night. In the morning they found her, half a mile away, in a deserted woodman's hut. The door had slammed on her, apparently. How she'd got there . . . what kind of a night she'd spent . . . it doesn't bear thinking of. Arabella blames herself, of course, but it wasn't her fault. The child had always been so good, you see: she'd never strayed before. And no one realized, at first, just how much harm it had done. It came on slowly, they say: a little worse every day. She got quieter and quieter . . . And then the screaming fits began. They go on and on. It's breaking my heart."

"I don't quite see what good you thought your cousin Liz would be." Dr. Brown was putting on his coat.

"Sarah needs caring for, I think, loving. Someone with her all the time. The local girls won't stay." And then, explaining: "They're so independent, our American girls. They'd rather work in the mill. And—it's worse than that. They're ignorant, superstitious . . . I heard one of them talking about witchcraft . . . about Salem. I got rid of her on the spot. The others we've tried were almost as bad. They just don't seem capable of the kind of patience—of caring that Sarah needs. That's what made me think of Liz."

"But your wife? Arabella?" Dr Brown picked up his bag.

"She seems to make her worse. And she blames herself so, it makes it hard for her. Besides, she has her own life to lead. She has to be at our Boston house a good deal; that's why we need someone we can rely on. I'm sorry. I'm keeping you, Doctor."

"No matter. I needed the rest. I'm an old man, Jonathan. This year's work, and, more still, today's has taught me that. As to your poor child, I'm sorry about Liz, but I've a suggestion for you just the same. Why don't you engage Mrs. Croston here to look after her?"

"Mrs. Croston!" There was nothing flattering about his amazement.

"Yes, Mrs. Croston. She's tired out, right now, with nursing your grandmother, and her husband before that.

And I watched her nurse them, Jon. I'd trust her with my own child, if I had one."

"Thank you." The girl raised her heavy head to look at him with a kind of weary sarcasm. "It's more than Mr. Penrose would. And I don't blame him. Look at what I did to his grandmother."

"Nonsense," said the doctor. "You might as sensibly blame yourself for what happened to Mr. Penrose's child. I tell you, Jon, you'll be a fool if you don't go on your knees to ask her to come. Besides, you're responsible for her. She risked her life to stay with your grandmother and nearly lost it too, by the sound of it." He moved toward the door. "If I were you, I'd get her safe on board ship just as quick as you can. There's all hell loose in the town by now—and talk of a counter-attack by the British, too. The 98th are on their way to Kingston, they say, straight from Bermuda and full of fight."

"The 98th?" Kate Croston's voice rose almost to a scream.

"Why, yes, so they say. But there may be nothing in it. Anyway, I must be going. I'll make arrangements for the funeral, Jonathan, when I've time, and then, my advice to you is to get back to the other side of the lake just as fast as you can. And take Mrs. Croston with you."

Left alone, they looked at each other for a long moment in a silence charged with doubt. Surprisingly she spoke first. "Mr. Penrose, would you take me? Could you?"

"Oh, I guess I could, all right. Chauncey's an old friend of mine. We sailed together once." No mistaking the doubt in his voice.

"But you don't want to. And I don't blame you. Oh, I suppose I'm mad even to ask it, but, Mr. Penrose, I must get away. There's someone—someone in the 98th. You heard Dr. Brown say they were coming? If I have to meet him again, I think I'll die." She was out of the chair now, her head hardly reaching his shoulder, her hands working together, her voice holding a threat of hysteria. And then, eyes eagerly searching his strong, unreadable face. "Suppose it was your daughter, Sarah, grown up: suppose she

18

was begging you like this? Or begging someone else? You'd want them to help her, wouldn't you? And, I promise you, I won't be a burden on you. If you take me away from here, I'll give my life to your Sarah. I'll be glad to. It's what I want, someone to care for."

"But I don't think you quite understand." There was something chilling about his tone and his cool gaze. "This is no sinecure, Mrs. Croston. This is no pet child to cosset. The doctors say it's hopeless. They don't pretend to understand the case, but they say it can only get worse. Myself, I refuse to believe them. Well, I'm her father, I remember what she was like—before. But I'm the only one. Even Arabella—" he stopped. "Well, it's no wonder; sometimes, when the screaming goes on for hours, even I despair. How could you cope with her, a little thing like you?"

Her chin went up. "Because I'd care, Mr. Penrose. You said that was what she needed, didn't you? Loving . . . caring. Don't you see, I've been lonely, been unhappy myself, for so long—" And then, impatiently, "But why should you see? Why should you listen? You know nothing about me."

"I know what Dr. Brown told me, but I confess I'm puzzled . . ."

"I don't blame you. Well then, let me tell you: here I stand, poor but honest. I'm not quite a pauper; I won't be a charge on you." Her tone of self-mockery came as a surprise to him. She might be a plain little shrimp of a thing, but she had character.

"My father was a clergyman," she went on. "In Sussex. I've lived there all my life. Till last Autumn—" She stopped, teeth biting into her lower lip, then went off at a tangent: "I taught Sunday school there; I'm not totally ignorant about children, though I had no brothers or sisters. My mother died—four years ago. I looked after my father till he died last year." Her voice shook on the words, and he was instinctively aware of immense gaps in her narrative. "I don't want to talk about that." She confirmed his guess.

"Poor Father, he'd been so unhappy . . . I can't talk about it."

"Never mind." Oddly now, he found himself wanting to make it easy for her. "But how did you come to Canada?"

"With Fred Croston. My husband. I married him. Well," she was looking back now, puzzled at herself, "there didn't seem anything else to do, then." She stopped, looking up at him hopefully, willing him to accept it as a complete explanation.

But he had another question. "And this man; what about him? The one in the 98th? The one you want to get away from so badly that you'll trust yourself to a stranger like me."

Suddenly, for the first time, she smiled, and he thought, with a little shock of surprise, why, she could be beautiful. "Oh, but I know all about you, Mr. Penrose. What do you think Mrs. McGowan and I talked about but her grandsons? And you were her favourite. The soul of honour, she called you, and her dear Jon." For a moment, her voice had been almost teasing, then her face changed: "Oh, poor old Mac! How can I be thinking about myself?"

It was his turn to be practical. "Because we must, I guess." Whether she had intended it or not, her reference to his grandmother had reminded him of the debt he owed her. But it was with a sensation of doubt amounting almost to panic that he heard himself saying: "Very well then, Mrs. Croston, if you really want to come with me, I'll see what I can arrange."

It was only much later, when he had got her safely installed in his own cabin on the *Madison* that he remembered she had never explained just why she was so anxious to get away from Canada.

TWO

THE NEXT FEW DAYS did nothing to make Jonathan Penrose feel any happier about the responsibility he had taken on. While the Americans systematically plundered York of anything that could be remotely considered as military stores, Kate Croston lay inert in the tiny cabin on the *Madison* with a marine on sentry duty outside.

"Don't worry." Dr. Brown, to whom Jonathan confided his doubts after his grandmother's bleak and hurried funeral, did his best to be reassuring. "The girl's worn out, that's all. It was no joke nursing Mrs. McGowan, I can tell you—and that consumptive husband before that. And that was an odd business, if you like. I never could understand how she came to be married to a mere sergeant. Something a bit havey-cavey about it, if you ask me."

"Now you say that!" Jonathan exploded into anger. "After I've committed myself to the girl, on your advice. And for Sarah, too."

"Well"—the old doctor refused to be roused—"you told me yourself you were in despair about finding someone for Sarah. Though why your Arabella can't look after her . . . but"—hastily—"never mind about that. To come back to Mrs. Croston; I've only known her a short time, but I swear to you, Jon, if she's got anything to be ashamed of, I'm not the judge of people I ought to be. No, no; in a year or so you'll be writing to thank me for persuading you. I'm sure—sure as I can be—that taking her is one of the best day's work you ever did. Besides, what else can you do?"

"Well, that's true enough," said Jonathan ruefully.

When the American troops re-embarked at last, Kate was still lying dazed and passive, somewhere between sleeping and waking. She hardly noticed the tumult above decks, nor the new routine of the stormy voyage across the lake, but slept, and waked, and ate the food she was brought, and gradually began to feel again. It was not pleasant; rather like the tingling discomfort of life coming back to a numbed limb. There was so much she must remember, so horribly much she would rather forget. And as for the future . . . well, at least the die was cast. Not much use now to regret the moment of mad panic that had made her thrust herself upon this unknown, almost hostile American. And, so thinking, she slept again and woke to an unusual sound of activity above decks and a new feel to the motion of the ship.

A friendly sailor, rousing her with a cup of strong black coffee, confirmed her guess. "Welcome to the United States, ma'am. We anchored in the night. And Mr. Penrose sends his compliments and asks how soon you can be ready to go ashore." And then, perhaps sensing something a little ruthless about this message to an invalid: "We're just east of Fort Niagara now," he explained, "and liable to sail again any minute for Sackett's Harbor, so you've no time to lose. I just hope you're up to it."

So did she. "Of course I am." She drank scalding, delicious coffee and thought, as she did so, that it was no wonder if British seamen were apt to desert to the American Navy. "Tell Mr. Penrose I'll be with him in ten minutes."

She was almost as good as her word. There was a minute, on the steep companionway, when the rancid smell of the between-decks hit her, and she thought for a moment she would faint. Then she set her teeth, held her breath, and clawed her way up to the blessed fresh air of the deck. It smelled rawly of spring, of dampness, and growth, and of something else she could not identify. She felt her strength coming back with every deep breath.

She needed it. Jonathan Penrose was pacing the deck, his eye anxiously on the telltale flag that told where the wind lay. "You're better? Good." It was rather a command than a question. "The boat's waiting for us. No time to be lost, I'm afraid, if you're coming with me."

She felt a flash of anger. What else could she do? But she was in his hands. "Yes, please. Unless you have changed your mind?"

"Of course not." He managed to sound almost as if he meant it. "This way then."

Following him across the busy deck, she fought resentment. Had he no thought for what this moment must mean to her? She was leaving everything she had ever known—for an enemy country. But then—she picked her way carefully over a pile of ropes—he had not asked her to come. Why should he think about her? She gathered up her skirts with a firm hand, grateful to Fred Croston, who had shown her how to use the bosun's chair without making an exhibition of herself.

Firm, friendly hands—not Jonathan's—helped her into the little boat. At last she had time to look about her. The day was overcast, with even a hint of late snow in the piled-up clouds, but as they pulled away from the ship the sun broke through for a moment to light up the wooded shore they were approaching. Where, before, all had been flat monochrome, she now saw great splashes of colour, the brown of last autumn's oak leaves contrasting with the deep green of pine and fir.

"I reckon you find that a mighty handsome sight, ma'am," said the very young man who commanded the boat. "You ain't got woods like that in the old country, I guess." He spoke with the same nasal twang as the other sailors, and she found herself surprised, for the first time, at her companion's lack of accent.

"It's beautiful." She forebore to say that the woods, in fact, looked very much like the ones on the other side of the lake, in Canada. "And it's spring!"

"Yes, ma'am. There ain't much to touch our American spring, I guess. What do you think of it?"

"It's beautiful," she said again, not quite sure to what his question referred, but grateful for his interest. "It's come on so fast." While she had been below deck rain and wind had washed away the last patches of snow, and now, as the boat drew nearer to the shore, she could see touches of brilliant green in the clearing where they were to land.

"Spring comes fast when it comes," said the young sailor. "But I reckon you'll have a rough journey of it, Mr. Penrose."

"I'm afraid so." How different his voice was. "This is the worst time of the year," he explained to her. "No snow for sleighing, and the roads still waterlogged. If you can call them roads."

"Perfectly good corduroy," said the sailor.

"Corduroy?" Kate had never heard of the phrase.

"They're made of logs." The sailor was glad to explain it to her. "Laid crossways. Well, stands to reason you won't get too smooth a ride."

"Goodness gracious, I should rather think not." And then, beginning to be aware of how sensitive these Americans were about any criticism of their country: "But what a miracle to have roads at all over all these miles of wilderness. How far is it to Boston, Mr. Penrose?"

"Quite a way, I'm afraid. We'll be lucky if we get there under three weeks, now it's thawed."

"Three weeks!" Her voice went higher than she meant. She brought it down a tone. "I had no idea. Stupid of me. I should have realized . . ."

"I suppose I should have warned you." No need to add that it was too late now.

"It's not that. I just hope I won't be a terrible trouble to you."

"Nothing of the kind." Impossible to tell whether he meant it. "Well, here we are. This is the landing for Fort Niagara," he explained. "But we're not going there. It's out of our way."

"Welcome to American soil, Mrs. Croston." The young American had lost his heart to her on sight and made a point of helping her ashore. He held her hand for a moment. "I reckon you're pretty average glad to have got safe away from that bloodthirsty Regent of yours."

"Oh—thank you." She had hardly looked on her adventures, or, for the matter of that, on the Prince Regent in this light, but felt a great surge of gratitude for his interest.

"We go this way." Jonathan had been watching the exchange with a slightly doubtful amusement. It was no part of his intention to have to set up as chaperon to his young companion, and, indeed, it had been a source of self-congratulation to him that she was such a quiet little thing and unlikely to attract much attention.

Now, watching the sailor press her hand in farewell and wish her a pleasant journey at rather excessive length, he was not so sure. "Come, Mrs. Croston, we've no time to waste." His tone as he cut short the interview sounded repressive even to him, and he tried to make amends as he took her arm to guide her up the rough track that led away from the lake. "I hope you don't too much mind our famous American curiosity?"

"They're wonderfully kind." She had expected hostility from the American crew of the Madison, and had met nothing but an oddly frank, friendly curiosity. Now, as they reached the turn of the track, a sailor who had just finished unloading stores from the boat ran to catch them up.

"Excuse me, ma'am." He sketched a salute. "But you're the first English lady I ever set eyes on. Tell me, do they really eat babies there?"

"Good heavens, no!" Impossible to resent the simple inquiry. But a relief just the same when he smiled broadly, said, "I reckoned it was just a tall story," and turned away. And yet his going left her feeling alone as never before. Fantastic to be walking along this wild trail with a total stranger.

"It's no distance." Jonathan Penrose might have read her thoughts. "We're going to the house where I left my wagon. The Masons are old friends of mine."

And indeed Hugh Mason and his wife Janet greeted them with warm relief and a volley of friendly questions. "And now, I suppose, you'll want to be on your way at once," said Hugh Mason, when the first explanations were over.

"As soon as we can. Yes, I'm afraid so. It's taken so long ... Arabella will be wondering—"

"She's bound to be." He had a quick look of curiosity and, she thought, sympathy for Kate. "Well, your wagon's all ready; your horse has been eating me out of house and home; you should be able to pick up the stage tomorrow, with luck. Lord, it's good to see you, Jon. Do you know, I was worried about you."

Janet Mason whisked Kate off to the surprising comfort of her upstairs bedroom. "Hugh says there is no need to live like savages, just because we have come to the west," she explained. "Of course, the first years, when we were still in the log cabin, were something else again." She watched as Kate took off her heavy blanket coat and combed out soft brown curls. "So you're going to have charge of poor Sarah ..." And then, abruptly: "What's Jonathan told you about Arabella?"

"Why, hardly anything. Do you know her?"

"Gimini, yes. Hugh and Jonathan have been friends since Harvard. Jonathan met her then, you know, on a visit to Washington. He adored her for years, quite hopelessly, it seemed. She was a southern beauty, with the world at her feet, and poor Jon was almost penniless."

"Was he?"

"Oh dear, yes. His father and grandfather lost everything between them, taking different sides in the War of Independence. Really, it was the most romantic thing. Jonathan went to sea, and made a fortune in the Western trade. They go around Cape Horn, and buy furs from the Indians way up in the northwest country, and then maybe a cargo of sandalwood from an island miles from anywhere, and so to China, for days of bargaining and a fortune in tea and willow pattern ware at the end of of it. You must get Jon to tell you about it some time. Anyway, he was soon captaining his own ship, and then, fantastically rich. He got back from, I don't remember, maybe his third trip, and went straight to Richmond, to Arabella. And there she was, beautiful as ever, proud as ever, and—single. That was a whirlwind

26

courtship if ever there was one. He worships the ground she treads on. Well, you can see for yourself how impatient he is to get home. And that reminds me, I should be downstairs getting something for you to eat. Only—I thought I should tell you . . ."

"Yes?"

"Well," she hesitated. And then, in a rush: "Of course, I've not seen her for years, but Arabella's a beauty, the golden kind you have in England. She was the loveliest thing you ever saw when they were married. But—now— well, there it is: she's not so young as she used to be. She must be all of twenty-eight. And from what I've heard she don't much like competition. Just look at all the trouble they've had finding someone to look after that poor child. I'm sure that's it partly. It's lucky you're small and dark."

"And plain." Kate rose from the glass, the flush in her cheeks suddenly making nonsense of her words. "Thank you for telling me, Mrs. Mason."

After Jonathan and Kate had driven off, Hugh Mason and his wife exchanged long, thoughtful glances. "Well," he said at last, "what do you think, love?"

"She's a plain little thing." She said it almost hopefully.

"That's what I thought at first. She'll do, I thought. Nothing there that Arabella could possibly object to. But then she smiled at me . . . Did you notice her smile? Something happens in those big brown eyes of hers. I tell you, something almost happened to me. I'd have taken on a dragon for her, if there'd been one handy."

"How lucky there wasn't," said his wife. "But I know just what you mean, Hugh. I felt the same, and I'm a woman. Oh well, let's hope Arabella doesn't notice, or Jonathan either."

"Jonathan won't," said Hugh cheerfully. "You know how he is about women. But I'm not so sure about Arabella."

At first, Kate's anxious thoughts circled around Arabella as they drove off down the narrow trail into the dark heart of the forest. But she was soon too tired and shaken even for anxiety. No doubt Jonathan Penrose, too, was thinking of his golden wife as he drove the light wagon relentlessly forward so that it bucked and jolted over the log road and Kate thought at every moment that they would overturn. But, "We must get to the Ridge Road before dark," he explained. "Hugh Mason has friends there, who will put us up tonight, and then, I hope, we'll pick up the stage in the morning."

She nodded speechlessly. They had been driving through deep forest for over two hours. Exhaustion had turned to nausea, and now, biting her lips, she fought down faintness.

"I'm sorry." Suddenly aware of her plight, he pulled the horses to a standstill. "You're not well. I should never have brought you."

"It's nothing." A gallant effort made the lie almost convincing. "I'll be better in a moment. I'm so sorry." She bent forward on the hard bench so that her head almost touched her knees, and felt reviving blood pound at her temples.

"I'm a brute," he said. "I should have let you rest a day at least. But you said you were better. And I've lost so much time already . . ."

"I know." With an effort she pulled herself upright and breathed deep breaths of the cool forest air. "I'm better now, truly I am. I wouldn't delay you for anything."

"The trouble is"—he was looking up, considering the position of the westering sun—"that it would take us almost as long to go back as to go on."

"Go back?" She would not think about the Masons' warm house. "Absurd."

"Good for you." For the first time his blue eyes met hers with a look of approval. "Well, in that case?"

"What are we waiting for?"

But she was dizzy with fatigue when they drew up, at last, outside the log cabin where Hugh Mason's friends lived. They were wonderfully kind. After the inevitable questions, and a quickly cooked meal of the tough fried salt pork she had learned to expect, there was, mercifully soon, a hard little bed where she slept the sleep of total exhaustion. Only once, waking to the howl of a wolf in the forest, had she a moment to think what a lifetime away she was from anything she had ever known. But that was what she had wanted. She turned, slept again, and dreamed of Arabella Penrose.

The stage coach from Lewiston to Rochester passed this isolated forest clearing early in the morning. "They can't do more than four miles an hour on these corduroy roads," explained Jonathan. "They make a very early start from Lewiston so as to reach the halfway house before dark. Ah, here it comes." He moved forward into the road as a strange, boat-shaped vehicle lumbered into view from among the trees. "They stop to bait and water the horses here anyway," he turned back to explain to Kate as the cumbrous-looking carriage lurched to a stop.

"Rochester?" the driver removed the quid of tobacco from his mouth and spat expertly between Jonathan's feet. "Wa-al, I don't just see why not. Not much business along the road today, as you can see. I reckon the rats as are going to run from the border, has run already, and the rest of us calculate to stay put a while, war or no war." And then, inevitably, "Where are you from, stranger, and what's the news?" He was busy watering his horses as he spoke and now turned back to address the four men who had spread themselves out comfortably on the three crossways benches of the coach that were intended to take three passengers each. "Move up in there, boys, we've got a lady passenger!"

To Kate's surprise, no one complained and no one seemed to find it in the least strange that she should be travelling alone with a man. She smiled her thanks and settled herself gratefully on the hard bench that had been vacated for her. Jonathan, she saw, was helping the driver harness up his horses. Hard to imagine an Englishman doing so. Now he climbed in beside her and pulled back the coach's leather curtains to improve her view. "Not that there's much to see but trees. There! We're off!"

And once again, as the four heavy horses lurched forward in their collars, Kate was aware of the tension in her companion, of how he longed to be at home. "I suppose you've not been able to let Mrs. Penrose know where you are," she said. "She must be anxious about you."

"I hope not." He turned away from her to lean forward and ask the driver what time he expected to reach the half-way house, and she, in her turn, turned quickly to look out unseeingly at the dark forest and fight back tears. Mr. Penrose did not discuss his wife with his servants. She would not forget her place again.

And yet it was increasingly difficult to remember it, in the easy camaraderie of the journey. She soon got used to the routine of the road, the huge fried breakfasts eaten at silent speed, the piling into the coach with, always, the best seat saved for her, and the long day's drive through the forest. Rochester, where they spent the second night, was nothing but a sprinkling of houses and a primitive inn, where the men slept huggermugger in one big dormitory but she, as the only woman, had a tiny room to herself, with a feather bed probably full of bugs. But she was too tired to care, too tired even for the nightmares that had haunted her since her father died.

They caught the Albany coach next morning. "We'll be there in ten days, if we're lucky," said Jonathan, helping her in. "The country's clearer from here on, so the roads should have dried out a bit."

And so they lumbered on, with a pause every five miles or so, to bait and water the horses, and a longer one, at some appointed way station, for a midday meal, which, like supper, was merely a repetition of the fried food served up at breakfast. Kate had learned by now, with relief, that these tobacco-chewing, tough-looking Americans were an abstemious race, at least by British standards. If they drank at all, it was in the bar of the little inns where they spent the night, rather than with their meals, and she was yet to see one of them the worse for liquor. It made a change, she thought wryly, from life in the British Army.

She grew used, too, to the independent, I'm-as-good-as-you-are attitude of landlords and their families, who always sat down at table with their guests, the daughters getting up, relucantly enough, to change the plates. She was even almost used to the incessant questions. In fact, without her quite realizing it, they were doing her good. Ever since the night her father died—the night she tried not to let herself remember—she had felt an outcast, a pariah, cut off from the fellowship of men. But it was impossible to go on feeling this among these friendly, inquisitive Americans, who wanted to know everything about her, from the price of her dress to what she thought of their country. It was only when the cross-examination turned, as, sooner or later, it was bound to do, to the past, to her background in England, that she would flinch and colour, and Jonathan Penrose would intervene to parry question with question and get her tormentors talking, as they were ready enough to do, about their own problems, about ground clearance, or the potash business, or the course of the war. Surprisingly, no one seemed to hold the fact that she was English against her. She remarked on this in one of her rare moments alone with Jonathan on the stoop of the little inn at Schenectady.

"Why should they?" He seemed surprised. "You have to understand about this war, Mrs. Croston. Nobody wants it. It's a folly—a lunacy. It almost died in armistice last fall— it will be over this year, if we New Englanders have any say in the matter. We've no quarrel with old England—or none that can't be solved by friendly discussion."

" 'Friendly discussion!' After all that's happened? Mr. Penrose, you don't understand. War—just the fact of war— changes things, changes people. I've lived with it. I know. Men—kind, ordinary men, with families, children—they turn into beasts, worse than beasts. Well, you were at York, you saw—"

"Oh, that!" With irritation, he remembered saying something like this himself. "That was barbarous, of course. And out of character. We're not that kind of people really, neither we nor you. We're civilized. It won't happen again.

31

Madison will apologize—you see if he doesn't. It will all blow over."

"I hope you're right." She shivered, haunted now by a new set of ghosts, by memory of the sights and sounds of the troop transport, coming over, with Fred Croston already coughing his heart out and hardly able to protect her from the more and more overt advances of his fellow soldiers. By the time they had reached York, even she, determinedly optimistic, had been able to see death in his face, and his closest friends had been drawing lots as to who should have her when he died. Soldiers civilized? "You don't know what war is," she said again. "What it does to people."

"Maybe not." He made his voice cheerful. "Albany tomorrow, your first real American town. You'll be glad of a rest." When she looked like this, haggard, and gazing back into an unbearable past, he wondered more than ever if he had not been mad to take Dr. Brown's advice without finding out more about her background. Once or twice, alone with her, he had nerved himself to ask her about the ghosts that haunted her, but he never managed to make himself go through with it. Wincing away from his first questions, she reminded him, somehow, of his own Sarah. He could no more persist in questioning her than he could slap Sarah for her bouts of hysterical screaming. And yet his anxious New England conscience gave him no rest. What right had he to trust his beloved child to this total stranger, who had only Dr. Brown to recommend her?

At least she had borne up gallantly under the fatigues of their journey, which was now entering its third week. He had watched, with an intense personal interest, the winning way she dealt with the often crass interrogations of the people they met. Quite unaware of it herself, she had a gift for making friends. The crossest landlady seemed, somehow, to relent when confronted with this child's gentleness. "Ladylike" was not a word much used in Boston, but whatever had happened to Kate Croston in the past, however she had come to marry a sergeant in the British Army, she was a lady, he thought, in the fullest sense. Watching her make friends with the hobbledehoy, mannerless children in the inns where they stayed, he found himself thinking: "She'll do. She'll do for Sarah." At all events, he was committed. He must just go on hoping he was right.

THREE

THE SPRING WAS RACING THEM as they travelled eastward. In Albany, grass on the hill below the town hall and chamber of representatives was vividly green, and here and there a tree was gay with new leaf. The sun shone brightly as they crossed the Hudson and turned into the long street that ran beside it, and Kate exclaimed with pleasure as she caught glimpses of the narrow streets and high, gable-ended Dutch houses of the old town. "It's almost like home," she said.

"Your highest praise? You're right, of course, though the influence here is Dutch rather than English. I remember thinking some of the streets in Amsterdam might have been taken bodily from here. Or—I suppose you would say—vice versa. Albany was Beverwyck when New York was New Amsterdam." He was beginning to enjoy explaining things to this eager listener. "It's one of the three oldest settlements in the Thirteen Colonies," he told her. "Of course we Bostonians think we're the oldest, but I'm not sure the Van Rensselaers would agree."

As usual, Kate was the only woman in the crowded dining room of Pride's Hotel except for the landlady and her daughters, and, as usual, nobody took the slightest notice. Most of these fast-eating, slow-talking men were actually residents of Albany, who preferred to dine in the hotel. "They get the news here, of course," Joanathan explained. Albany, he said, was in close touch with New York since Mr. Fulton's steamboat, the *Clermont*, had begun a regular service up and down the Hudson in 1807. And indeed the news room at Pride's Hotel had Boston and New York newspapers only a few days old. Kate longed for a glimpse of these, but this, evidently, was something that an Ameri-

34

can lady was not expected to do. She had to be content with the dinner-table comments on the news.

It seemed to be gloomy enough from the American point of view. How odd, she thought, sawing away at a particularly tough bit of beefsteak, to find herself getting used to the American view of the war. A fat Dutchman who seemed, from his conversation, to be a fur dealer, had launched forth into a jeremiad about the state of the nation. "Terrible." He filled his mouth with a huge bite of ham, chewed and swallowed it with formidable dispatch, and returned to his gloomy theme. "Boney's beaten, by the sound of it. We could have told him to mind out for the Russian winter, if he'd asked us. They say he left his army to die in the snow and hurried back to Paris to get himself another one, but how long are the French going to stand for that, I ask you? And if they give in, what happens to us? Answer me that!" He addressed this to Jonathan, but did not wait for an answer. "And what does poor Jemmy Madison do? Does he build us a navy? Does he even prepare to defend Washington? And the British ships in Chesapeake Bay, too! No sirree, he summons an extra session of Congress and goes about to tax us out of existence. I tell you it's more than a man can stand. Taxes on salt, on licenses, on spirits, carriages, auctions, sugar refineries! There's no end to it, sir!" He paused once more for a huge mouthful of hot bread.

This time, Jonathan took the chance to intervene. "Maybe it's a good thing," he said. "Maybe it will give the country the courage to turn against this lunatic war."

"Ha!" The Dutchman pointed a dinner knife at him. "You're one of those Yankee Federalists, ain't you? I did hear that your Governor Strong thinks Jemmy Madison's been unfair to England and partial to France. O'course I'm just a businessman, and don't reckon to understand these things, but that sounds mighty close to treachery to me. And your Josiah Quincy, too. Did you hear what he said?"

"No. What was that?"

"Bless me, if he didn't up and say Lawrence's sinking the

Peacock was 'not becoming a moral and religious people.' What do you think of that, sir? One of our few victories in this war and he wants us to act ashamed of it! It's not the way they did in New York, I can tell you. I was down there on business when Lawrence got back in March, and, by cracky, he had a hero's welcome. And quite right too. A few more like him and Chauncey—and a few more ships for them to captain—and things might look a shade better for us. You see, ma'am," he turned to Kate. "We've proved over and over again, that man to man and ship to ship we can outshoot you British, yes, and outfight you, too."

What in the world could she say to that? Luckily he did not expect an answer, but had turned away already, to help himself lavishly to pie. Just the same, it was a relief to escape, as soon as she decently could, to the comparative solitude of the porch that overlooked the River Hudson.

"I'm sorry about that." Jonathan found her there a few minutes later.

"It's all right. I'll get used to it. It's only . . . you none of you understand; you talk as if it was all some kind of game. Not real; not real people, fighting, dying, drowning . . ." her voice rose dangerously and she steadied it with an effort. "I hope you never learn."

"I hope we never need to." His dry tone reminded her of how much he disliked any display of emotion. "But the question now is, are you quite worn out? Should we rest here for a day?"

Every bone in her body ached to say yes, but how could she? "Of course not. I know how you must long to be at home."

"I shall be glad to get there certainly." Once again his tone made her regret her proffered sympathy. "That's fine then. I'll go right out and order us an extra exclusive for tomorrow."

"Extra exclusive?" Here was a phrase she had never heard before.

"A coach to ourselves. It's the quickest way of finishing the journey."

"By ourselves?" She regretted it instantly.

"Why not? You're not in England now, Mrs. Croston. I remember how absurd I found it to see how your young women are hedged about with restrictions—as if they had no sense. We have more confidence in our girls here, I'm glad to say. But of course if you don't like the idea—"

What a genius he had for getting her, quite accidentally, on the raw. Did he really think she might be scared to travel alone with him, when he noticed her merely as a necessary piece of extra baggage! She could not help an angry little laugh. "Nonsense, Mr. Penrose. I feel as safe with you as I would with my grandfather. But Mrs. Penrose—" She was remembering Janet Mason.

"Arabella? She'll think nothing of it. Why should she?"

Why indeed? Why should not Jonathan Penrose, of Penrose, bring home the new nursemaid?

But he had moved toward the porch door. "That's settled then. I'll order the coach now and we'll start first thing in the morning."

"How much longer now?" Suddenly she wished this journey would go on forever.

"Only two days, I hope. But we've no posting system here, as you have in England, so we'll have to spare the horses."

"Of course." If not the passengers, she thought with a little spurt of anger.

The extra exclusive coach turned out to be merely a rather battered specimen of the usual boat-shaped type, with a surly driver who amazed Kate by asking no questions. But he knew his business, and took them up the winding, precipitous road over the Green Mountains without mishap. It was, to begin with, a silent enough drive. Pride's Hotel, though more luxurious than the little inns where they had stayed before, had also been a great deal noisier. All night, it seemed to Kate, bells had been ringing, parties coming and going, horses whinnying and harness jingling in the yard below her bedroom window. This on top of the cumulative fatigue of the journey left her, this morning, almost beyond speech, her eyelids gravelled with sleep, the mere action of sitting upright on the hard seat a conscious effort.

Jonathan, too, seemed preoccupied, brooding, no doubt, about the two days that must still separate him from Arabella. Or was he feeling the awkwardness of this enforced *tête à tête*? She certainly did. She was not going to forget again that she was in his service, not even a governess, but the lowest kind of nursemaid, and dependent on him for everything. And, worst of all, she had thrust herself upon him. Suppose Arabella or, worse still, little Sarah should take a dislike to her? Suppose, as Jonathan himself had suggested, she found she simply could not manage Sarah. What then? She had spoken boldly enough, back at York, of having money of her own, but the bills she had seen him paying along the way had taught her how little it was. Was he, perhaps, as he sat beside her, silent and withdrawn, wondering whether he had wasted his money, wishing he had never agreed to bring her?

She had turned on the hard seat to look at him sideways and try to read the expression of the closed, brown face that gave so little clue to what he was thinking. Now, disconcertingly, he turned from gazing at the hills ahead, and the piercing, sea captain's blue eyes met hers directly. Absurd and irritating, to feel herself colour under the calm, impersonal, and yet somehow questioning gaze.

Had he, too, felt that the silence was drawing out too long between them? Certainly, what he said was commonplace enough. "You will begin to see a change in the landscape, I think, when we're over the mountains and into New England."

"It's changing already." She, too, could play at general conversation. "It's good to be in country that's been cleared awhile, away from the forest, with those forlorn tree stumps left standing, and the pall of woodsmoke over everything. But will it be tidier in New England?" More than anything, so far, she had been impressed by this element of untidiness in the landscape. However grand the remoter prospect might be, the immediate neighbourhood of the road seemed always

38

to be marred by evidence of man's carelessness. And it was the same in the towns. Even in Albany, the capital of New York State, pigs had roamed the streets at will. "They're the best street-cleaners we have." It had evidently seemed sufficient explanation to Jonathan Penrose.

"Untidy?" Her comment had surprised him. "I suppose it is. Yes, I remember your English countryside: those neat hedgerows and landscaped parks. And how do you do it? By what's as good as slave labour—starvation wages and soup doled out graciously by the lady of the manor. I tell you, Mrs. Croston, we've too much to do here, and too independent a citizenry for that kind of refinement. You must take us as you find us."

"Of course." Somehow a new warmth in his tone made it possible to ask the question that had been haunting her all morning. "But that's not the point, is it? It's how you take me. Mr. Penrose, I must ask you, have you regretted bringing me? Will I do, do you think?"

Now again, and more disconcertingly than ever, he turned to gaze at her with deep-set eyes that seemed to see everything. "I hope so," he said at last, after a silence that had seemed to her interminable. "It all depends . . ." And then : "No, that's not fair. To be frank with you, there have been moments when I have wondered whether you have the strength for the job. Whether I have not done you an injustice in bringing you so far from your friends."

"Friends? What friends? That's what worries me, Mr. Penrose. I'm so afraid of turning out a useless charge on you. Just think what I've cost you already !"

"Cost me?" The heavy eyebrows drew together. "You mean the expenses of this journey? Absurd ! I've got more to worry about than what you cost me." And then, more gently : "Don't worry about the future. If it doesn't work, and God knows it's a forlorn enough hope, I'll look after you."

"That's not the point ! Why should you look after me? I persuaded you to bring me. I had no right—"

Her voice rose on the last words, and the driver turned

around in his seat to give her a curious glance. "Coolly does it, Mrs. Croston." Jonathan's imperturbability was more galling than anger. "When you speak like that, I do find myself wondering whether you will have the patience for my poor Sarah. And yet," thoughtfully, "who knows? Maybe it will be a good thing. Perhaps if you scream right back at her . . ."

"Scream?"

"She does. Endlessly, meaninglessly, dreadfully. Perhaps I should have made more of it. It's as if she were in a world of her own, poor lamb, with an invisible barrier between us. We're just not there to her, most of the time. And then, if something goes wrong—or, more often, for no reason one can understand—she starts to scream. It goes on and on; she's like a mad thing. Biting, kicking, scratching. My little Sarah who wouldn't hurt a butterfly. I don't really blame the girls we've had for leaving. I won't blame you." He paused, remembering all his own doubts about her. On the *Madison*, he had been afraid she might sink into a state almost like Sarah's. But, after all, she had not quite broken down, and therein, for what it was worth, lay a gleam of hope. Might she not, perhaps, understand Sarah out of a kind of fellow feeling? Searching for a scrap of comfort as much for himself as for her: "Did you know you were singing in the coach?" he asked abruptly.

"Singing? Oh, dear; *Greensleeves!* It seemed to go with the motion, but I thought no one could hear me."

"Don't apologize. I like it. And if you'll just sing to Sarah . . . You sing as if you cared. And she loves music. I've seen her, when my wife has guests, creeping as near as she dared to the door of the room, just to listen. Her face comes alive again . . ." And then, with one of his sudden changes of subject: "You must let me exchange your English money for you. I shall be able to get a better rate than you would."

"Thank you." She had not wanted him to know just how little she had. "But will you be able to?"

"Able? Oh—you mean because of this war? I've told you

40

before, Mrs. Croston, we don't believe in it in Boston. I reckon there's about as much English money as American circulating in town right now. When you came through Lower Canada, you must have heard of the lively trade in provisions that goes on between there and Maine. I'm not sure I'd do it myself, but some of my friends say they'd rather hold the English Government's bills than our own."

"But that's treachery! It's as bad as Benedict Arnold!"

He laughed. "You should hardly be calling him a traitor, Mrs. Croston. After all, he betrayed my country to yours. But what I'm trying to explain to you is that this isn't like that war. This is just a mistake, an absurdity that our two countries have been lured into by Napoleon. He's the enemy. He's the one we ought to be fighting, side by side, like the friends and relatives we really are. You'll see; there'll be peace before the year is out."

"I wonder . . . Do you remember something you said to that militia captain at York? It struck me at the time. 'The fires you've lit today,' you told him, 'will be paid for sometime, in blood and tears.'"

"Did I really say that?" He looked back at the absurdity with humorous resignation—"I was provoked that day; upset, you might call it, by poor old Mac's death. All nonsense, of course. You'll see, Mrs. Croston. And, in the meanwhile, you'll let me change your English money into dollars. Not that you'll need them." Had he sensed her anxiety? He was sometimes disconcertingly acute. "We live mostly out at Penrose—Sarah exclusively so. You will have no expenses there. Arabella uses the Boston house a good deal; for parties, the theatre . . . I prefer Penrose myself. Well, the manufactury is there, for one thing."

"Yes." She was too tired to speak. He had warned her that it would be a long day crossing the Green Mountains, and she was beyond enjoying the rolling panorama of field and river when they reached the top of Mount Hancock, almost beyond thought when they arrived, at last, at Northampton.

"Another long day tomorrow, I'm afraid." Jonathan helped her to alight stiffly from the coach. "But home at the end of it."

Home? Not hers. Kate shivered a little as she followed him into the main room of the inn, which she had learned to call the news room. She was used by now to the routine of waiting with the baggage while Jonathan arranged about rooms with the barman, but here things went differently. They were hardly indoors when her companion was the centre of a hand-shaking, back-slapping crowd. "Jonathan!" "Jon Penrose!" "Where in tarnation did you spring from?"

Laughing, and returning their greetings, he contrived at the same time to settle her in a comfortably inconspicuous corner by the door. "Canada." He answered the last question and, inevitably loosed a perfect storm of further ones. But by this time the proprietress herself had come forward to greet him as an old and valued friend. "A room to herself for the young lady?" Here a very sharp glance for Kate. "Well—" the monosyllable spoke volumes of curiosity.

"Mrs. Croston has kindly consented to take charge of my daughter." This was the sea captain's voice. "She is English and used to privacy." It was settled.

That evening gave Kate a whole new light on her companion. He had told her he was rich, but he had given her no inkling of the position he held in Boston. Now, watching the deference with which he was treated by even the older men among these free and easy Americans, she began to see him as a man of power as well as of wealth. They were eager for his opinion not only of events on the border but of what had gone on in Boston during his absence. When he spoke, they listened. Was it because he was a Penrose of Penrose— a descendant, Mrs. McGowan had told her—of one of New England's oldest families? Must she revise all her views of this vociferously egalitarian society? Sitting quiet at her corner of the supper table, she rather thought not. The deference paid him was a tribute not to his ancestry but to the man himself, to Jonathan Penrose who had succeeded to a dwindled estate and made a fortune. She smiled to herself; the almighty dollar again. But that was not fair either to Jonathan Penrose or to the men who were cross-questioning him eagerly now about the command on the Canadian front. It was his judgment they respected, and rightly.

FOUR

MASSACHUSETTS WAS CHECKERED green and white with rolling fields and blossoming orchards. Kate knew better by now than to tease her silent companion with exclamations over glimpses of white wild cherry by the roadside or an orchard foaming uphill to its group of white-painted farmhouse and huge red barns. Willows by the Connecticut River gleamed golden in the morning light with their first shimmer of leaf, and from time to time as the heavy coach rolled on, more smoothly now, over well-made roads, Kate leaned forward to get a better view of a patch of flowers, brilliant purple or white against one of the gray walls that bounded these neat New England fields.

Jonathan, apparently, noticed nothing of this new splendour of flower and leaf. This last day of their journey found him silent, withdrawn, with new shadows etched under his deep-set eyes, so that Kate wondered whether he, too, had spent an anxious and wakeful night. His impatience to be home manifested itself in an occasional suggestion to their taciturn driver that his horses might make better time now they were out of the mountains.

The driver's only reaction was to go, if possible, a little slower and to dally interminably when they stopped for their midday meal at the thriving little town of Worcester.

"At this rate, we won't be home before dark!" Jonathan turned impatiently to Kate as they stood watching the driver deliberately harnessing up his horses.

"It's maddening for you." She forgot her own anxiety in a wave of sympathy for his.

"Oh well," he shrugged. "Better late than never, I suppose."

It was hot today; flies buzzed around the patient horses

44

and tormented Kate. The afternoon dragged out endlessly. She was beyond caring for views of snug village greens arranged round white-spired churches, and when Jonathan roused himself from his brooding to tell her that the first of these New England churches was said to have been designed by Sir Christopher Wren, she could only nod wordlessly.

Jonathan had been right. It was almost dark, with lights showing here and there in cottage windows, when he leaned forward to give an order to the driver. "We turn off the Boston road here," he explained. "Not much further now. I hope you're not quite worn out."

"Of course not." She sat up a little straighter. "But I confess I'll be glad to get there." Would she? Suddenly, she was fighting panic. Suppose Arabella refused to have her . . . Suppose little Sarah took an instant dislike to her . . . With a hand that would shake, she tucked rebellious strands of hair closer under the brim of her bonnet.

"Don't worry." He was too good at reading her thoughts. "Just remember how badly we need you."

"Oh, thank you." It would be absurd to disclaim anxiety. "I'll feel better when I've met Sarah."

"I hope so." It was not altogether encouraging.

It had rained a little just after sunset, and the leather sides of the coach were still up, but she could feel that they were beginning to climb. She leaned forward to peer out into the gathering darkness. "I wish I could see."

"It's the beginning of the Gray Hills. So far, the road's kept close to the Charles River, but now we've turned off to go over the ridge. Penrose lies on the far side, on the Penrose River. You English would no doubt consider it a romantic situation, since the house is just above the falls. I look on it as a good one, as they provide the power for my mill."

"Is it so bad to be romantic?"

"It's an expensive luxury, that's all, and one we Penroses have not been able to afford since my grandfather took the romantic line and stood out for God and King George—poor old lunatic."

"You mean your grandfather?" Irritated suddenly, she mistook him on purpose.

"No; King George." He refused to be drawn. "Though, mind you, Grandfather was crazy enough. Anyone with half an eye could have seen what the upshot of that war was bound to be."

"And can you foretell the result of this one as easily?" She was too tired to conceal her irritation.

"A draw, of course." Her tone of challenge at once roused and amused him. "We will agree to differ, or differ to agree, if you prefer it like that."

"I think you are talking a great deal of nonsense." It came out sharper than she had meant, and she turned it off with a question. "Where does your land begin?"

"On the top of the ridge. We used to own the whole section. One of these days I'll buy it back—I hope. There, we're over the ridge now; we're almost home." He was leaning forward eagerly. "There—there it is. Those are the lights of Penrose. I'm sorry you should see it first in the dark." He spoke with automatic courtesy, his thoughts already at the house.

Penrose was a blur of lights, hazy through a new fall of rain that blew into the crevices of the leather curtains. Then the carriage wheels found smooth surface. "Ah," said Jonathan, "that's better. I had the drive gravelled last year. Can you tell the difference?"

"Yes, indeed." The lights were very near now. The driver pulled up his horses. Penrose.

She was aware, as Jonathan helped her down, of the looming bulk of a big three-storey house, its shape defined against the sky by a scattering of illuminated windows. Now the front door swung open and light from inside showed a handsome pillared portico with three shallow steps. An elderly coloured man advanced to meet them: "Welcome home, Mr. Jonathan."

"How are you, Job? How's everything?"

"She's fine, Mr. Jonathan. She's missed you, I think."

46

"Not speaking?" Now, belatedly, Kate realized that they were talking of Sarah.

"No, nor smiling neither. Not since you left, sah." He spoke, Kate thought, the most beautiful English she had heard since she crossed the border. Could he be a slave? Surely there were none in Boston?

"This is Mrs. Croston, who has agreed to take charge of Sarah." Jonathan guided her across the threshold into a wide, well-lighted hall. "Mrs. Penrose?"

"In the drawing room, sah."

"Good." He moved toward one of the closed doors that opened off the big hall. "We're famished, Job, and tired. Food—and warming-pans."

"Yes, sah. I'll see to it at once, Mr. Jonathan."

"Thank you." Jonathan threw open the door and ushered Kate into a room whose elegance amazed her. So far, her experience of American living had been limited to the Masons' house in the wilderness, Pride's Hotel, and the makeshift discomfort of the other inns they had stayed at. But here was a room that might have graced the most luxurious English country house she knew. She had seen furniture like this in many a lady's drawing room when paying calls with her father, and thought he had told her it was made by a Mr. Chippendale in the previous century. Each detail of the elaborately carved chairs, cabinets, and sofas shone with polish, as did the floor, where it showed around the expanse of crimson carpet. Crimson damask covers on the chairs and sofas echoed the carpet's sumptuous colour and formed a striking contrast with white curtains and the white dress of the tall woman who had risen to greet them. The whole room served as a foil for her blonde, full-blown beauty, and might have been designed to do so.

Following Jonathan across the desert of carpet, Kate felt horribly at a disadvantage in this glowing room, conscious of her drab bonnet and sober pelisse and of the long day's heat and dust. And still the beauty stood silent, watching them from amber-coloured eyes under heavy brows, while

Kate wished passionately that she could have avoided being the unwanted third at this meeting.

"How are you, Bella?" Jonathan's question seemed oddly inadequate.

Now, at last, Arabella took a step forward to greet them. "About as you'd expect." Her voice was deep, beautifully pitched, and angry. "I was beginning to despair of you, Jonathan." And then, to Kate: "Were you so hard to persuade, Miss McGowan?"

The dislike in her voice was worse than anything Kate had imagined: "I'm not . . ." Impossible to go on in face of that coldly hostile gaze. She stammered to a halt and listened wretchedly while Jonathan explained about Liz McGowan.

"Not Miss McGowan?" Arabella summed it up, eyebrows arched over those extraordinary amber eyes. "How do you do, Mrs. Croston? I hope, as an Englishwoman, you will not find us quite barbarous here. As to your work; you have experience, I take it, in dealing with children?"

"A little—"

Once again Jonathan cut short Kate's stumbling approach to explaining herself. "She has what I hope will prove more valuable—sympathy." They were discussing, Kate thought, a great deal more than the mere words suggested. "Job says Sarah is just the same," he went on.

"Job would." Weary impatience in the beauty's voice. "He's like the rest of you; won't see what's before his eyes. She's worse, of course; it's been intolerable; screaming fits night after night. I thought I'd go mad. If I'd known you'd be gone so long, I'd never have agreed." And then, turning to Kate, "I wonder if my husband has warned you just what you are in for," she said. "Has he convinced you that a little 'sympathy' is all that the child needs? I don't suppose he told you that the doctors find her case hopeless."

"Yes, he did." Kate was surprised to hear herself speak so firmly. "But he said he didn't believe it."

Dark eyebrows rose over scornful eyes. "So you can speak up for yourself? Well, that's something. Yes, Job?"

"Tea is ready, Miz' Penrose."

"Tea? Oh—you've not eaten, Jonathan?" Wearily graceful, she led the way across the hall to a crimson and mahogany dining room, and sat watching them eat with a sultry indifference that took away any appetite Kate's exhaustion had left her. She had grown so used to the American habit of asking questions that she was actually disconcerted by Arabella's silence, but Jonathan seemed to notice nothing. He had questions of his own for his wife, about the manufactury, the news in Boston . . . Her answers were oddly negative, Kate thought, harping always on how she had been tied to the house by Sarah's bad behaviour.

It was an awkward enough meal, and Kate was deeply grateful when Jonathan, saying, "Mrs. Croston's exhausted. I'm afraid I have brought her across country at a monstrous speed," gave her an excuse to escape.

Arabella rang a silver handbell. "You won't mind, Mrs. Croston, if Job shows you to your room? I have the migraine, a little. And—we keep early hours here in Penrose, you will find. Prue—the girl's in bed long since, and I would not ask Mrs. Peters."

Jonathan was on his feet. "I will take Mrs. Croston up," he said. "We might look in on Sarah as we go."

"I wonder you've waited so long." Something very strange in her tone, but Kate was beyond analysis.

Sarah's room was on the second floor, next door to her father's. "Arabella's over there." Jonathan pointed to a door at the far end of the red-carpeted hallway. "You are to be upstairs, I believe, in the chintz rooms . . . I had meant—" he stopped, gestured for silence, and eased open the door of Sarah's room.

It was dark inside, cool and quiet, with only a faint glimmer by the bed where a night light burned under a glass shade. "I said she must always have light," he whispered. And then, "Sarah, love, are you awake?"

A listening silence in the room, and the faintest possible stirring under the bedclothes was all his answer.

"It's Father, love. I'm back." This time the only response

was a definite movement down among the bedclothes. He sighed, moved forward to tuck in a loose sheet, bent to kiss the quiff of dark hair that showed against the pillow, and came back to Kate, who had stayed quietly by the door. "She's always worse when I've been away," he said, closing it behind them. "Sometimes I let myself think that's a good sign."

"Yes." Thoughtfully. "I see what you mean. She does notice—"

"Exactly." He had turned to lead the way to a steep flight of stairs that went up from the centre of the hallway. "Mrs. Penrose has had you put on the upper floor," he said, with a trace of apology, "we will have to see—"

The servants' floor? But he answered the unspoken question by pointing to a door at the head of the stairs. "The servants' quarters are through there, if you should need anything. They have their own stairway. These are your apartments. I'm sorry Arabella is not well enough—"

"But it's charming!" The opened door revealed a snug low-ceilinged sitting room lit by candles above the hearth where a newly lit fire burned brightly. The chintz curtains and chair covers had evidently given the room its name.

"The bedroom's through there." The door stood ajar and she glanced in to see a bed, hospitably ready, and her carpetbag standing in a corner. It was all of a sudden an oddly awkward moment. "I hope you have everything—" he had stayed with his hand on the door handle.

"Absolutely. It looks like heaven. And I could sleep for days." A yawn fought with the words. "Good night, Mr. Penrose."

Downstairs, Arabella had poured herself a glass of madeira and was sitting, elbows on table, lazily sipping it. "Did she greet you with open arms?"

"No." He would not let her see how the mockery hurt. "She was asleep." He moved over to stand with his back to the handsome carved chimney piece. "You might have been more welcoming to Mrs. Croston."

"Might I?" Indifferently. "A poor little brown thing. How you imagine she will contrive to cope with Sarah . . . But that's your affair, Jonathan. I shall go into Boston tomorrow."

"No, you will not." The snap in his voice brought her eyes up from her wine glass to meet his. "You will stay here, Arabella, and play the hostess a little more successfully than you did tonight."

"The hostess? To my nursemaid? Don't think, Jonathan, because I tolerated her in here tonight that I shall do so in future. As long as she holds a servant's position in my house, she shall be treated as a servant. We did not sit down at table with menials in Richmond."

"What you did, or did not do, in Richmond has no bearing on the case. And—perhaps you have forgotten, Arabella? This is my house."

"Pray, what do you intend me to understand by that?"

"Just this. I have great hopes of Mrs. Croston. She may be a little brown thing, as you so elegantly put it, but she has courage, spirit, warmth . . . I've watched her on the journey, fighting exhaustion, gallantly refusing to admit how tired she was, because she knew I wanted to get home. I wonder what you would look like, Bella, after travelling non-stop for three weeks, staying at the kind of inns we have. You'd have something more than an imaginary migraine to look weary about then."

"Imaginary! That's what you think! If you knew what I've been through with that child! Dirt, spilled food, screaming fits, the sullens . . . It's past bearing, and the sooner you admit it and have her placed in a home where she can be properly looked after, the happier we shall all be. I tell you, I'm ashamed to have her about."

"Ashamed!" He stopped himself with a furious effort. "I tell you, Arabella, if Sarah leaves this house, I go too. How ashamed would that make you?"

"That would depend . . ." she tried to make it sound light, but he had shaken her.

"Depend? On what, I wonder. What would the Quincys

51

say then, or the Lowells, or the Otises, or any other of your fine old families? Don't try me too far, Arabella, or you may regret it. As for Mrs. Croston, she is a lady and will be treated as one in my house. After the way you received her, I doubt very much whether she will wish to sit in your drawing room, but she will eat with us, whether she likes it or not. Perhaps, after all, it is better that she should have quarters of her own, away from the rest of us. Because, let us have this clear from the start, I intend her to stay. Is that understood?"

"Do you?" She yawned gracefully behind a white hand. "What's that to do with me? I had no share in hiring her; she's no affair of mine." And then, with a sudden change to the warm, winning voice that had captivated him once: "Jonathan! Try and see it my way. Try and understand what it's like for me, out here by myself all day . . . every day . . . what it was like last year, while you were in England. Buried here, week after week, at the back of beyond. It's the loneliness, Jon. With no one to talk to but the servants, nothing to do—"

"Nothing, Bella?" But his tone was milder. "There's the housekeeping, surely?"

"You know perfectly well that Mrs. Peters does it much better than I could—and wouldn't much relish my interfering, either. And we weren't brought up, in Richmond, to spend all our lives on jams and jellies. Oh, Jon, do you remember how gay life was there? The balls, the parties, the laughter . . . Do you wonder if I need to escape, sometimes, from this dull old house? To get to Boston and remind myself that life still goes on? If only you'd try to understand what it's like to be a woman, tied to one place . . . It's all very well for you: you go to England, to Canada, wherever you please. And I? I stay at home, with chores for company."

"And your child, Bella. Aren't you forgetting her?"

She shivered, as if a ghost's hand had touched her, and gulped madeira. "Must you keep reminding me? You know I make her worse. And what do you think that's like for me, for her own mother? Jon, don't you see, that's why I want to get away, not to watch this girl making herself at home with my child. Taking my place! A stranger, a nobody, from God knows where . . . Perhaps worse than a nobody. How do we know?'

"Stop it!" At first, he had been in a fair way to being sorry for her, but her reference to Kate's past caught him on the raw. He had wondered about it too often himself. "We won't talk any more about Mrs. Croston," he went on more mildly. "As to your going to Boston; time enough to think of that in a week or so."

"But, Jonathan!" Too late. He had already left her.

Back in Sarah's room, he stood, for a long time, silently by the bed, where, now, she lay asleep and asked himself, over again, all the old, despairing questions. At last he turned away, sighing, to shut himself up in his own room at the far end of the hall from Arabella's.

Upstairs, Kate was asleep already. Much later, she woke with a start to the sound of a child's frantic screaming. Sarah! She was out of bed in a flash, feeling in the dark for her dressing gown, then paused, hesitating. What good, after all, could she do, a complete stranger? She could hear movement downstairs, a door opening . . . The screams were louder, desperate, an agony to hear. She felt her way to the door of her room and opened it a crack. Now she could hear Jonathan's voice, a soothing murmur against the harsh persistent tremble of the screams. That settled it. She closed the door as quietly as she had opened it and found her way back to bed.

The screams went on and on. In the morning it was hard to believe that she must have fallen asleep through them. Broad daylight warned her that she had slept late, and she was out of bed in a bound and hurrying into her clothes. On the floor below, a glance into Sarah's room showed it empty and quiet, the bed already made up. She passed the closed doors of the other bedrooms and hurried on down the main stairway to the hall that ran from front to back of the house. There was no sound or sign of life. A door at the far end was open onto morning sunshine, and she moved instinctively to it and looked out on a broad stretch of rather shaggy lawn that fell away toward the river. Not a sign of life anywhere. Feeling oddly lost in this silent landscape, she walked across the rough grass to the wall that edged the river. A gravel path ran along her side of it, and she turned to follow it upstream toward a small building that had caught her eye among the trees that bordered the lawn. It was, illogically, a relief to get away from the sightless windows of the house. She had a curious feeling of flight as she approached the gray building and saw, with a little shock of surprise, that it was a miniature imitation of a Greek temple. The kind of folly one might have expected to find in an English garden, it seemed oddly out of place here. Hard to imagine Jonathan Penrose spending his money on such a frivolity. But Arabella perhaps?

Arabella? Mrs. Penrose. At last, reluctantly, she made herself remember last night's hostile reception. It had hurt horribly at the time, but now she could see that there might be plenty of reasons for it. Facing them, she sat down a little forlornly on the marble bench in front of the temple, castigating herself as she did so, for a coward. She ought to be in the house, finding Sarah, finding servants, asking for breakfast, asserting herself. In a minute, she would go . . .

The minute drew out. It was pleasant here in the sun, with unknown trees in young leaf around her. It was good, after the fatigue of the journey, just to sit for a while and think about as little as possible. It was too peaceful to last. Suddenly, her head went up at the sound of running footsteps. A moment later, a child burst into view on a path that wound away through the trees in the direction of the house. She was running like a mad thing, head down, hair flying, small fists clenched. A small child. Five years old? Six? Sarah, of course. And now Kate heard a voice—Arabella's deep, unmistakable voice calling impatiently from the direction of the house: "Sarah! Sarah! Where are you, child?"

Sarah had almost reached the temple. Surely she was not heading for the river? But on the cold thought, she stopped, panting, outside the temple, looked up, and saw Kate. Instinctively, Kate neither moved nor spoke, but merely sat there, calmly smiling, one hand held out in—what, greeting, propitiation? Their eyes met and held, the child's gray and steady for a moment before they shifted to look, oddly, to somewhere behind Kate's left shoulder. And then, nearer, Arabella's voice, angry now: "Sarah! Sarah!"

The child was watching Kate sideways, to see what she would do. She did nothing, but merely sat there passive, hoping she looked as friendly, as compassionate as she felt. At any rate, Sarah seemed to have come to a decision. She edged around, keeping as far from Kate as she could, and then, with a last glance—pleading, perhaps?—dived into the little temple and hid with the ease of long practice in a corner behind the altar.

And only just in time. Arabella now appeared at the corner of the path, her mouth open to call again: "Sarah—oh!" She saw Kate. "You!" And then, formally. "Good morning, Mrs. Croston. I hope you slept well." It was more reproach than question. "I'm looking for Sarah. Wretched child; never there when you want her. I hope you realize what you have taken on, Mrs. Croston."

"I think I am beginning to." Odd to feel so violent a relief that she had not been asked point blank whether she had seen the child. It seemed as if she could feel terror behind her in the little temple. And yet—this was Sarah's mother. Fantastic not to tell her at once where the child was. But she was not going to.

"It's just a question of time," Arabella went on. "It will become impossible. It's bad enough already. You must have heard what went on last night. How can I invite guests to the house when that kind of scene happens two nights out of three? There's an admirable asylum in Boston . . . But I don't mean to discourage you, Mrs. Croston. Do your best —I am sure you will—and when you are beaten, tell my husband. Perhaps he will believe *you*." She turned away, elegant in her dark blue morning dress, and called again. "Sarah! Sarah! Come here this instant!"

Kate sat very still on her bench, watching the tall figure move away toward the river. Aware of a little stir of movement behind her in the temple, she automatically held out a warning backward hand. Shocking to be doing this.

Arabella was coming back. "It's just too bad." She shrugged trim shoulders. "I had meant her to have the treat of driving out with me. It would have given you a morning's peace, at least; but there it is. You might as well see at once how things are. I wish you joy of your charge, Mrs. Croston."

"Thank you." But already Arabella had turned to sweep away, skirts fastidiously held up from the damp grass.

And Kate, who had risen to speak to her, sat down again on the cold marble, trying to control a spasm of rage. How could a mother speak thus of her own child? Appalling, too, to think that Sarah had heard it all. But then, how much did she understand? Here, at least, was a chance to find out. "She's gone now." She said it casually, without turning around, and was answered by a stir of movement behind her. Turning, she saw Sarah emerge from her hideaway behind the altar. Her face and gingham dress were filthy and her thin arms bore red marks to show how desperately she had squeezed herself into the cramped space. She stood there for a moment, silent, gazing, as she had done before, at a point somewhere behind Kate's head. Instinctively, Kate too said nothing, but smiled and held out a reassuring hand. Sarah moved sideways, as if to edge around her and escape. It was, somehow, a crucial moment. What was the right thing to say, to do?

Very gently, very smoothly, as if this was a small wild animal that must not be startled, Kate rose to her feet and moved one step backward so as to give the child free passage, if she wanted it. At the same time, she still held out that encouraging hand. "Come with me, Sarah?" she asked.

The girl stood, poised for flight, huge eyes asking a question. What a graceful little creature she was, Kate thought, for all her strangeness. But the next move was hers.

"To the river, perhaps?" she said. "I love running water. Do you?" And she made the slightest possible movement away from the house. "We'll wait, shall we, till the carriage has gone?"

A sudden sparkle in the wide gray eyes told her that Sarah had understood. She moved forward, seized Kate's hand, and pulled her hard toward a path that led away behind the temple.

FIVE

THAT WAS THE BEGINNING of a fantastic day. Sarah never spoke, and though Kate had established that she could, in fact, understand what was said to her, she often seemed simply not to hear it. She lived, as her father had said, in a world of her own. Of course, Kate told herself, all children must do so to a certain extent. Perhaps this was merely an extreme case. Following instinct, she submitted, that morning, to the child's whim. Surely, back at the house, they must have connected her own disappearance with Sarah's? She hoped that they were not worrying, but felt deeply certain that the contact she had achieved with Sarah was too important to be risked. Today, at least, she would follow where she was led.

They went first to a small waterfall among the trees a little above the house. A rough pile of rocks by the wall just above it provided a convenient perch from which to watch the plunging water, and Sarah climbed it, sure-footed, evidently taking it for granted that her companion would follow. The stones hurt Kate's feet through her soft slippers, but she hitched up her skirts and climbed just the same, to settle on cold and slimy stone with a silent prayer for her worn gray worsted. Sarah, watching the swift rush and fall of the water, seemed to have forgotten everything else. Presently, she began very quietly, almost in a whisper, to sing. Kate remembered something Jonathan had said to her. Casually, she too began to sing, her own favorite song, *Greensleeves*:

> "Alas, my love, you do me wrong
> To cast me off discourteously—"

Instinctively, she made as little as possible of the words.

For the moment, she was sure, the tune was the thing. The child had stopped her own singing and was looking at her cautiously, sideways, out of those big, strange gray eyes. Kate sang the first verse over again, but humming it this time, without words. Then she stopped. Water rushed and gurgled beside them. Sarah's voice picked up the first phrase of the song and hummed it in perfect tune. It seemed to Kate a tiny miracle, and she turned, smiling, to the child. For a moment, their eyes met directly, for a moment it seemed that Sarah was going to smile back. Then, once again, her eyes slid away.

Impatiently, she scrambled down from the rock, and Kate, following more slowly, wondered if she had spoiled everything. But Sarah was waiting for her, was holding out a small brown hand. Kate took it and followed along a woodland path that led still further up the narrowing river, noting, as they went, how gracefully the child moved. Already, she was beginning to agree with Jonathan Penrose whose optimism about the child's condition had previously seemed to her merely the hopeful self-delusion of a devoted parent. But now—could there really be anything seriously wrong with this bright-eyed, graceful little creature?

Of course, her continued silence was disconcerting, and so was the odd sliding way her eyes refused to meet one's own . . . If only she knew more about children . . . Following Sarah into a secluded hollow of the woods, Kate promised herself that she would learn. Here, the ground was carpeted with violets, not only the blue ones she was used to in England, but big yellow ones as well. She bent, with an exclamation of pleasure, to smell them, only to exclaim again in disappointment. They were scentless.

Sarah had been watching her. Now she turned to lead the way to a coolly shadowed nook among boulders where grew a glossy-leaved, pink-flowered plant Kate had never seen before. This time, it was Sarah who bent, in almost comic imitation of Kate's gesture, to sniff ecstatically. Following suit, Kate was rewarded by a delicious fragrance, at once sweet and spicy. "It's heavenly," she said. "Thank you, Sarah." And then, hopefully, "What's it called?"

No answer. Losing interest in the flowers, Sarah had picked up a handful of sticks and was laying them out in a line across the little glade. She seemed happy and occupied, and Kate settled herself on one of the stones to watch and wonder about her. But sunshine, creeping across the gray boulders, reminded her that they must have been out a long time. She jumped to her feet and held out her hand. "Time to go home, Sarah. I'm starving." And then, on an inspiration she was slightly ashamed of, as the child hung back, eyes lowered, mouth drooping: "The carriage must have gone long since. Won't you show me the way back to the house?"

No question but Sarah understood everything that was said to her. She looked through her bundle of sticks, chose one, dropped the others, and turned to lead the way down yet another well-trodden path. To Kate's relief, it left the river and cut through the woods to bring them quickly back to the shrubbery near the house. The back door still stood hospitably open, and Sarah suddenly darted ahead and in, to be greeted with angry affection by a woman's voice: "There you are at last, Sarey. Where in the world have you been? Oh—" She looked up from the child and saw Kate in the doorway. "Mrs. Croston? You found her? I hoped you must have."

"Yes—Mrs. Peters, is it?" She liked the looks of this tall, calm-faced woman. "I'm so sorry if we've frightened you. Sarah took me for a walk along the river. I hoped you'd realize . . ."

"Took you for a walk, did she? A stranger?" Mrs. Peters digested this for a moment. "Well, I do declare; wonders will never cease. Anyways, I reckon you was dead to rights to go, in that case, and if you won't mind my saying so. She don't often take a shiner to strangers, not our Sarey."

"She's very quick to understand—aren't you Sarah?" Every instinct in Kate rebelled at this discussion of the child in her presence as if she had been negligible, a thing.

"But she won't speak, will you, love? That's what makes her ma so mad. Pure orneriness, Mrs. Penrose calls it, and I don't know what else. But she's gone out to lunch now, Sarey-lamb, clear into Boston, and there's no one here but me and Prue—and she's out back doing the washing—so come get your breakfast, there's a good girl, and you too, Mrs. Croston. I'm mortal sorry I wasn't about when you came down, but we were all at sixes and sevens looking for the child. Job thought he'd seen her going out the front way, see, so we reckoned she might be down to the mill looking for her pa, which Mr. Penrose won't have on any account. Because of the machinery, you know. She's such an active little bit of mischief, our Sarey."

Just for an instant, as Mrs Peters spoke, Sarah's eyes met Kate's in a look of such pure child's mischief, that Kate knew she had gone out by the front door on purpose to mislead her pursuers. Nothing, surely, stupid about that?

And yet, over breakfast, she found herself compelled to reconsider. With the appearance of food, a devil seemed to enter into the child. Kate tried to laugh at herself for the notion, but failed. Sarah began by upsetting her milk, apparently by accident. Then, while Mrs. Peters was mopping this up and Kate was pouring her own coffee, she took a jug of maple syrup and poured it, slowly and deliberately, in a trail along the side of the table.

"Oh, lawks, Sarey, look what you've done now!" Mrs. Peters' tone made it all too clear that this was no surprise to her. "And I thought you was going to be good today, for Mrs. Croston. Now you just move over here and try and eat your ham like a good girl while old Peters cleans up this mess. No, ma'am," this to Kate, "don't you stir yourself. You must be plum famished. I'm used to it."

"I see." Kate was beginning to see a good deal. Sarah, who had moved obediently enough to the other side of the table, was occupied in arranging the little pieces of ham Mrs. Peters had cut for her in a neat line across her plate. So far, she had eaten nothing.

"Do you like ham, Sarah?" No answer, but a quick, side-

61

ways flash of the eyes showed Kate she had been understood.

"She don' like nothing, Mrs. Croston, but bread and milk, and her pa says she'll never grow big and strong on that."

"Perhaps not," said Kate, "but could she have it for a treat, because it's my first day? I'll talk to Mr. Penrose about it later."

"Of course, if you say so, miss—ma'am, I should say. I'll fetch it directly. That will be a treat, won't it, Sarey?"

Again the child took no notice. She was busy now, lining up salt cellars and other bits of crockery across the table, and Kate, who was indeed famished, was glad to leave her to it and hurry on with her own meal. She had almost finished when Mrs Peters returned with a steaming bowl of bread and milk. "Ummm—that looks good," she moved over to sit beside Sarah. "Shall we pretend you're my baby and I'll feed you? Would that be fun, Sarah?" And then, when the child merely looked past her with wide, uncomprehending eyes. "My mother used to have a game she played with me. Let me see how it went." She dipped the spoon in the steaming bowl. "Here's a bite for Lord Nelson"—the child swallowed it—"and one for the Queen —A bite for Lord Chatham. Wherever he's been—" She laughed. "I shall have to make up a new one for you, Sarah. Let's think—" as she talked she was spooning bread and milk into the passive mouth. "No good thinking we can find a rhyme for President, is there?" She did not expect an answer, and went straight on, as if talking to herself. "Here's a bite for your father, and one for his mill. A bite for your mother—" Sarah's teeth clenched on the spoon and she spat bread and milk all over the table. "Oh, Sarah!" But instinct warned her not to lose her temper, and she managed, quite cheerfully : "What a mess ! Let's mop it up, shall we?" congratulating herself, meanwhile, that Mrs. Peters had vanished with a disapproving glance as she began on the first rhyme.

While she was busy cleaning up the table, Sarah contrived to spill most of the rest of the bowlful down her front, but Kate refused to be drawn. "Had enough, have you? Right; then let's go up and change that sopping dress." She pulled back Sarah's chair, making a mental note to ask Jonathan Penrose if there was not some more practical place and way of feeding the child than at this polished dining table. In the meantime, Mrs Peters would doubtless draw the gloomiest conclusions from the state in which they left the room, but that could not be helped. Sarah was her job—and no sinecure. She took her hand and felt it writhe in hers, the child desperately braced against her, ready for flight.

Fatal to give in now. She stooped and swung Sarah up into her arms. "My father had a game he played with me too." She began to sing: "Ride a cock horse/To Banbury Cross," swinging Sarah in her arms in time to the music. Sarah struggled for a minute, wildly, then just as suddenly burst into a shriek of laughter that Kate found almost as disconcerting as her previous resistance. But never mind, they were halfway upstairs.

In Sarah's room, she delved in closets and drawers, to find what struck her as an immense and unsuitable wardrobe for a child so young. Hard to imagine wayward little Sarah dressed up in these frilled and flounced muslins. The checked gingham she was wearing seemed eminently more suitable, and Kate found its twin lying in a drawer. But Sarah stamped her foot, her lip trembling.

"You don't like it, Sarah? Well, pick one you do like."

At once, the child dug to the very bottom of the drawer and brought out a well-worn dotted muslin.

"That one? Do you think it's big enough for you? Let's try it anyway." She had got used now to the fact that Sarah never answered her, and was already suiting the action to the word. The dress was a tight fit, but not, she thought, actually an uncomfortable one. At any rate, Sarah was obviously pleased, taking a few almost dancing steps across the room, skimpy skirts held out. Kate half expected her to run to the looking glass, but when she led her there, the child showed no interest, merely pulling Kate out of the room and downstairs again. Outside, the sun was now shining brilliantly with all the warm promise of early summer. Kate held back for a moment. "Let's have a picnic, Sarah." After all, she must be hungry. And then, when a mutinous look and a further tug of the hand suggested that here was a word Sarah did not understand: "We'll get some cake or something from Mrs. Peters and take it out in the garden. Where's the kitchen, Sarah?"

The child stood stockstill, puzzled, wary, but luckily at this moment Mrs. Peters appeared from a door halfway down the hall, and Kate explained what she wanted.

"A picnic? I don't see why not. I forgot to tell you, miss, that Mr. Jonathan left a message. Just to say he was sorry not to see you before he left, but he'd have to be at the mill all day. He mostly lunches there. He looks forward to seeing you at dinner, he says."

"And that's?"

"Late. Seven o'clock, if you'll believe it. It's an idea Mr. Jonathan picked up in foreign parts. Well, I reckon it does fit in well with his business." It was the grudging approval of an old retainer.

"You've been with Mr. Jonathan a long time?"

"Just about forever, I reckon. And his father before him —oh, I've seen some times . . ."

"And Job?" She had been wondering where the old coloured man had got to this morning.

She snorted. "Oh, he's just a newcomer. Mr. Jonathan brought him back one year he was at Harvard. He'd been down to Washington with a friend of his for his Christmas vacation. I guess they went down into Virginia to one of those slave auctions they have there, and Mr. Jonathan just couldn't bear it. I know there was ructions when he got home, on account of all the money he'd spent on Job—and only to free him, of course. Though I reckon Job earns his keep at that. He's a powerful fine coachman and never had a spill yet. And waits at table when there's company, and valets Mr. Jonathan . . . We don't have the kind of house-

64

hold you've likely been used to in England, miss." Here, suddenly, was the heart of the long speech. "Just me and Prue, and Job and the boy, but we'll do our best to make you comfortable."

"I'm sure you will, Mrs. Peters, and I'll try to be as little trouble as possible. I'm not a bit used to being waited on. My father and I only had one daily girl toward the end." She had never thought the day would come when she would speak of her father, and face the old nightmare of his death, and what followed it, so easily. It all seemed at last, mercifully, a long time ago.

The present was Sarah. Here was a challenge, something worth doing. For already she found herself wholeheartedly in agreement with Jonathan Penrose. She could not believe that whatever ailed Sarah was beyond cure. If only she knew more about how it had started. Surely there must be some clue there?

On an impulse, she asked Mrs. Peters about it, as they wrapped up pound cake and cheese and dried fruit for the picnic. Sarah had retreated to the far end of the big kitchen to kneel in a big rocking chair, rocking violently and singing to herself—a tune that Kate recognized, almost with triumph, as *Greensleeves*.

"It's been a year?" Kate was comfortably certain that Sarah was paying no attention.

"Since it happened? Just about—and getting worse all the time, poor lamb."

"Were you here when it started?"

"Yes, but *they* weren't. Mrs. Penrose had taken Sarah to Saratoga Springs with her," she explained. "When they came back, I noticed at once the child was quiet—it seemed to come on from day to day; awful to watch it was. She was such a lambkin, Mrs. Croston, before and now . . . (she looked over her shoulder and lowered her voice) sometimes it seems as if the devil was in her, and I have to remind myself it's our Sarey. There's some in the village, though, won't come near her. I've heard talk, once or twice, that's frightened me."

"And no one knows what started it?"

"Not rightly. It was that night, of course—the one when she was lost, poor little lamb, and locked up in that awful shed, in the dark. And how she came to stray so far from the hotel is more than I'll ever understand; she was such a good little thing. Do always try to remember that, when she kicks and screams and bites, and you think you'll go crazy too. And nothing they can do, the doctors say. It fair breaks your heart."

"Well, I'm going to try—" she stopped. What was she going to try?

"You do that, miss. You never know. She's certainly taken a rare shine to you, which is more than I've seen happen since . . . Mind you, she cares about her father, all right; you can see that plain enough, if you just use your eyes." She stopped, suddenly aware of the implication with regard to Arabella. "Well, there's your picnic, and I hope it keeps fine for you."

Though it was still only the end of May, the sun was shining as brilliantly as in full English summer, and Kate found herself envying Sarah her cool muslin dress as they took the path that led to the violet hollow. This, she was sure, was the place for their picnic, since it was clearly a favourite of Sarah's. The sun was high overhead by the time they got back there, but she did not open their parcel of provisions at once. The kind of scene Sarah had made over breakfast must be bad for her; she would delay their meal until she had hunger on her side. So she began picking bunches of violets, separate ones for each colour, and for a while Sarah joined in enthusiastically. But soon she tired of this, and instead of arranging her flowers in bunches began laying them out in long trails across the clearing, a line of white, a line of yellow, a line of blue. Kate, carefully wrapping her own bunches in damp moss, tried to persuade her to do the same, but it was no use, the child merely shrugged in a curiously adult way, and went on with what she was doing.

Kate finished her own bunches, laid them down carefully in the shady spot where she had put their lunch, and looked up at the sky, wishing she had a watch. The sun was well past the meridian now and she, for one, was hungry. Without saying anything to Sarah, she moved about the clearing, picking large leaves and laying them out on a flat gray stone to serve as plates. Sarah laid a line of blue violets so that it passed close by this improvised table. In a moment she was watching as Kate opened Mrs. Peters' neat packets and put a slab of cake, a lump of cheese and a little handful of dried fruit on each "plate."

"There," Kate said at last, arranging a wreath of violets around the little feast. "I'm hungry!" And she sat down by one of the pieces and took a hearty bite of pound cake without apparently taking the slightest notice of Sarah.

For a moment, the child hung back, but she had had nothing to eat all day except a few spoonfuls of bread and milk. Suddenly she was beside Kate, frantically pushing alternate mouthfuls of cheese and cake into her mouth. Kate took no notice, but went on eating her own food with what she recognized as slightly exaggerated neatness. Naturally, Sarah finished first, and Kate was aware of her casting longing glances at her own pile of dried fruit. Without saying anything, she reached into her satchel for another helping. This, too, vanished at such speed that she began to understand the child's gaunt, large-eyed look. She was close to starvation.

It was a relief when Sarah stopped suddenly, halfway through her third helping. Too much, on top of such a long course of undernourishment, might well be worse than too little. Sarah was rubbing her eyes with a dirty little hand. She was visibly dropping with sleep. And no wonder. Kate remembered the night's endless screaming. She took off her shawl, spread it on a patch of last autumn's dry leaves, arranged the satchel for a pillow, and picked up Sarah bodily to lay her on the improvised bed. For a moment, the child was tense as a wild little animal, then, as Kate laid her down, she went limp, her face turned into the lumpy pillow. Almost instantly, she was asleep.

Kate sat down by the driest bit of rock she could find to watch and think about her. Time passed slowly, restfully. Birds made strange, hoarse noises in the trees. Some insect kept up a perpetual, almost mechanical, whirring, creaking sound. A tiny brilliantly green lizard came out and basked in the sun on a rock on the other side of the clearing, and she thought of snakes and wished she had not. She, too, was tired. Her head drooped back against the rock; the noises merged into a summer lullaby.

She woke with a start, shivering. The clearing was in shadow. She must have slept for a long time. And the child? A pang of pure terror was instantly allayed by the sight of Sarah, curled up in a ball, like a hedgehog, fast asleep. Waking her gently, Kate was filled with bitter anger at herself. What kind of guardian was she to bring this wild little creature out into the woods and then fall asleep and leave her unprotected? But there was no time to waste in self-blame. That could come later. She only hoped they could get home before the alarm was out for them.

But Sarah would not hurry. Refreshed by her sleep, she darted this way and that from the path—after butterflies, wild flowers, anything, nothing . . . Kate longed to pick her up, but remembered how she had resisted this before. Instead, she held out her hand: "Have you ever seen soldiers marching, Sarah? Take my hand, and I'll sing you one of the songs they march to." And then, as Sarah still hung back, she began to sing:

"The Campbells are coming, oh ho, oh ho,
The Campbells are coming to bonny Lochleven . . ."

and walked faster, with a swing in her step, in time to her own music. At last the child fell into step beside her. Their swinging hands touched, and Kate caught hold of Sarah's, pulling it high in the air on "Bonny Lochleven." For a moment, she was afraid it would not work, but then the hand that had felt for a moment like a snared bird relaxed in hers.

So they were marching hand in hand to Kate's singing,

68

when they came out on to the big lawn and saw Arabella
Penrose standing tall, elegant, and furious on the porch.
Kate's voice dwindled into silence, and as they crossed the
lawn, she regretted with useless passion that she had not
paused to tidy the two of them a little before they hurried
home. Sarah's ill-fitting muslin was creased and stained, her
own durable worsted little better. They must look a proper
pair of tatterdemalions. She could feel Sarah's hand pulling
away from hers and held on tighter as she met Arabella's
frowning look. "I'm so sorry we're late, Mrs. Penrose, I hope
you've not been worrying."

"Worrying! What d'you think I've been doing?" As
Arabella's wrath exploded, Kate instinctively let go of
Sarah's hand and watched her dart away round the side of
the house. Arabella drew a deep, angry breath. "Do you
know what time it is?"

"No, I'm afraid I don't, but I know it must be dreadfully
late. We took a picnic, you see, and I'm afraid, afterward,
we both fell fast asleep."

"Asleep?" Scornfully now. "In charge of a mentally de-
ficient child, and you take her out into the woods, God
knows where, and 'fall asleep'!"

"It was inexcusable of me," said Kate quietly. "I can only
say I'm sorry. And it won't happen again."

"It certainly won't," said Arabella. "I'll see to that. What
did my husband say he would pay you, Mrs. Croston?"

"He hasn't said. But you can't mean—"

"To dismiss you? Why not? Can you give me one good
reason why I should trust you with Sarah after this?"

"Yes." The deep, sun-drenched sleep had done Kate good.
Her head felt clear at last; her voice was steady as she went
on. "I can see now what Mr. Penrose means about the child.
I cannot believe that her condition is incurable."

"And you propose to cure her by falling asleep in her
company? You know so much better than the doctors?"
The scorn in her voice should have been crushing, but Kate
found it merely a challenge.

"Well, after all, they do admit that they know next to nothing about what ails the child. If only there was some clue as to what started it. I mean—of course, it would be terrifying for a little thing like her to spend a night shut up, alone in the woods, but still it doesn't seem enough, somehow. You were there, Mrs. Penrose. Wasn't there anything else? Anything that would help me to understand—help me to help her?"

"That's enough!" Arabella erupted suddenly into a rage that was all the more horrible because she kept her voice low and controlled. "You bitch. You—" She used a word Kate had heard often enough in the army, but never from a woman. "That's your game is it? To suggest it's all my fault! To come into my house, a drab, a slut, a bit of army refuse, and try and turn my husband and child against me. Yes, I saw you urge Sarah to run away from me. Don't think I'm stupid, Mrs. Croston." And then, on a new note. "Is it Mrs. Croston by the way? Did my poor, gullible Jonathan ever think to ask for your marriage lines before he engaged you? Camp follower with the British Army seems nearer the mark! I wonder what made you so anxious to get away. Yes"—she saw this had struck home—"you don't much like to be asked that, do you? Well, Mrs. Croston"—this time she made the title an insult—"I'll make a bargain with you. We won't go into that. Your shabby past shall be entirely your own affair. So long as you are packed and out of the house in half an hour."

Half an hour. Before Jonathan came back. Kate put out a hand to steady herself on the porch railing. "I'm sorry, Mrs. Penrose, but your husband engaged me. He will have to dismiss me. It's true enough. He did trust me without seeing my papers. There's no reason why you should. I'll bring them down when I've put Sarah to bed."

"Don't trouble yourself. What's a piece of paper, after all?" Arabella's tone had changed to one of mere indifference. "We are both being absurd, Mrs. Croston. You cannot wish to live here in this dead-and-alive hole. I don't know what your reasons were for wanting to leave Canada—I don't want to know—but you've succeeded. There's no need to stay here, slave to a child who becomes crazier every day, may be dangerous any moment. Jonathan didn't tell you the doctors said that, did he?"

"No. And I don't believe it. She might just possibly, from what I've seen of her, do herself an injury, out of—I don't know—not caring. But I've spent the day with her, watching her. Do you know she goes out of her way to avoid treading on a worm? A butterfly lit on the cake she was eating this afternoon. She'd been chasing them all morning. She could have had it easily. She smiled and blew it away. Mrs. Penrose, I know I've made a bad start, but, please, give me another chance. I truly think I might be able to help Sarah. Did you see? She was holding my hand just now?"

"Yes. I did see. She won't hold mine."

Suddenly, Kate was sorry for her. She made a stumbling attempt to say so. "I'm sorry, Mrs. Penrose. I hadn't thought what it must be like for you. But she'll get over it, I'm sure she will."

"Thank you!" Savagely. "Do you propose to 'understand' me too, as well as my child?" She changed all of a sudden from anger to condescension. "I won't keep you any longer from your duties. Or do you think feeding Sarah less important than understanding her?" Moving away, tall and graceful, into the shadowed hall, she turned back for a last word: "We will discuss your leaving when Mr. Penrose gets home."

Kate found Sarah in the kitchen, eating cookies under the benevolent eye of Mrs. Peters.

"I'm glad you sent her in to me, miss—ma'am, I should say. She don't much like scenes, our Sarey."

There was a question somewhere in the short sentences, and Kate decided she could not afford to ignore it. "I'm afraid I'm in dreadful disgrace for staying out so late. I hope Mr. Penrose won't be too angry."

"Angry! Mr. Jonathan? When I tell him Sarey drank two glasses of milk right off? Well, if he is, ma'am, just send him out to me. She looks better than she has for weeks, and will sleep like a log tonight, I reckon, and what's more important than that?"

"Thank you." Tears she had fought while confronting Arabella were dangerously close behind her eyes.

"Don't you mind anything, love." Mrs. Peters bent toward her. "Just remember it's the child that counts."

The child. Kate swallowed tears, and managed cheerfully: "My goodness, Sarah, high time for your bed."

Sarah went to bed without a murmur. Safely tucked in, she looked up just for a moment, directly at Kate. Surely there was the faintest glimmer of a smile in the gray eyes before they slid aside to gaze away into the corner of the room. Bending to kiss the now unresponsive face, Kate made her a silent promise; she would not abandon her if she could help it.

Downstairs, Kate found, with a sinking heart, that Jonathan and Arabella were already deep in talk in the drawing room. Arabella stood erect and magnificent in crimson satin, her back to the huge gold-framed looking glass over the chimney piece, so that to Kate's anxious imagination it seemed that two of her were dominating the room. Jonathan was leaning, long and loose-jointed against the window-frame, his daytime black in contrast with his wife's magnificence, his face shadowed, impassive under the fair hair that always looked wind-blown. Disconcertingly, he stopped talking at sight of Kate and the two of them awaited her in chilling silence.

Nothing for it but to plunge right in: "I'm extremely sorry, Mr. Penrose, about today. It won't happen again." No excuses. He must know how exhausting their journey had been. She was not going to refer to it. But the silence dragged out, as if each of them was waiting for the other to speak. At last Kate went on. "I brought down my marriage lines, Mrs. Penrose." And then, when Jonathan merely shook his head impatiently, and Arabella turned away to study her own profile in the glass as if the whole subject was profoundly indifferent to her: "Sarah went to bed like an angel. I truly think her day in the open has done her good. She's got a little colour—"

"And so you think she's cured!" The two Arabellas shrugged marble shoulders. "You come into our house, turn everything topsy-turvy, break all our rules for the child, give way to her in everything, and then talk about a cure! And to crown it all, you fall asleep out in the woods leaving her exposed to God knows what danger. It's no good, I tell you, Jonathan. I won't have a quiet moment."

"You're so anxious about the child?" Jonathan's tone surprised Kate.

"Of course I'm anxious about her! Do you think I don't suffer when I see her as she is? Don't mind when she runs away from me? D'you think I've no feelings, Jonathan? Besides, it's not safe for her here, running wild the way she does."

"It's just about as safe here as anywhere," he said reasonably. "I've taken care she can't get off the place. And with Mrs. Croston to watch out for her. If you think you're up to it?" No mistaking the doubt in his voice as he spoke to Kate directly for the first time. "Maybe I shouldn't have let you persuade me you could do it . . . Well, that's my fault. You see now, it's not just a job, it's a whole life. No reason why we should expect you to take it on." And then, as she made to protest. "No—wait a minute. I brought you here, and I'm responsible for you. No way of getting you back to England right now, I'm afraid, but this war won't last for ever—not beyond this fall, or I miss my guess. It should be easy enough to find you work in Boston till then."

"But I don't want to work in Boston! I don't want to go back to England, come to that. Please, Mr. Penrose, give me another chance. I want to try. I want the kind of life I could have with Sarah. She's what I need . . . I told you . . . someone to love . . ." She stopped, embarrassed at her own vehemence.

"Love!" Arabella broke in. "Because her mother doesn't? If you only knew the nights I've lain awake, listening to her scream, knowing it would do more harm than good to go to her—"

"But, Bella," put in Jonathan, "be reasonable. Someone's got to look after Sarah." And then, wearily. "Lord knows, we've been through this often enough before. You've got to face facts, Bella. You can't; Mrs. Croston thinks she can. Well then, I say, let's give her a trial. If you're really sure you're up to it, Mrs. Croston?" Again that note of doubt.

"Of course I am. Mr. Penrose, I don't know how to thank you. All I can say is, I promise I'll do my best."

"Promises!" said Arabella. "From a complete stranger, picked up God knows where in the train of the British Army. No, Jonathan, I won't hush! What do you know about women? No mother; no sisters; it's no wonder if you are a fool for a tale of woe and a pitiful face. I won't say a pretty one. And it's my child you propose to turn over to this—"

"Young lady," he intervened grimly as she paused for a word. "And—our child, Arabella."

"Yes. Our only—" For a moment it seemed that she would say more, then she moved away to pull the scarlet bell rope, merely throwing back over her shoulder: "Well, Jonathan, don't say I didn't warn you." And then, when Job appeared: "I'll need the carriage first thing in the morning, Job. I'm going back to Boston." Her defiant tone was belied by a quick sideways glance for Jonathan. Goodness, thought Kate, is this what she has been aiming at all the time?

Jonathan took it coolly enough. "Maybe you're right, my dear. It will give Mrs. Croston time to find her feet. And that reminds me. There is one other thing, Mrs. Croston. This question of giving in to the child. I don't like that. She must learn, poor lamb, that she cannot always have her own way."

"Of course she must—when she's well enough. At the moment she's thin as a rail and nervous as a scared colt. I want some weight on her, and some colour in her cheeks before I so much as think about discipline. I tell you, Mr. Penrose, if I'm to do anything for Sarah, I must have a free

74

hand. If not—" She stopped, appalled at what she seemed to be saying.

He was looking at her with the amazement of a lion ferociously attacked by a mouse. "Well, I'll be—" It was the first rumbling of an explosion and she nerved herself to face it. Then, surprisingly, he laughed. "You might be right at that, Mrs. Croston. I wouldn't call in an expert at the works, and then tell him how to go about his business. Why should I do it to you? Very well. You're the expert. Yours shall be the decision, and, mind you, yours the responsibility."

"Thank you." She was breathing like an exhausted runner.

But it was Arabella who had the last word. "Responsibility?" she said. "After what happened today? My poor Jonathan."

Her taunts echoed, that night, through Kate's recurring nightmare. They had opened up the old wound. Once again, in the mounting terror of her dream, her father fell dead across the table, once again Charles Manningham—she woke there, sweating, and lay for a long time, eyes open to stare blankly into the darkness, trying to convince herself that it was all over, all past, to be forgotten. What had happened, had happened. The present, and Sarah, were what mattered now. Because she was almost sure that there was something she could do for Sarah. This was more important, surely, than the old disaster? And, thinking of Sarah, she smiled and slept quietly at last.

SIX

AGREEING TO GIVE KATE A TRIAL, Jonathan had not speci-
fied how long it should be. At first, inevitably, he was full
of doubts, which Arabella's harping on the mystery of
Kate's past had exacerbated. It was true that he knew nothing about women. His own disastrous marriage was proof
enough of that. Memories thronged to mock him; of how
he had adored Arabella, of sleepless nights, pacing the deck
of the ship he had named after her, dreaming of her, aching
for her. Well, he thought bitterly, at least he would never
make such a fool of himself again.

And yet—he had taken Kate on trust. He ought, he knew,
to have looked at her papers that first night when she had
offered them. He ought still to ask her about her background, but always when it came to the point, when he saw
her flinch away from the first hint of a question, he could
not bring himself to do it. And, besides, there had been something oddly convincing about the way she had turned on
him, that first evening: "If I'm to do anything for Sarah, I
must have a free hand." It had shaken him—he was not
used to being crossed—but it had also given him hope—a
hope that time was to strengthen. Kate's instinctive understanding of the child was worth any amount of doctors'
theory. The two of them were inseparable, spending most
of their time out of doors as the brilliant New England
summer days ripened toward fall, and already both of them
looked the better for it.

Sometimes he asked himself, as he watched them chasing
each other across the lawn and in and out among the locust
trees by the river, what it was they had in common. Something there was, he felt sure. Kate was good for Sarah because of some deep need of her own that complemented

Sarah's. Or was he being absurd? Very likely. But his rash act was justified a thousand times by results. Sarah had actually put on a little weight; the bones were less obvious in her face, and her bouts of senseless, horrible screaming were rarer.

Kate remarked on it timidly, over dinner one still night of early September. "Don't you think she's better?"

There was something rather touching about the appeal for praise. "I really think she is. A little." He reproached himself, afterward, for his caution. Why not give her the encouragement she deserved? After all, she had been with them three months now. It was time to stop thinking in terms of a trial and make a permanent arrangement. If only he could bring himself to ask her about her past, to clear up the nagging little doubt that recurred every time he found her poring over the newspaper accounts of the war.

Of course it was natural enough that she should do so. But always, when he tried to tell himself this, he was stopped by memory of her frantic tone, back in York, when she had begged him to take her away. "There's someone . . . someone in the 98th. If I have to meet him again, I think I'll die." Surely no innocent relationship could have left such a legacy of terror?

And yet—did he really want to know about it? Was it this, in fact, that dried the questions on his lips? Whatever shadow lay over Kate Croston's past, there was no question that in the present she was what Sarah needed.

But it irked him. It was against all his practical business-man's instincts. Problems should be faced, doubts resolved, issues brought out into the open. He was brooding about this as he walked the short way home from the factory next day. Usually, Sarah would come flying out when she saw him, with Kate smiling behind her. Today there was no sign of them and he knew one of those instant pangs of almost unbearable fear to which he had become accustomed since Sarah's illness. He took the porch steps at a bound and was instantly aware of bustle in the house, of a distinctive, heavy perfume in the air. Arabella.

"Well, Jonathan." She was standing, golden, impassive, more beautiful than ever, in the wide doorway of the drawing room.

"Well, Arabella?"

She looked him up and down with that mocking half-smile of hers. "Don't you think, my love, that a speech of delighted surprise would be in order?"

He looked down the hall. No servant in sight, but still no need to conduct this conversation so publicly. He ushered her into the drawing room. "Surprise, certainly. But if you expect delight . . ." He closed the door. "I thought we agreed, when you insisted on going, that you would stay in Boston until I advised your return."

"Yes." Her voice was mocking. "So we did. To give Mrs. Croston a chance to get acquainted with Sarah. I think I must be very stupid, Jonathan. It had not occurred to me that I was giving her a chance to get acquainted with you."

"Oh?" He looked at it for a moment from all angles. Then, "Someone has been gossiping? Mrs. Peters, I suppose."

"Gossip!" She made it a challenge, then seemed to think better of it. "Based on nothing, of course. You only have to look at the poor little mouse." A sideways glance enjoyed her own reflection in the big looking glass over the fire. "No; Mrs. Peters has said nothing; to me, at any rate. Frankly, I should think better of her if she had. But there's talk in Boston just the same. A good deal of talk. I value our good name too highly to let it go for a nothing, a poor little drab of a nursemaid. So I've come to ask you to face the facts, at last, about Sarah. It's hopeless, and we must admit it. God knows we've tried everything. They think your mad journey to Canada quite romantic in Boston. Miss Quincy was saying so just the other day. But it's no good, Jonathan. Dr. Smedley says so: 'Tell him to stop breaking his heart over the impossible,' he said. And he knows a thoroughly genteel place in Salem, Jonathan, run by a widow lady of his acquaintance. Only a few patients, you understand, and the very best of care. Jonathan!" She was pleading with him

78

now, the big eyes seeming almost ready for tears. "You know—we must face it, you and I! it's she—poor crazy child—who's come between us. Only send her away and you will find everything as it used to be. We will be happy again, Jonathan. How can we be, with things as they are now? With her screams always in our ears?" She put out a white hand to touch his shoulder appealingly. "Remember what it used to be like?"

"Yes, I remember." He brushed the hand away like a spider. "I was mad for you, if that is what you mean—and I suppose it is. Until you turned me out of your bed after Sarah was born because you'd 'never go through that again.' I suffered then. I don't think you're capable of understanding what I suffered. And now—am I to understand that you are offering to bribe me with your 'favours' "—he made the word sound obscene—"if I will agree to send Sarah away to some genteel madhouse kept by friends of that ass, Smedley?"

"But Jonathan," the huge eyes held real tears now, "you know you always wanted an heir—a Penrose to carry on the name."

"Yes, so I did. It's hard to imagine. As for your offer, it's too late. That's all over: dead as yesterday. You can't bring back the past, Bella. We have to think of the future now, and Sarah."

"Sarah!" She spat it out. "Never anything but Sarah. I warn you, Jonathan—"

"Yes? Warn me? Do you, perhaps, wish to change the terms of our bargain?"

"Bargain? What do you mean?" She was shaken now, wary.

"Oh—a tacit one, of course, but a bargain nevertheless. Granted, I did not understand at the time that you were marrying me for my money, but that was my fault. You've said yourself that I don't understand women. Well, you should know! I was a young fool when I met you, believing a thousand impossibilites a minute. I'm older now, wiser

79

perhaps, but the bargain holds so long as you keep your side of it."

"Which means?" She had given up the attempt to charm him, and moved away to gaze moodily out the window at evening mist rising from the river.

"That you continue to behave like my wife. And—so far as you are able—like Sarah's mother. And that, by the way, involves courtesy to Mrs. Croston, whom we will be meeting for dinner. Otherwise—" He left it to hang ominously in the air.

Kate and Sarah had spent the afternoon picking huckleberries in the big meadow that lay on the far side of the carriage road, and Kate had been congratulating herself, as they walked contentedly homeward through lengthening shadows, that the child really did show an improvement. Oh, nothing spectacular. She did not speak, and would not meet your eyes, but she seemed to understand more of what was said to her, and better still, she seemed more able to concentrate her energies, to go on contentedly doing the same thing. A month ago, it would have been quite impossible to spend a whole afternoon like this one, peacefully filling their baskets with the crisp, shining berries. Not that Sarah had picked steadily, when there was so much wild life to distract her—a chipmunk chattering at them from his vantage point on a wall, a snake's cast-off skin glimmering by the path, and, as always, her favourite butterflies to chase. But these had been the activities of any ordinary child. It was only as the shadows lengthened that she began to play that strange and, to Kate, ill-omened game of laying out sticks and stones and anything else she could find in an endless line.

Seeing this, Kate had picked up her basket at once. "Time for home, Sarah."

They had walked back cheerfully enough, Sarah dragging behind a little, needing to be sung to, one of the marching songs she loved. "Some talk of Alexander . . ." Oddly inappropriate, Kate thought wryly, here in the New England countryside in the second year of her war with old England. But in this sun-drenched late summer landscape it was easy to forget the war and think only of today, and the improvement in Sarah. Something heart-warming, something to tell Jonathan Penrose over dinner.

Disconcerting, then, to go in by the kitchen door with their berries and recognize instantly crisis in the air.

"Huckleberries?" Mrs. Peters, who had urged the project that morning, promising pie, now sounded as if she had never heard of such a thing. "Oh . . . yes, thank you." She put the big and the small basket down side by side and went back to her pastry. "Mrs. Penrose is home." It came out oddly flat. "You'd best hurry, Miss Kate, if you're to get Sarey to bed and be changed for dinner."

"Yes, I will have to, won't I?" Kate was very fond of Mrs. Peters by now, and found her habit of calling her "Miss Kate" as if she had been an unmarried daughter of the house particularly endearing.

It was one thing to intend to hurry; quite another to succeed. That was one time when Kate could almost have believed in diabolical possession. Where was the cheerful child who had hummed the refrain of *The British Grenadier* on the way home? Mrs. Peters, apparently anticipating trouble, had produced Sarah's favourite supper of bread and milk, and Kate, aware of thunder in the air, had begun the meal with a favourite counting rhyme:

"Here's a bite for the *Frolic*
And one for the *Wasp* . . ."

It was no use. The bite for the *Frolic* was merely spat out, but the next one was snatched and thrown across the room. And then, while Kate was retrieving the spoon, Sarah picked up the whole bowlful and poured it on the floor at her feet.

Kate was tired too. In an instant of pure rage, she seized the child, ready—to do what? Controlling herself, she merely tucked her, with firm gentleness, under her arm. "No supper, then, Sarah? Right, then it's bedtime." Thank goodness she had insisted that Sarah have her meals in the

81

little, unused morning room where she could clear up the mess at her leisure.

That moment of near-violence seemed to have had a chastening effect on Sarah. Getting her to bed was often a battle, but tonight she was almost alarmingly docile, and Kate got upstairs to her own room in plenty of time to wish she had something more elegant than a well-worn India muslin to put on for dinner.

She wished it even more when she finally got up the courage to join Arabella Penrose in the drawing room. She found her alone, a striking, sullen figure in a blaze of deep green satin, and was not sure whether she was glad or sorry that Jonathan was not there to mitigate the meeting.

And yet it went off easily enough. "Ah, Mrs. Croston." Arabella hardly looked up from the book of fashion plates she was studying. "I believe I am to congratulate you on an improvement in Sarah. Does she speak?"

"I'm afraid not. Not yet."

"Not yet! I admire your optimism. In what, then, does this 'improvement' consist?"

"She's"—how difficult it was to put a finger on it—"I don't know, easier, more friendly . . ."

"Friendly! I take it you like having bread and milk thrown at you. I'm sorry, Mrs. Croston, but I looked into the morning room just now. The scene there hardly suggests improvement to me."

"It's true; she was a little difficult tonight, but I hope it's just a temporary setback."

"You hope! Well, of course, so do I." She bent once more over her book, and Kate moved across the room to settle herself uncomfortably on the edge of a straight chair, feeling both angry and unwelcome.

Mrs. Peters had excelled herself, and dinner was a very much more formal meal than Kate and Jonathan were used to sitting down to, but Arabella, picking a morsel here and there, contrived to suggest that it was hardly worth eating. She addressed such remarks as she made exclusively to her husband and ignored his efforts to bring Kate into the conversation, so that it was with a sigh of relief that Kate escaped to her own room as soon as the meal was over. If this was what life with Arabella was going to be like, she could only hope that she would return to Boston at once. Or—she settled by the lamp with the dress she was making for Sarah—persuade Jonathan that she would prefer to dine by herself? But then—if his wife did go back to Boston—it would be almost impossibly difficult to rejoin Jonathan. And—face it—the evenings with him were an important part of her day. Without these easy discussions that ranged from Sarah's behaviour to his labour troubles at the factory and so—inevitably—to the news of the war, she would be hard put to it to keep any sense of proportion after the exhausting days spent with Sarah.

The trouble was, there was no one else to talk to in Penrose. Jonathan Penrose had at once explained and apologized for this before they had even got there. "It's a tiny village—a hamlet really. I'm afraid you won't find much society."

It had been, she had found, a massive understatement. The factory workers lived in a huddle of cottages below the factory, where one shop, owned and run by an elderly, gossiping spinster, provided for their simple needs. Kate's greatest disappointment had been that there was no church. She had counted, more than she knew, on the society of a minister and his family. But the faithful of Penrose had to row themselves across the Charles River to church on Sunday. Jonathan had apologized for this, too. "My grandfather planned to build a church," he explained. "He even had the plans drawn—and then came the Revolution. Well, there it is . . . It was all my father could do to keep a roof over his own head . . ."

"And you?"

He had laughed. "I had quite forgotten you are a parson's daughter, Mrs. Croston. Well—when this war is over, perhaps I will spend some of my profits on a village church. It might be a good investment at that." And then, quick to see the change in her expression. "I'm sorry. That offends you."

"It's not that" (but, of course, to an extent, it had been)

83

... "It's just ... it seems so horrible to make a profit out of this war."

"Not so horrible as to make a loss." It had been characteristic—and unanswerable. Thinking of it now, as she sewed fine tucks in the muslin dress she had copied from Sarah's shabby old favourite, Kate thought she would never understand the New England character, with its mixture of shrewdness and ideals, its factories and its Unitarianism. It was just like Jonathan Penrose to plan a church out of his wartime profits—and think of it as a good investment.

What was that? The sewing dropped from her hands and she ran to throw open the window and lean out. Sarah's room was on the same side of the house as hers, and now she could hear the screams clearly. It was more than a month since Sarah had had one of these fits of endless, senseless screaming and Kate had hoped they were a thing of the past.

Pausing in the doorway of Sarah's room, she saw that Jonathan was there already, bending over the screaming child.

"Good." He looked up and saw Kate as she hesitated there, wondering whether to leave him to it, since he was often the best medicine for Sarah. "I hoped you'd come. This is a bad one, I'm afraid."

It was indeed. Sarah was rigid on her back, a mindless, screaming thing, more animal than child. And yet—she had seen Kate, her eyes flickered a little wider open, almost, it might be, in an attempt at a greeting, a recognition. But all the time the screams continued, piercing, mechanical, horrible.

"You try." Jonathan had seen that flicker of recognition and got up to make way for Kate on the chair by the bed.

Kate sat down and gathered the rigid child in her arms. "It's all right, Sarah, my pet; it's all right, my honey." She crooned it over and over again, rocking the child to the rhythm of the words. She knew, by now, that in one of these fits, Sarah was beyond reasonable appeal. She would go on screaming until exhaustion plunged her into sleep; the soothing movement and rhythmic chant might just possibly speed up the process.

Jonathan was looking a question. For a moment, she stopped her chant to answer it. "I'll manage," she said. No doubt he wanted to join his wife downstairs.

Sarah's eyes had flown open. The screaming intensified. At least it meant that the singing was doing some good. Still rhythmically rocking the child, she had a question of her own. "What started it?"

"God knows."

But downstairs, he crossed the drawing room to stand over Arabella. "What did you do to her?"

"Do? I? Nothing at all."

"But you were in there."

"Nothing of the kind."

Should he believe her? She was always most convincing when she lied. "At all events," he said, "I think you had best go back to Boston tomorrow, Arabella."

"And if I say no?"

"I shall stop your allowance. But why should you? You always say you are bored to distraction here. As for your talk of rumours about Mrs Croston and me—surely the worst thing we can do is to seem to take them seriously. You'd much best go back to Boston and the parties you enjoy."

"But that's just it. Everyone who is anyone has been out of town for ages now. Those who aren't at Saratoga are at Ballston Springs. There's hardly a soul I care for left."

"Why don't you go too?"

"Because I've no money, Jonathan. I don't know where it's gone to this quarter. If you could see your way to advancing me my October allowance?"

"So that's it. You've outrun the constable again, have you? How much are you in debt, Arabella?"

"Oh nothing! The merest trifles. You know I promised you..."

"And I know what to think of your promises. No, Arabella, I will not advance you your next quarter's allowance. That way lies bankruptcy for us both. You must learn to

85

live within your means—God knows, they're lavish enough."

"Lavish. Don't make me laugh! Do you know what one has to pay for French gloves these days? And as for their silks . . . why, it's almost prohibitive."

"But not quite? Blood money always comes high, you'll find."

"Blood money? What do you mean?"

"Has it really not occurred to you that goods from France must run the blockade, at God knows what cost in life and dollars? Of course they come high. I can only suggest that you try the effect of American gloves—and as for silk—when you next need a new dress, come to me, and you shall have the choice of what my factories can produce."

"You're joking."

"Nothing of the kind. As a patriotic American you should be ashamed to be pouring your money into Napoleon Bonaparte's pockets."

"Oh, Jonathan." She despaired of him. "What has patriotism to do with what I wear?"

"Everything." But he knew he had no hope of convincing her. "How much in debt are you?"

"It's nothing—a couple of hundred dollars at the most of it."

"By which I reckon I had better understand five hundred. Very well, let me have a note of the amounts in the morning, and I will pay them for you. Debt, as you know, is one thing that I will not tolerate. But as for an advance on your allowance, that is out of the question."

"What a pity. Then I shall just have to stay here and scrimp, shall I not? It's a shame I have such an upsetting effect on that poor mad child upstairs. I merely opened the door of her room and looked in to say good night, and she set up that caterwauling that's gone on ever since. A fine way for a child to greet her own mother."

"I knew it." His hands were clenched at his sides. "I knew you were at the bottom of it." And then, with an effort. "Very well, you win. You shall have your advance—

or rather, I will pay your board, either at Ballston Springs or Saratoga, whichever you prefer, so long as I have your promise that you will keep away from here."

"Thank you, dear." She smiled her sleepy cat's smile. "I knew we should understand each other in the end."

SEVEN

SARAH REFUSED TO GET UP NEXT MORNING, but lay huddled deep in her bed, the quilt drawn up around her face, so that all Kate could see was a tangle of brown hair. She seemed perfectly well. Her forehead was cool under Kate's anxious hand. She just would not get up. This was something that had never happened before, since the problem was usually to keep her in bed. But then, she had been awake late the night before; a rest would do her no harm.

"All right, honey, I'll bring you your breakfast in bed— we can have a picnic here in your room." When Kate got downstairs at last, she found the house quiet.

In the kitchen, Mrs. Peters was picking over the huckleberries they had brought. "Had quite a night of it last night, didn't you? Made herself ill, has she, poor lamb?"

"I don't really think so. She just won't get up. I don't quite know what to do." It was a relief to confess this to Mrs. Peters, who could be relied on for a quiet and practical sympathy in any problem of Sarah's.

"Not much you can do, I reckon," she said now. "But give way to her. Not when she's got something fixed in her mind. Breakfast in bed won't hurt her, once in a while. She'll get tired of it soon enough, if I know her." She stopped work on the huckleberries and moved over to survey her well-stocked larder. "I wonder what would go down best— she must be famished, mark you, after all that crying last night. We could hear it clear up in our quarters. A good thing the house stands by itself." She came back into the room with her hands full of dishes. "I thought you'd want to take her out today, Miss Kate, after all that carry-on, so I made a couple of meat pies, very first thing, and some of

88

those spice cookies she likes. Why not give her those? They won't make half so much mess."

"You're an angel, Mrs. Peters. And I'll have the same. She always eats better that way."

"I reckon she's right down fond of you, Miss Kate, so don't you go worrying about a thing. It'll all come out right, I guess . . . Oh—" on a carefully casual note. "Mrs. Penrose goes back to Boston today."

"So soon?" Their eyes met in an unspoken question and answer.

"Yes. Job's to have the carriage out front at eleven sharp. First to Boston and then on to Saratoga, as I understand it. I reckon she just came home for her country clothes."

"I see." This was the nearest they would ever get to discussing Arabella.

But, carrying their odd breakfast upstairs, Kate could not help wondering about the brief visit; about Arabella and her husband; and, inevitably, about the possible connection between her arrival and Sarah's screaming fit.

At least, Sarah was prepared to eat. A meat pie and half a dozen cookies later, Kate said casually, "You'd best get up soon if you want to say good-bye to your mother. She's off to Saratoga this morning."

Of course, she did not expect the child to answer, but neither did she expect her to plunge out of bed, scattering cookies broadside over the floor. Usually it was something of a struggle to get her dressed, but today she dived into her clothes as if her life depended on it.

When she was ready, she took Kate's hand and pulled her toward the door. Then she stopped and looked up at her, the big eyes holding an incomprehensible plea.

"What is it, lamby?" It was on these occasions that Kate most hoped Sarah might suddenly burst, almost despite herself, into speech. "What do you want?"

But Sarah's mouth had turned straight and obstinate. Still holding Kate's hand, she opened the door very quietly and peered out into the hall. Everything was quiet. Arabella's bedroom door was still shut. Then, from the driveway below Sarah's window they heard the crunch of carriage wheels, and Job's voice talking to his horses. And, simultaneously, from Arabella's room, the jangle of the handbell she used to summon Prue. Sarah pulled loose from Kate and rushed helter-skelter down the stairs. Kate heard the screen door of the porch slam, but when she reached the porch herself there was no sign of Sarah in the garden. Remembering their first meeting, and how she had hidden in the temple, Kate hurried across rough cut grass still wet with autumn dew to peer in.

This time there was no crouching figure behind the altar, and she had to fight down a moment's panic that would have driven her to the edge of the river, set her calling wildly for Sarah. She would not do it. There had been times like this before in the early days, not many of them, but enough to convince her that the excitement of hearing herself shouted after was the worst possible thing for Sarah. Very likely she was watching now from some secret hiding place, liable to be panicked into further flight. So, with a great effort, Kate made herself shrug her shoulders and drift casually back to the house.

She found Arabella standing in the hall, shaking out a silk parasol and looking cross. "Where in the world is everyone?" She looped the parasol over a slim wrist and picked up reticule and gloves. "I can't keep the horses standing much longer. Where's Sarah, Mrs. Croston? Surely she intends to say good-bye to her mamma?"

"I'm very sorry." Kate was amazed to hear herself lie. "I didn't know you were going. She's run out into the garden somewhere—it's such a beautiful day."

"Beautiful! Hot, you mean. If I delay much longer, I'll die of it. A pity you 'didn't know,' Mrs. Croston. I only hope you know what you are doing with Sarah." She picked up crisp muslin skirts and turned toward the front door. "If no one's here to say good-bye, I may as well be going." And then, just as Kate was beginning to feel a pang of sympathy for her: "I hesitate to teach you your business, since you seem so sure of yourself, but do you really think it wise to let Sarah loose in the garden as you do? There is a river, you know ..."

"Sarah has a great deal of sense, Mrs. Penrose." How she hoped she was right. "She'll come back when she is ready. At times, I think, we all need to be alone—even children."

"A very convenient belief. I hope you are right." She turned and swept gracefully down the shallow steps to where Job awaited her at his horses' heads.

Kate, too, turned sharply away into the shadows of the further hall, fighting a fierce anger that only half masked her anxiety. Was it this kind of barbed remark that had caused Sarah's terror of her mother, or was there more to it? What had really happened that day at Saratoga? Was it mere coincidence that Sarah had run away this morning after her own mention of that unlucky place? She sighed and ran upstairs to fight anxiety by a rigorous tidying of Sarah's room. Time passed. The last cookie crumb was swept up from the brightly coloured rag rug, the ruffled bedspread neatly adjusted, the whole room was shining, and fresh, and ready.

Ready for what? At last anxiety boiled up in her. She had a vision of Jonathan Penrose, his drowned child limp in his arms, bringing her up to lay on the tidy bed. Absurd. But her fingernails were biting deep into the palms of her hands. It was almost intolerably hard not to rush out and raise the hue and cry. Right now, this very minute, Sarah might be over the wall, looking down into the swift water, half-hypnotized, ready for the plunge. And if she was, would not the sounds of a search be the worst possible thing?

Deliberately, she made her hands go limp, made herself go casually downstairs, pick up her sewing, and drift out into the garden, to settle conspicuously on a wooden bench by the river wall. Sarah would come back when she was ready. She must believe this, believe it so hard as to make it true.

She could make herself sit, but she could not make her shaking hands sew. She willed them to lie idly in her lap, then started at the sight of Jonathan emerging from the wooded path that led down the river to the factory.

"Where's Sarah?" That his question was inevitable made it no easier to answer.

But he, at least, must have the truth. "I don't know." She faced him with it squarely. "She's hiding somewhere. Has been all morning."

"And you're not looking for her? Not anxious at all? Just taking the morning off and sitting in the sun?" She had not imagined him capable of this cold anger.

At least it touched a warming spurt of answering rage in her. "Just so. I think it the worst possible thing for her to be shouted after, panicked over. I am making myself sit here like this."

"No doubt a mighty effort."

"I find it so. After all, I am responsible for her."

"And I'm her father."

"Yes. And she's running away from her mother. She was afraid, I think, that Mrs. Penrose would take her to Saratoga with her." There; it was out. If she had not been so angry, no doubt she would not have said it.

He took it well. "You think so?"

"I'm sure of it." But she would not tell him of that first occasion—of Sarah hiding, obviously terrified, in the temple. "Why did you come back this morning if you were not afraid of something of the kind?"

"Yes." It was neither affirmation nor, quite, denial. "But what are we going to do now?" Tone and question alike were an implicit apology for his earlier anger.

Now she was on her feet, eager to share the burden of anxiety with him. "Oh God, I wish I knew. Suppose I'm wrong? Suppose we ought to be shouting and searching? But I've the most dreadful feeling that it might push her into doing something . . ."

"She wouldn't otherwise? I see what you mean." He did, completely. "How long has she been gone?"

"All morning. I'm worried to death." The admission increased her fear. "What shall we do?"

"I'll go and call her casually, as if I'd just come home by chance. No harm in that, surely?"

"No . . . no, of course not." She seized on it. "Do, Mr. Penrose—quickly. Up along the river. She likes to sit on that big rock; where you can see over the wall. I'll stay here." No need to say that this bench commanded the widest view of the same river.

She could hear him calling as he moved away upstream. Lightly, casually, "Sarah, my monkey, where've you got to?" And then, further off, "Sarah . . . Sarah . . ."

She must fight the temptation to run after him, to share his anxiety. Because—face it—this morning Sarah had run away from her, as well as from her mother. It must mean that somehow she had failed her . . .

Here was Mrs. Peters, plodding heavily across the grass. "There you are, Miss Kate. It's lunchtime. I made johnny-cake for Sarey. But—where is she?"

"I don't know. She's been gone all morning. Mr. Penrose is looking for her."

"Oh." Mrs. Peters thought about it for a moment. "I reckon it weren't your fault. You've been like a mother to her. We all know that." She stopped, aware of how much she had said. "I'll keep lunch hot. Don't you worry, Miss Kate. Mr. Penrose'll find her, you'll see if he doesn't. And, even if not, who's to say it wouldn't be all for the best . . ."

"No!" Explosively. And then, more gently. "No, Mrs. Peters, you mustn't ever even think like that. Sarah's going to be all right. Quite all right." Lunatic to speak with such confidence, today of all days, and yet, just having done so made her feel better.

The older woman shrugged. "Just as you say, Miss Kate." And moved off toward the house.

How long had Jonathan been gone? She could not hear his voice any more. He must have gone clear up to the Boston road. This brought a new line of fear. The road . . . a panic-stricken child rushing madly out under a horse's hoofs. Or—why did the idea of a kidnapping leap to her mind? Who in the world would want to kidnap Sarah?

93

She could not sit still any longer. After all, it would be perfectly reasonable to call Sarah to her lunch. She laid her sewing down on the bench, rose to her feet, and moved across to the shrubbery, calling low and casual, as Jonathan had, "Sarah! It's lunchtime." Once again she stopped to look well into the shadows of the little temple, but of course there was nothing there. She moved on along the path through the trees, calling at regular intervals, peering about her in all the shady corners where a child might hide.

From time to time, almost despite herself, she moved over to lean against the low containing wall that ran beside the river, and peer down into its secret waters. Sarah had never, to her knowledge, tried to climb this wall. Could she, if she tried? Kate thought not; it was quite as high as a small girl and had been built carefully on Jonathan's orders, its gray stones smoothly held together with mortar so as to provide no toehold.

And yet—a desperate child, running out of the house as Sarah had wildly run? Kate could hear Jonathan Penrose calling again now—far off at the other side of the wood, toward the road. Reasonable or not, she would walk along by the wall.

The ground had been cleared when the wall was built, but already a thick growth of barberry and wild rose and tangling grapevine was coming back, and at times she had hard work of it pushing far enough through the undergrowth to make sure the wall was still smooth and unclimbable. Mrs. Peters had taught her to avoid the brilliant green of the poison vine, and she had noticed that Sarah, too, was automatically careful of it. There was a good deal of it along the wall. Sarah would never have pushed through here. She was wasting time, vital time, as, it seemed to her, she had been all morning. She would turn back at the next bend of the river.

But when she got there it was to find a complete change in the vegetation along the wall. Here was a stand of small, sturdy oaks and surely, running in among them, the faintest trace of a path. Was this, perhaps, one of Sarah's secret places that she had never been shown? Certainly it was a path more suitable for a small girl than a woman. She had to bend almost double to push her way through the stubby little oaks. But the path led directly to the wall—and to a place where mortar had crumbled away among the rocks, leaving what looked almost like a flight of steps.

No time now to blame herself bitterly for not having found this place sooner. The sense of urgency that had been driving her all morning was stronger than ever. She should have been here hours ago. Too late? The crickets were chanting it around her. No time to find Jonathan Penrose. Besides, if the truth was as bad as she feared, it was the least she could do to face it alone.

Leaning over the wall, she could see nothing at first but scrubby bushes sloping away toward the river, which was quite far below her here, running smooth, deep, and deadly. Then she saw that the path continued on the far side of the wall, turning sharply downward into a tangle of small oaks and stunted firs. The rocks crumbled a little as she climbed the wall, and she thought with horror of Sarah doing this. But a broken ankle was the least, now, of her worries.

Why did she not call? Not, she knew, because the nearby rush of the river might drown her voice. No, quite simply, she was afraid to. And in a moment she knew that in this, at least, she had been right. She was in among the oaks now, looking down the steep slope to the river, and halfway down, on a little ledge just the width of a child's body, lay Sarah, quite still. A fall—a rattlesnake—a sudden illness . . . The horrid possibilities flashed through her mind to be dismissed in favour of a certainty that was almost as bad. Sarah was fast asleep. If she turned over or woke suddenly, she would roll down into the river.

No time even to think of fetching help. Kate was already working her way down the slope, grateful for the toughly rooted blueberry bushes, which, taken in painful, prickly handfuls, provided a chancy support in the climb. She left the path at last, to work her way straight down a little to

95

the left of where Sarah lay, and then, very silently, very cautiously, along below her. There was just enough hand and foothold if she was lucky. If not, she must remember, at all costs, not to make a noise as she fell.

But she would not fall. One foot on a firmly rooted little oak, and the other pushed deep into dry earth, she stood still at last, her head almost on a level with Sarah's. Now, one arm firmly entwined in a prickly bush, the other ready to catch Sarah if she fell, she dared speak. "Sarah." Very gently. "Time to get up." It was the way she called her on the rare occasions when she woke first in the morning.

And it worked. Sarah's head merely lifted a little, her eyes opened, vague, puzzled . . .

"Don't move, lamby, or—carefully. I don't want you falling on me. That's it." Sarah had stretched, stirred, and sat up all of a piece on the path. Now what? Don't mention Arabella. So—"Guess what, Sarah," she said. "Your father's home for lunch. And Mrs. Peters has made johnny-cake." As she spoke, she felt the oak tree beginning to give under her weight. No panic: don't even feel it; it's the most catching thing in the world. "I'll race you to the wall, Sarah. One, two, three: go!"

Sarah took off with a little spurt of gravel which almost blinded Kate. At the same instant, the oak root under her gave way, and she threw herself upward with a push of the other foot that sent a shower of earth and little stones splashing into the river below. But she was up, lying on her face sideways across the path, just where Sarah had been a moment before. "You've certainly won!" She kept her voice steady as she rose first to her knees, then to her feet, and pushed her way upward along the little path.

Sarah was sitting astride the wall looking down at her with that unfathomable wide-eyed stare of hers that seemed to take in at once everything and nothing. And—Kate was shaking like a leaf. Better not pretend. "Do you know"—she was level with the child now—"I was afraid for a minute I was going to fall. Just look at me. Isn't that ridiculous?" And she held out a shaking hand for Sarah's inspection.

The child's reaction was as surprising as it was heartwarming. She leaned down from the wall and held out her own small brown hand to pull Kate up.

"Thank you, lamby. I'll be glad to get home for my lunch, won't you?" As they set off together down the winding path, Kate wondered what to do about Jonathan. The less Sarah was aware of the fright they had had, the better. And yet, he must not be left in his anguish a moment longer than she could help.

The problem was solved for her, as they neared the little temple, by the sight of Jonathan's tall figure approaching down another path. No need to call to him; he had seen them. "Let's wait for your father, shall we? He's been looking for you too." Now she had time to wish that she had warned Jonathan about alarming the child over this adventure. But Sarah had let go of her hand and darted off to meet her father, who swung her up on to his shoulder. "There's my girl." Kate need not have worried. He sounded as casual as if they had only parted five minutes before. And yet it seemed to her that the morning had left new lines in his tanned face.

"You found her." His tone made it the fullest possible speech of thanks. And then, at sight of Kate's torn dress and scratched and bleeding face and hands. "But, good God, where in the world?" And to Sarah, giving her a reassuring jiggle on his shoulder: "Are you riding comfortably, love? Is your horse behaving?"

He was rewarded by one of her delighted squeals, as she wound her arms more closely around his neck, but his eyes were for Kate. "Where?" he asked again.

"She was over the wall, the naughty little thing." Kate's tone made it sound the mildest of misdemeanours. "And, would you believe it, fast asleep on a ledge above the river. I had to get below her before I dared wake her. I must be a mess."

"You are." He kept his tone light to match hers. "And, I

rather think, a heroine, Mrs. Croston. But there will be time for thanks. A lifetime—Sarah's." He gave the child a loving squeeze with his free hand. "Climbed the wall did you, minx? Well, I'm the father who's going to see that's never possible again, so we need say no more about it. But—how?"

"The mortar's gone, up there among the bushes. It was too easy. I think she had been there before—often. I'm ashamed not to have known."

"Don't be." Almost brusquely. "You can't be with her all the time. It wouldn't be good if you were. The wall shall be fixed today."

For the first time since they had arrived, Jonathan stayed home all that afternoon. "Sarah and I," he announced after lunch, "are going for a walk. Sarah is going to show me her path over the wall. And you, Mrs Croston, are going to sleep."

"To sleep? In the daytime?"

"Does it seem so fantastic? Well—shame on me—I suppose it might well. You should have reminded me that you have been working twenty-four hours a day since you got here. I don't know any other of my employees who would have stood it. You need lessons in American independence, Mrs. Croston. You should have complained."

"Complained?" It surprised her. "Why should I complain? I've been happy here, Mr. Penrose."

His answer was disconcertingly off point. "I think it's about time you took to calling me Jonathan," he said.

EIGHT

"DO YOU THINK we could have the piano tuned?" Kate asked it over breakfast one dark November morning, when massed clouds threatened the first snow.

"Arabella's piano? Of course, if you wish it." Jonathan had got back from Boston late the night before and was busy sorting through a pile of letters. "I should have thought of it myself. I'm afraid this place is dull for you."

"It's not for me—or at least, not mainly, though it's true I should like to be able to play. But I thought I might have a try at teaching Sarah."

"Sarah!" His surprised glance rested for a moment on the child who sat between them systematically eating the line of bread fingers Kate had arranged for her. "I know she's wonderfully better, but if she can't read?"

"What has reading to do with it?" Kate found herself increasingly impatient with the household's habit of taking Sarah's condition for granted, as something immutable. "The piano is different. She can learn from watching me, if she doesn't want to be bothered with the notes. Can't you, Sarah?" One never knew whether the child was in fact listening or not, but she made it an absolute rule to behave always as if she were. Today, Sarah justified her, by looking up, smiling her vague, entrancing smile, and humming a snatch from her favourite tune, *Greensleeves*. "You see," Kate said. "She has a natural aptitude for music. I think it might be a beginning . . . Besides, the days are so short; we need something to do in the evenings, don't we, lamb?" No answer of course, but Sarah went contentedly on with her breakfast. She was stuffing rather more bread into her mouth than it would comfortably hold, but Kate knew better than to interfere. The fact that she was feeding herself was triumph enough to be going on with.

"I reckon you're the world's most confirmed optimist." Jonathan helped himself to buckwheat cakes. "I'll send Job for the tuner today. I should have done it long since; I don't know what Arabella would say if she got home and found it out of tune."

Sarah spilled her milk. "Oh dear!" Kate jumped up to fetch the cloth she kept handy for such emergencies. "Too bad, honey, but you've finished, haven't you? Take your dishes out to Prue, would you? She's in a hurry this morning. It's her day off and she wants to get down to the village before it snows." Would it work? This running of errands was a new thing in Sarah's life, and a wonderfully encouraging one. But today, after the reference to Arabella?

Sighing inwardly and mopping up milk, Kate asked herself whether she ought to force a discussion of the problem of Arabella. But how could she in face of Jonathan's resolute silence? And, after all, Arabella had never come back since the day Sarah had disappeared. Kate had learned from Mrs Peters that she had gone straight from Saratoga to the Boston house and apparently planned to spend the winter there. Since then, Jonathan had made a practice of spending one or two nights a week in Boston too. "He worships the ground she treads on," Janet Mason had said.

Sarah was still standing, swinging to and fro against the back of a chair, watching her with the straight, mutinous mouth she had come to know so well. Let it go? Make an issue of it? She had to make these decisions a dozen times a day, but remained passionately convinced of the importance of getting each one right. "Hurry up, lamb," she said now. "Then we'd better go out too, before it snows. I'll give you one hundred swings." Surely this would work. The swing—her idea—had only been finished a few days ago, and Sarah loved to be swung in time to one of Kate's counting rhymes. But she still hesitated, looking at once obstinate and pleading. "I'm sure your mother will let us know before

100

she comes home," Kate went on. "So we can get things ready for her. Won't she, Jonathan?"

"Of course." And then, as Sarah flashed Kate a quick, almost conspiratorial smile and left the room: "You think it's as bad as that?"

"Yes, quite as bad."

"I see." He put down the letter he had been reading. "That rather settles it then. We were talking about Christmas yesterday," he explained. "Arabella and I."

"Yes?" Kate, too, had thought about this.

"Arabella was thinking of a party out here. Once the snow packs hard it's an easy sledge ride. We used to have them every year. Before . . ."

"Yes. Before." What in the world could she say?

"You don't like the idea?"

"It's none of my business." She could not help a little spurt of anger at the way he was leaving the burden of objection to her. And yet—Sarah was her responsibility. "You saw Sarah just now," she went on. "And she's been so much better."

"I know. But that's just it, you see. I told Arabella she was better. Of course she would like to be home for Christmas, to have things as they used to be. It's difficult . . ." Painful to see him fumbling for a way to put it. "But you're sure?"

"That it would do harm? Well—you saw." She was not going to make his decision for him.

"Yes. Right. We'll have the party in Boston. It's lucky I've got a man I can trust, now, to see to things at the factory. I'm afraid it will mean a quiet Christmas for you and Sarah, but we can make up for it in January, for her birthday. Yes, thank you"—he was glad to have it settled—"one more cup of coffee, and then I must be off to the factory. We've a huge new order—winter uniform cloth. Now! In November! And no doubt Wilkinson's army up there in the north country in their summer ones. Not that anything can excuse what happened at Chrystler's Farm. Two thousand Americans beaten by eight hundred English! I tell you,

Kate, I'm almost ashamed to be an American. It's no wonder the English won't accept the Czar's offer to mediate. Why should they? Gallatin and Adams and their 'Peace Commission' have about as much chance of success as that poltroon Wilkinson has of pulling out of his winter quarters and taking Montreal. Imagine giving him the command—a coward and bungler; maybe worse. Do you know, Kate, sometimes I wonder whether I should not—whether it's not my duty to take a hand in politics?"

He made it a question and her reaction was instantaneous. "Oh, I wish you would! It all seems such a muddle. But—what would you do, what would you say?"

"Not, 'Peace at any price.' Be sure of that. Do you remember how we argued, last spring, on the way back from York? Well, I can see it now; you were right and I was wrong. War's a monster, a juggernaut. Once it's started, everything's different. We can't—whatever they say in the Massachusetts Assembly—we simply cannot afford to submit now. We just wouldn't be a country any more. We may not be anyway. Do you know the Federalist papers in Boston are urging that the New England states secede from the Union, and make their own peace? How can they, after all that's happened? And in Boston, particularly, after seeing the *Shannon* destroy our *Chesapeake* last summer? Do you remember how the crowds rushed out to the beaches to watch poor Lawrence's glorious victory? And what they saw?"

"Yes. It was just after we got here. But remember, just the same, how people were stirred, even here, by Lawrence's last words." It was merely part of her fantastic position that she should be encouraging him about the course of a war against her own country.

"'Don't give up the ship'? Yes, it makes a good slogan, I admit, but I'd rather have Perry's any day: 'We have met the enemy and they are ours.' A few more victories like his, and we would be in a position to negotiate from strength. Particularly if Napoleon keeps you British busy in Europe." And then, on a different note, remembering how the news of Napoleon's victory at Dresden had hit her. "Forgive me. It's so hard to remember . . ."

"I know. It doesn't matter. It's all horrible, whichever way you look at it. I don't believe I even know what I want any more. Except the piano tuned for Sarah."

"And that you shall certainly have."

December was a lonely month. Snow deepened around the house, and Jonathan spent more and more time in Boston, no doubt busy with arrangements for the party. Even out at Penrose, they felt the stir of the preparations for it. Mrs. Peters was making puddings and mincemeat and sorting out jars of preserves for Job to take into Boston. Prue was hard at work making ornamental garlands on instructions sent out by Arabella. The whole house smelled deliciously of spices, and Sarah was happily occupied helping them. It left Kate with more time on her hands than she wanted, time to wonder if she had not been a fool to take so firm a line about this party.

Restless and miserable, she wandered about the house, wondering what it would be like filled with a gay Christmas crowd of guests. Arabella had sent out for the bronze slippers that matched her most spectacular evening gown of tawny velvet. Job was busy brushing imaginary specks of fluff from Jonathan's black broadcloth evening coat. "He won't wear knee-breeches, won't Mr. Jonathan," he told Kate. "Not even Miz' Penrose could make him do that."

Jonathan had not been home for seven days now, and it was surprising how the time dragged without him. Inevitably, on Christmas Eve, Kate found herself thinking about the party as she tiptoed into Sarah's bedroom to fill her stocking with candy and nuts, the gingerbread man Mrs Peters had baked, and her own exquisitely sewn rag doll. That safely done, she moved over to the window to gaze out at moonlit snow and think about poor Arabella, who could not be with her child at Christmas.

Poor Arabella? Nonsense. This very minute she was doubtless standing to receive her guests, magnificent in golden velvet, with Jonathan at her side. Poor Arabella? For a moment, she nearly thought, poor Kate, shook herself instead, and went to bed.

Jonathan returned, as he had promised, in good time on the evening of Sarah's seventh birthday. She had rushed downstairs at the sound of the sleigh bells and now watched with eager eyes as Job followed his master into the house, almost invisible behind a huge package carefully wrapped in sacking.

Jonathan laughed, and kissed her, and shook snow off his hat and overcoat. "It's your Christmas present, honey," he said, "and your birthday present too. What do you think, Kate? Shall she open it now?"

"I don't see why not." Kate bent down to help Sarah remove the wrappings and reveal a magnificent scarlet toboggan.

"Oh!" The child drew in a great breath of excitement, and for a moment Kate thought she would speak, but instead she ran over to hug her father.

He felt in his overcoat pocket and produced another parcel. "And this is from your mother, honey."

The glow faded from Sarah's face and she watched listlessly as Kate opened the parcel for her and revealed a doll, splendid in tawny golden evening dress.

"How beautiful!" For a moment, Kate imagined Arabella sewing those tiny seams, but Jonathan's next words dispelled the illusion.

"She had her dressed by her own dressmaker," he explained. "Out of the pieces from her ball gown. Isn't she a beauty, Sarah?"

But Sarah's only answer was to drop the doll and run headlong from the room. Kate followed far enough to make sure that she had gone upstairs and not, as, for a cold moment, she had feared, straight out into the snow.

When she returned, Jonathan greeted her ruefully. "I thought she was so much better. Besides—what else could I do?"

"Nothing. Don't look so anxious. She'll get over it. And

she is much better. Six months ago it would have meant a screaming fit. Now—"

The sentence was finished for her by Sarah, who reappeared carrying the rag doll Kate had made her, sat down on the floor and began to dress her in the new doll's elegant, unsuitable apparel.

Jonathan had still another tiny parcel. "And this is for you," he told Kate. "From Sarah."

"Oh—" Kate breathed her delight as she undid the wrappings to reveal a beautifully plain gold lady's watch. "You shouldn't have—"

"Not I. Sarah."

Kate bent to hug the child. "Look what you've given me, Sarah. Isn't it beautiful?" Her hand shook a little as she pinned the watch to her dress, and thought, oddly, of the lines her father had had carved on their sundial. "I only tell the sunny hours." Sunny? Memory of her last Christmas rose to choke her.

Did Jonathan see that she was near to tears? He changed the subject. "You've not asked me for the news."

"Is there any?" She bent down to help Sarah with the fastenings of the velvet dress.

"Yes. From Europe at last. Good news for you. But not for us. Napoleon's beaten. The Allies crushed him at Leipsic last fall. Now, by what I hear, it's only a matter of time. Fantastic, isn't it, that it should be bad news. The end of one of the greatest tyrants the world has known—and the beginning of the end for us."

"You're so sure it is the end? Napoleon's got himself out of tight places before now."

"I doubt if he can this time. There's trouble even in France, by all reports. No, we must face it; we'll have Wellington and his Peninsula veterans here by summer. And then what hope is there for our bungling generals?"

"Wellington?" said Kate thoughtfully. "I wonder if he would come?"

"Mr. Madison seems to think so. He's had letters from

Castlereagh, offering direct negotiations. Our Peace Commissioners will have something to do at last."

"He'll accept?"

"He'll have to. And take what terms he can, and be grateful if it's in time to save the Union."

"You mean, 'Peace at any price' after all?"

"What else can we do? With the full strength of the British Army against us? And their Navy? You know what the blockade's like already. Remember how they sailed up the Potomac last summer without a shot fired against them? And those were just the ships they could spare from blockading the whole of Europe! No, this defeat of Napoleon has altered everything. I just pray God, Adams and Gallatin lose no time. But it may be spring before their instructions even reach them. And God knows what may not have happened here in the meantime. You've heard about Newark?"

"Yes." She had wondered when he would bring himself to speak of this wanton act of violence, when the American general, McClure, forced to retreat from Fort George, had burned the helpless village of Newark before he went.

"You don't say you told me so?"

"What's the use?"

He turned to make sure that Sarah was still busy dressing Kate's doll. Then back to her. "I don't like to tell you, but there's worse."

"Worse?"

"Yes. The English have stormed Fort Niagara. Its—vengeance, I suppose. They're burning and harrying from Lewiston to Buffalo."

"Oh my God! And the Masons?"

"I've heard nothing. Well, there's hardly been time. One can only hope—and pray. Their house is secluded—a little way from Fort Niagara. But—it's the Indians. The English have let them loose. You were right, Kate, about this war."

"I wish I hadn't been." Horrible to remember Janet Mason's kindness, her simple pride in the comforts of her home. Where was she now? "And in this weather too." She shuddered, looking out at steadily falling snow.

"I know. And—Kate—I expect you would want to know." She had known somehow that there was still more to come. "The 98th were there."

"The 98th!" He might as well have hit her. "Oh—thank you." Absurd, but what else was there to say?

Once again—aware of her distress—he changed the subject. "How are the piano lessons going?"

"Do you know"—she seized on it—"I hardly dare begin to tell you. It's—I feel almost superstitious about it. She takes to it like an angel. I think she'd spend all day at the piano if I'd let her. And I'm sure, the other day, I heard her trying to sight-read from that book of carols you sent us. I've certainly never played her *The Holly and The Ivy*."

"Reading music, you mean, when she can't read words? But how in the world?"

"I simply can't imagine. Of course, she's watched me, but I've never tried to teach her."

"Perhaps that's the answer," he said. "Well, God bless you, Kate, at least there's something hopeful, one bit of good news in a black winter. I don't know how to thank you."

"There's no need. You know how happy it makes me." But there was a glow of pleasure, just the same, for his praise.

"And when I think I had my doubts about bringing you!" he went on. "I don't know what I'd do without you now." And then, quickly, as if to get it over with: "I have to go back to Boston at the end of the week. There's a meeting I must attend. You'll be all right, you and Sarah?" It was only just a question.

"Of course." She swallowed something bitter. The glow of pleasure had turned, all of a sudden, to one of rage. A meeting, indeed! Why could he not be honest and say he was going back to his wife? "No need to trouble yourself about Sarah and me," she said. "We wouldn't dream of keeping you from your politics." And then, aware that she had not managed quite the casual tone she had intended, she made a business of looking at her new watch. "Goodness! It's late. Sarah! Time we were changing for dinner."

As a great treat, Sarah was to dine with them that night, and Kate was glad of it. With Sarah there, sitting bright-eyed between them, following everything they said, their conversation must inevitably keep in the shallows, and that was where she wanted it. While she talked, and laughed, and told Jonathan about the snow castle she and Sarah had built down by the river, she was wrestling with an emotion at once familiar, horrible and strange. She was jealous. Jealous of Arabella.

She would not think about it. Jonathan had been over to the factory before dinner and was retailing a long story of his overseer, Mr. Mackintosh, and his battles with the inde-pendent, outspoken factory girls. "But he's a good man, Mackintosh. I'm lucky to have him."

"Yes." And lucky to have me, so you can spend your time in Boston, dangling after Arabella. Stop it, she thought, and plunged into a story of her own about Prue and her brothers. But Sarah was too observant. Sarah had recog-nized the strain in her voice, and was looking at her with big, puzzled eyes. Sarah's mouth was beginning to quiver.

Kate took a last bite of huckleberry pie. "You're tired, honey, aren't you? It's been such an exciting day. You'll excuse us?" To Jonathan.

"Of course. But you'll join me for coffee when Sarah's in bed."

"I don't believe so. Not tonight. If you'll forgive me? I'm a little tired myself." And he would never know what it cost her to say that.

Luckily, Sarah went to bed without a murmur, and at last, safely tucked in, with her rag doll beside her, she held up demanding little arms and pulled Kate's face down for a touching, unpracticed kiss, her first.

Hugging her warmly in return, Kate swallowed tears with an effort. Sarah knew something was wrong and was offering her comfort. "Good night, honey," she said, "it's all right, bless you."

And, alone at last in her room, faced just what she had said. In effect, she had promised Sarah that nothing should change. She had promised to stay. And how could she, now she knew that she loved Jonathan? She ought to go, any-where, anyhow. She made up the fire with a shaking hand. She could not go. That quick kiss of Sarah's had settled it. Sarah needed her. Nothing else mattered but that.

Or was she deceiving herself, snatching at excuses to stay in Jonathan's house? Impatiently, she moved over to gaze into the glass that hung over her dressing table. Huge eyes, pale face, softly curling hair . . . a perfectly good face . . . one to be forgotten, to be taken for granted, as Jonathan Penrose took her for granted. There it was. She made herself conjure up the imagined face of Arabella behind her own. Golden Arabella with the honey-coloured hair and amber eyes. Arabella, whose spell drew her husband back to Boston even from the daughter he adored.

Well then, what she, Kate, did was surely, her own affair. If she chose to stand by Sarah; to fight this feeling that had grown in her without her knowing it, there was nothing to stop her. In fact, there was nothing else she could do. It was not only that she had, quite simply, nowhere to go; there was another problem; how could she explain her going? She imagined it and blushed with rage. "Mr. Penrose, I've fallen in love with you. I must leave." Impossible . . . intolerable even to think of it. But what other explanation would satisfy him?

So; fight it, conquer it. Of course she could. And oddly, comfortingly, an early memory of her father came back to her. It must have been a long, long time ago. Mother had been alive, had been sitting in her low armchair, pouring tea, while Father paced to and fro across the little room and talked about the sermon he was writing. "Man decides for himself," he had said. "That's what distinguishes him from the other animals."

Strange to remember so clearly. Mother had put down the teapot and looked up with that wistful smile of hers. "Decides right?" she had asked.

He had stopped his long-legged pacing to look down at her with the smile he kept for her alone. "Ah, if we could be sure of that," he had said, "we'd be angels, wouldn't we, love?"

And Kate had thought this curse, this jealousy a new thing. Now, remembering that smile of her father's, she knew it of old—as old as childhood. Her father had never looked at her like that. And she had tried so hard after her mother had died, tried to have everything as he liked it; tried, with a child's passion and a girl's diffidence to keep things the same in a household where everything was horribly changed.

Of course she had failed. "Man decides for himself." Poor Father. Had he seen himself deciding to forget his sorrow in drink, to let it all go . . . Sermons botched up anyhow, parish duties neglected, his daughter . . . Stop there. And yet, looking back, she thought that probably she had done her best. A child's best, where a woman's was needed. And it had all led gradually, horribly downhill to Charles Manningham.

She turned back to the glass, fighting thoughts that shamed her. He found me attractive, she had caught herself thinking. Odious . . . disgusting . . . attractive? The haggard face mocked her from the glass. Nonsense. So; man decides for himself. And I decide to stay with Sarah. After all—but it seemed a long time ago now—she had decided, once, to be dead. In a sense, everything, since that night, was unreal, post-mortem. I'm a ghost, she told herself, what I do now, concerns me alone.

But her sleep that windy January night was haunted by the old nightmare. Whose hands were they this time? Charles Manningham's, or—unspeakable—Jonathan's?

The Penrose House in Boston was in Mr. Bullfinch's Adam-style Tontine Crescent, where so many of Boston's leading Federalists lived. Jonathan had bought it for Arabella from Mr. Bullfinch's creditors early in their married life, when nothing was too good for her. Now, facing her across her Chippendale dining table, he found it hard to remember himself as that infatuated young man. "I'm sorry

I was late again," he said patiently, "the meeting ran longer than I expected."

"They always do." Arabella's mouth had taken a sulky turn this winter, and there were new lines around her eyes. "Politics ... politics ... politics! Can you think of nothing else? You're even neglecting the business for them, and I never thought I'd see that day. And your precious Sarah, for the matter of that."

"Sarah's all right; Mrs. Croston sees to that. She's improved beyond recognition this winter."

"Certainly beyond mine." There was a new bite to Arabella's voice. "Since I am not permitted to see her. My own child!"

"Do you wish to?" He asked it quietly enough, but his eyes held a challenge.

"Well ... of course ... a mother ..."

"A mother who thinks her child would be best in an asylum? I don't care what tales you tell your friends, Arabella, but don't waste them on me. It's not to see Sarah that you want to go out to Penrose. Nor yet for the pleasure of my company. So—why? Except, of course, as a means to blackmail."

"Blackmail! That's not a pretty word."

"It's not a pretty thing." He poured her a glass of madeira. "Come, Arabella, we're beyond quarrelling, you and I. We made an agreement last fall. Your allowance increased if you stayed away from Penrose till I gave you leave to return. And, to prevent the talk that troubles you so, I would come into Boston at least once a week. Admit, I've kept to my side of it."

"Of course you have, since there have been these dreary political meetings for you to go to."

"These dreary political meetings, Arabella, may decide whether the United States are to remain united or not."

"Oh, I know that." Impatiently. "It's the common talk. Mrs. Quincy was saying only the other day—"

"I'm sure she was. Do you think, if it was secret, that I would mention it to you? But the fact that the likelihood

111

of the New England states' seceding from the Union is public knowledge makes it more important, not less. I know you care nothing for politics, Bella, but had you thought of the practical aspects of secession?"

"Practical? What do you mean?" She did not sound much interested.

"Why; just this. You like money, don't you? Then think for a moment where it comes from. My entire production at the manufactury is turned over to government stuff now—to uniform cloth and blankets. If we secede and make a separate peace, who's going to buy them? And where will the money for your French silks come from then?"

"You could sell to the British."

"Never! Oh yes, I know about the brisk trade in corn and cattle that goes on across the northern borders, but don't delude yourself I'll ever join in anything of the kind. Just because our farmers feed the English troops, don't think I'm going to clothe them. I'd rather go bankrupt. And you wouldn't like that, would you? Where would your black-mail money come from then?"

"I wish you wouldn't use that word!"

He cracked two walnuts against each other in the way that had always annoyed her. "Do you know, Bella, you're getting a terrible trick of frowning. It will mar your looks if you don't take care. Where do you drink tea tonight?"

"Nowhere." She flounced to her feet. "Who invites a woman whose husband never accompanies her!"

"Good gracious." He was a man of mild expletives. "Times are changed indeed. I can remember the day—and not long past, either—when you positively urged me to stay at home and rest after my day's work. What's the matter, Bella? Are your devoted swains turning coy? I can't believe they've gone off to the wars."

"Well—have you?"

He laughed and rose to his feet. "You win, as always. So—since it seems to be all I'm good for—if you will excuse me, I will return to my politics."

NINE

"'The spring's on its way at last." Jonathan had just returned from Boston and was stamping snow from his boots under the front portico.

"Yes, that's what Job says." Kate followed Sarah, who had run headlong downstairs to throw open the front door and jump into his arms. "We found a green plant where it's thawing by the river," she went on. "Job says it's called skunk cabbage. Of all the unromantic names for the first green sign of spring!"

Jonathan laughed. "You ought to know by now, Kate, that we're an unromantic lot, we Americans. And none the worse for that. I remember one time when I was in England, I happened on a book of poetry called *Lyrical Ballads*, and a fine lot of nonsense it was, too. Though come to think of it, there was one about a sailor that had something to it. What was it called?"

"*The Ancient Mariner*, I expect. It's one of my favourites. But what's the news in town?"

"Bad—for us." He hung his heavy overcoat in the closet beside the front door. "And good for you. The last word is that the Allies crossed the French border in January. God knows what has happened since then, but it can only be a matter of time till Napoleon's beaten, and then; God help us Americans."

"As bad as that?" And then, aware of the listening child: "Sarah, honey, run upstairs and fetch your father's slippers."

"I think so. Well; you're English. You must know. So far, they've been fighting us with their hands tied behind their backs. Once the whole British Navy is free to turn its attention this way, we're finished. Anything may happen. I

113

even wonder whether I should not send you and Sarah away. Inland somewhere."

"No!" It came out louder than she intended. "No—" more calmly now. "Don't do that. Surely they'll not attack Boston, of all places?"

"Probably not. God knows it would be a gamble. To read the Boston *Patriot*, or listen to the talk in town, you would think our citizens would welcome them with open arms. And a fine reversal of our Boston Tea Party that would be! But it might so easily work the other way. An English landing on American territory might unite the country against them as nothing else could. Even here, I doubt if Pickering and his friends would sit quietly by and watch the redcoats take over the town. Certainly, if you saw the fortifications going up, and the militia at their drill on the Common, you'd think we meant to strike a blow for ourselves. But when you read the papers!"

"You've told me often enough not to take them too seriously. Anyway, even if the worst should happen, Sarah and I should be safe enough out here." She was angry with herself as she said it. Here was her chance to get away, and what was she doing? "I'm sure it would be bad for Sarah to move her," she went on. "She's coming along so well. Do you know, I think she can read?"

"Read when she can't talk? Are you serious?"

"Not can't talk; won't. I'm sure she could if she wanted to. And as to reading; it began with the piano, of course. She doesn't even pretend now that she can't read music. Why, that book of songs from the opera you brought back from Boston last month—she was playing them through two days later. Before I'd learned them myself. Most of our music is songs; I can't think that while she's learned the notes she's taken no notice of the words. And, another thing. You know I always read aloud to her when she's in bed? I've never known how much of it she takes in, but it seems to soothe her, to help her get off to sleep."

"Yes. We've not had a screaming fit for ages."

"No, thank God. Yesterday, just when I'd sat down with

The Pilgrim's Progress, Prue called me away. There was a travelling peddler at the door and Mrs. Peters was having trouble getting rid of him. It took me a little while, and I expected trouble when I got back, tears at least. But there was Sarah curled up as snug as you please in bed, looking as if butter wouldn't melt in her mouth. And two pages had been turned in the book. It was an exciting bit we were at; the Hill Difficulty. I think she just read on. Of course, I pretended to have noticed nothing, and picked up where I had left off. And, do you know, just for a moment I thought she was going to say something, to tell me she had got further than that. But of course she didn't—she just wriggled a bit while I read it all over again. I'm sure she can read. And I'm sure we should do nothing to set her back. Just think of taking her away from her piano . . ."

"I know. I've thought of that. Well, for the moment, we'll chance it. But have things packed for the two of you, so that if there should be a landing, I can get you away at once. I've a cottage near Northampton you could go to. And— just think what the sight and sound of fighting might do to her—quite apart from the risk. I don't need to tell you . . ."

"No." Her hands clenched at the memory of old Mac lying on the cold ground; at all the memories.

"I'm sorry: I'm a wretch to remind you. Whatever happens, you and Sarah shall be spared that."

"Thank you." Suddenly, his consideration was more than she could bear. "Sarah!" She turned away to hide a quick start of tears. "Where are those slippers?"

Only much later, lying sleepless while the wild March wind blew sleet against her window, had she time to be angry with herself. Here had been the perfect chance to get away, and she had dodged it. And don't pretend it was for Sarah's sake, she told herself, because I won't believe you.

The anniversary of the taking of York came and went. Soon, Kate would have been a whole year at Penrose. "The best year of Sarah's life," said Jonathan, commenting on this over dinner one mild night early in May. "But it's fantastic that you have never even seen Boston in all this time. Now the snow has gone we really must arrange it. Sarah used to love driving into town with me. Do you think, now—"

"I don't know." She was certainly not going to mention Arabella before he did. "It's going so well; why chance spoiling it? And, truly, I don't in the least mind staying quietly here. It suits me."

"It certainly does."

"Oh—I didn't mean." Blushing angrily, she wondered if he really thought she had been fishing for the compliment. But, of course, it was true; her glass told her that she was a different creature from the haggard, anxious-eyed young woman who had arrived here a year ago. "It suits us both," she said now. "I'd as soon not make any changes till Sarah begins to speak."

She thought that had settled it, but a few weeks later he came home from the mill with a different suggestion. "What would you two think of an outing in the carriage to-morrow? Not Boston—" What had he seen in Sarah's face? "I'm driving up to Lynn to look at a shoe manufactury that's for sale there. If you ladies cared for a look at the sea we could drive on across the beach to Nahant, dine at the hotel in Lynn, and still be home not much after bedtime. It will mean an early start, of course, but I know early rising is nothing to you two. My business at Lynn won't take me more than an hour or so, and, if you liked, the carriage could take you on for a run on the sand. You always loved that, didn't you, pet?"

For a moment, Kate really thought Sarah would answer him with words as well as with the glowing smile that lit up her face.

Jonathan, too, waited for a moment before he went on: "That's settled then." If he was disappointed, he took care not to show it. "We'll start at six and have a second break-fast at Lynn. You'll like that, won't you, Sarah?"

Silence again, and the beaming smile. "The trouble is," he said later to Kate, "she manages so well without speaking.

Do you sometimes think that we make it too easy for her? Should we drive her into a position where she must speak?"

"No." Violently. "I think it might be disastrous. Leave it to time, Mr. Penrose, I beg of you."

"I thought you were to call me Jonathan."

"I'm sorry; I quite forgot." And that was a lie, if ever there was one. She had hoped to slip back, without comment, into a more formal relationship. Sour consolation to tell herself that he would never have remarked on it if he had had the slightest idea of how she felt about him.

Luckily, he had found a batch of newspapers awaiting him, and it was an accepted thing that on these occasions he would read his way through dinner, pausing from time to time to give her the more striking bits of news. So tonight, she was free to be angry with herself, as she had all day, because instead of trying to avoid tomorrow's expedition, she was looking forward to it. She ought to plead headache, illness, anything to avoid the insidious pleasure of a whole day with him. But—Sarah. Impossible to deny her the treat to which she, too, was obviously looking forward. And unlikely that Jonathan would take her alone. So, once more, there it was, an impossible situation which might just as well be enjoyed. After all, there would be the rest of her life to be miserable.

In fact, there was delicious excitement in the breach of a year's routine. She and Sarah were up in the half-light, and Sarah, usually a dawdling dresser, was like quicksilver, managing buttons and bootlaces with an easy assurance that would have amazed Mrs. Peters.

They found Jonathan already in the dining room, drinking coffee by candlelight, and Kate was soon smiling at the sight of Sarah feeding herself fried ham and buckwheat cakes as if it was the most natural thing in the world. She caught Jonathan's eye. "We must do this more often," he said.

"Yes . . ." A shade doubtfully. "Maybe. If all goes well."

"Pessimist! Of course all will go well. We're going to have a splendid day, aren't we, Sarah?"

117

It was delicious to drive off into a morning still glistening with dew, and wreathed, here and there, in early mist. Women and children were pouring into the factory when they passed it, and Kate was aware of curious glances, and of Sarah, equally curious, staring back. "Goodness me, some of them are no bigger than you, Sarah!" And then, to Jonathan. "Poor things, do they work all day?"

"Most places, yes, but not here. My friends think I'm crazy, but I have a schoolmaster for the little ones. They have two hours off a day for lessons, and I reckon it pays me one hundred per cent. We have fewer accidents than any factory in the district, and fewer absentees too. A little learning works like a charm, I find, and pays dividends."

The carriage was rattling downhill now, along beside the Penrose River, and already they were beyond the limit of Kate's and Sarah's walks. Sarah, sitting on her father's knee so as to see out better, was singing quietly to herself, a sure sign of excitement and happiness, but Kate could not help a pang, as they passed an orchard in full blossom, to think of the excited exclamations that should be bursting from her.

Perhaps today . . . She deliberately suppressed the thought. Even to think about it seemed somehow, to be putting pressure on the child, and pressure, she was sure, was the worst possible thing for her.

"We'll be in Cambridge soon." Jonathan settled Sarah more comfortably on his knee. "I wish we could stop to show you Harvard College, Kate, but that will have to wait for another time. The sooner we get to Lynn, the sooner you'll be on the shore, eh, Sarah?"

But he called to Job to slow down the carriage as they drove through Harvard Square, so that Kate could have a glimpse of the college yard, with boys' figures hurrying this way and that among the trees. "Late for prayers, I expect," said Jonathan. "And there's the Charles River—named for your King Charles, Kate. It makes our Penrose look a mere stream, doesn't it? And if you keep watching you'll soon

118

see Trimountain Hill, the one that gave Boston its old name. We keep to this side of the river for Lynn, though. You'll be glad of your second breakfast when we get there, won't you, puss?" He tweaked Sarah's ear and she giggled up at him delightedly.

It was high morning when Job set Kate and Sarah down on the edge of the golden, sandy beach. "The spouting horn's down that way, Miss Kate," he said. "Over the rocks. Or if you don't want to bother with that, I'll just look for you here when I've fetched Mr Jonathan."

"Yes, do, Job. We'll have plenty to do here, I'm sure." Sarah had already darted off across the smooth, hard sand. "Is it safe, Job?"

"As houses. The tide's falling, I reckon, and you've not a thing in the world to fret over. Now, later in the season, it would be quite another matter. This is a great summer jaunt for the nobs; they even talk of building a big hotel out there on Nahant point. But this time of year you'll have the place to yourselves. And no need to be looking for us for a couple of hours or more; I know Mr. Jonathan said he'd only be half an hour, but he's always longer than he says, is the master."

"Thank you, Job. We'll be happy as larks, won't we, Sarah?" She had darted back with a handful of shells. "Good-by, Job, don't hurry back on our account."

The sun was high overhead now and already it was as hot as the best kind of English summer day, the fierceness of the sun tempered by a fresh breeze off the sea. "Look, Sarah, there's a ship, a big one. I wonder what she is?" Strange to think she was probably English, waiting to pounce, as the *Shannon* had on the *Chesapeake*. But Sarah was not interested in anything so distant as the graceful, white-winged ship. She had discovered that a kind of cradle-shaped shell was plentiful on the beach and was busy collecting them to lay out in one of her long, purposeless lines. Then, suddenly tiring of this, she came tugging at Kate's hand to persuade her down to the very edge of the sea, where big Atlantic breakers came screaming in and she had to run away, with squeals of joy, to escape getting her feet wet.

It seemed a hazardous pastime to Kate, so she found them a couple of flat pieces of driftwood with which to dig. This was an immediate success, and they were soon both absorbedly at work building a castle: "Like Doubting Castle, Sarah, in your picture book."

A flash of Sarah's big gray eyes showed that she had understood the reference to the picture in her *Pilgrim's Progress* and she began molding turrets on the solid base Kate had helped her build. She was exquisitely happy, absorbed . . . She needs to make things, Kate thought . . . I must think of something like this for her to do at home.

They were both of them extremely sandy by the time the castle was finished. Sarah's hair was a mass of tangled curls and Kate did not think her own could be much tidier. "Now, shall we find some shells and seaweed to decorate it with, Sarah?" Her own back was aching with the unaccustomed stooping, and even active little Sarah was obviously glad to straighten up and move away toward the sea, picking up here a bright green strand of seaweed and there a delicately whorling shell.

It was wonderfully peaceful on the beach. They had not seen a soul all morning and Kate felt the winter's tensions easing in her as she drifted here and there, further now from Sarah, making a pleasant pretense of hunting for shells. With the sun hot on her back and the sea for music, it was easy to forget everything in a delicious, unreasoning surge of happiness. Vaguely, contentedly, she began to sing one of the nursery rhymes Sarah loved so, *Oranges and Lemons*.

"Here comes a candle to light you to bed,
    Here comes—"

She stopped. What was that other noise, mixed up in the roar of the breakers? A horse—horses—driven fast. Surely it was early still for Jonathan? Much more likely that someone else had had the same idea as they. She began to move back toward Sarah, who was some way off on the far side of their castle, when a chaise emerged onto the beach, driven tandem and at breakneck speed.

"Sarah! Stay where you are!" Had the child heard the carriage over the sound of the sea? Absurd, of course, to be frightened—with miles of golden sand spread out before it, why should one chaise be a danger to Sarah?

But she did not like the way the driver was handling his horses. There was something at once ruthless and flamboyant about his use of the whip. Ah—Sarah had seen the carriage and was standing quite still, watching it. That was all right then.

Or—was it? Another crack of the long whip, and Kate saw that the chaise had changed direction and was heading straight for their castle, and—Sarah had seen too. Suddenly she darted forward, with the speed of a mad thing, to stand, a tiny dauntless figure, directly between chaise and castle.

Kate, much further off, was running forward, was screaming at once to Sarah and to the unknown driver. Had he even seen Sarah? Would he stop? Could he stop? Was he even trying to? For an endless, horrible few moments it seemed that he would drive right over the motionless child, then, at the last instant, he swerved his horses sideways, pulled them to a stop, and shouted furiously at Sarah.

Kate could not hear the words, but their purport was obvious enough; he was in a blind rage at the risk he had run. His companion, a woman, leaned forward apparently to intervene, and then stopped, gazing in amazement at Sarah.

"Sarah!" As she approached at a breathless run, it was the first thing Kate heard, in Arabella's unmistakable voice.

Then she stopped, to stare, in a kind of tranced horror at the driver. "Nearly killed the lot of us," he was saying, his fury emphasizing an English accent. "Blithering little fool." And then, becoming aware of Kate: "Why don't you keep your idiot child in some kind of control, my good woman?"

It was odd to feel oneself tremble, to know one was white as a sheet. Never, in all her nightmares had she imagined a meeting like this. He had not recognized her yet. Was there any hope, any chance that he might not? Her name, after all, was different. But . . . Arabella?

"Well, have you nothing to say for yourself? You might have ruined as good a pair of bays as you'll find this side of the Atlantic; you and that cretin of yours."

"Not mine." What an absurd thing to say. "Mrs. Penrose's." And then, with stiff despair. "How do you do, ma'am?"

"I've never had such a fright in my life!" Arabella, too, was furious. "What in creation's name are you doing here, Mrs. Croston? It's not your fault that the child wasn't killed!"

And are you sorry she was not? The thought went through Kate's mind like angry lightning. But she managed to speak coolly enough. "Mr. Penrose is to pick us up here; he has business in Lynn." What else was there to say? Not for anything would she apologize, when she knew as well as Arabella must that it was only her companion's obstinacy that had endangered the child. "Sarah and I built that castle," she went on with a calm she was very far from feeling. "I think she loves it a little."

"Loves it!"

But Arabella's scornful outburst was interrupted by her companion. "You're English," he said. "You're—Good God—" At least he was as appalled as she. "Miss Ffynch."

"No, Captain Manningham, Mrs. Croston." Surely, for his own sake, he would say nothing. So—to Arabella: "Captain Manningham and I were very slightly acquainted in England."

"Very slightly!" His sneer was familiar as despair. But—he must have been thinking fast. Now, at all events, he took his cue. "Yes," he turned to Arabella. "I knew Mrs. Croston's father—a little." His tone dismissed Kate as beneath his interest, and he turned to look at Sarah, who appeared to have forgotten all about them and was busy arranging her collection of shells along the castle's battlements. "So this is the poor child?" Contempt mingled with curiosity in his tone. But more significant to Kate than either was the familiarity with which he spoke to Arabella.

"What are you doing here?" Kate's question to him came out with a bluntness that surprised herself.

"What business is it of yours?" This was Arabella, her colour becomingly high, her eyes flashing.

But Charles Manningham merely laughed and freed one hand from the reins to put it over hers in an oddly intimate gesture. "No need to fly into a pet, Mrs. Penrose. Your estimable nursemaid doubtless thinks she has caught me red-handed, a spy unmasked. Though it raises, does it not, a rather interesting question of your own allegiance, Mrs. Croston? I might well return your question. If I were interested, which, frankly, I am not. Your affairs are—your affairs." His bright eye, fixed on hers, seemed to make of this at once a threat and a promise. "As to me: you see me before you that miserable creature a prisoner of war. I was taken, by pure bad luck, at Fort Niagara."

"Niagara! You were there!" Anger in Kate's voice reflected her memory of Mrs. Mason, who was still gravely ill from shock and exposure.

"Yes, for my sins." He laughed his boyish laugh. "My dear Miss Ffynch—I beg your pardon, Mrs. Crosway—don't tell me you have turned Yankee since last we met."

How could he refer to that night? Angrily aware of a sudden rush of colour and of Arabella's eyes on her, she said merely, "I cannot imagine that my ideas are of the slightest interest to you, Captain Manningham."

"No. Why should they be?" Arabella leaned forward, her eyes bright with anger under the plumed hat that matched her riding habit. "And now, Mrs. Croston, if you have quite satisfied yourself that I am not helping a prisoner to escape, or whatever melodramatic notion you have been entertaining, perhaps you will be so good as to pay a little attention to the child so that we may be on our way in safety. The horses will take cold, standing so long." And then, a casual afterthought: "Best, perhaps, that we say nothing of this affair. Sarah seems to mind you—God knows why—and I do

123

not particularly want to get you dismissed, which must be the outcome if I tell Mr. Penrose how careless you are with her."

Was this a threat, or a bribe, or a bit of both? Kate gave her look for look. "I shall tell Mr. Penrose myself," she said. "He must do what he thinks best for Sarah."

"Of course." And then, with malicious carelessness: "But if you'll be advised by me, Mrs. Croston, you'll at least comb your hair—and the child's—before Jonathan joins you." And as an afterthought. "How are you, Sarah?"

Kate's nails bit deep into the palms of her hands. Even through the shock of this meeting she had been aware of a deep undercurrent of delight because Sarah had borne it so well. Now, would her mother's direct address spoil everything? But Sarah merely lifted her eyes from her busy hands to look past Arabella for a moment with that strange, unfocused stare of hers that seemed always to see something on the far horizon, then bent again to her work of decoration.

Arabella shrugged. "You see what I mean," she said to Manningham. "Quite hopeless."

"Poor little thing." He said it entirely without interest. Then, with the nod that dismisses a servant: "Good-by, Mrs. Crossley. I doubt if we will meet again." He whipped up his horses without giving her a chance to reply and drove off at the old furious speed across the beach.

Kate's first thought, even now, was for Sarah. But—miraculous sign of the extent of her recovery—the meeting seemed to have made little or no impression on her. She was already hard at work smoothing out the horses' tracks, which crossed the patch of sand she had designed for her castle's garden. Helping her, with hands that trembled, Kate's thoughts whirled chaotically through the implications of this horrible meeting. Charles Manningham, the devil of her nightmares, here. Even if he said nothing of what had passed between them, was not she in honour bound to do so? Of course she was. She heard her own voice, clear and satisfyingly steady: "I shall tell Mr. Penrose myself."

But—what would she tell him? She put gritty hands to her hot cheeks. If she could not bring herself, except in those nightmares, to think of what had happened, how imagine telling Jonathan? And yet, face it, somehow, she must make him see that Manningham was no companion for Arabella.

Memory, flashing from scene to scene, brought up now the picture of Manningham's hand set firmly, possessively, on Arabella's. He was sure of her. Well, there had never been any doubt about Manningham's charm—or his looks, for the matter of that. She remembered—she would rather not remember how she had felt about him, once, herself. But no doubt about it, he and Arabella had made a striking pair and had been, it was subtly evident, pleasantly aware of this themselves.

Well then, was it not already too late to warn Jonathan? Was not the kindest thing to say nothing, to spare him the knowledge of betrayal? Here was a temptation worthy of Bunyan's devil. Let it go; do nothing; stay quiet; least said soonest mended. Might that not really be best? But no, here her own honesty brought her up against a crucial point; Manningham might have charmed Arabella, but that, at present, was as far as it went. The hand on hers, the little liberties he had taken with her were those of a hopeful, not of a successful lover.

So; there it was. It was still possible to save something for Jonathan. For Jonathan, who despite the calls of the factory and his affection for Sarah, had gone so faithfully all winter through snow and storm to see his wife in Boston. Jonathan whose very silence about Arabella must spell adoration. And why not? Another of those devilish little pictures sprang into Kate's mind; Arabella in Manningham's chaise; her dark green riding habit setting off her golden hair, the plume of her hat throwing up the clear colour of her cheek. No wonder if Jonathan adored her without reason. And no doubt either; no doubt, at least, worth allowing oneself, of where her duty lay.

She would tell him, of course; but not all. Surely that she might spare herself? And, in the meanwhile, she remembered Arabella's parting words and called Sarah: "Come here, love. It's time we tidied ourselves a little. Your father should be here directly. Won't he be pleased with our splendid castle?"

For once, Sarah submitted patiently to the combing of her tangled, wiry curls, and let Kate brush the worst of the sand off her muslin. But: "We're a pretty pair of raga-muffins, I'm afraid," said Kate ruefully, surveying her own reflection in the tiny glass she carried in her pocket. "Never mind, love; I don't suppose your father will notice."

Although she had taken the whole incident so calmly, it had had its effect, and Sarah clung close to Kate from then on, her bright spirits dimmed. The carriage arrived at last—very late, as Job had predicted, with Jonathan cheerfully apologetic. "I had a good notion, though," he told Kate. "Job has procured us the makings of a picnic luncheon which we can eat here on the beach, or on the way home if you'd rather. I thought you ladies might prefer it to the Lynn Hotel?"

"What a splendid plan." Among her other worries had been the idea of Sarah confronted with the noisy dining room of a small hotel. Besides, they might even meet Arabella and Manningham there before she had a chance to speak to Jonathan.

Instead, they found a secluded spot on the edge of a blossoming apple orchard and ate cold ham and rolls and spicy apple turnovers among the whirr of insects new-awake for spring. To Kate's relief, the morning's air and exercise had given Sarah such an appetite that she fell to with a will. But her father had noticed the change in her, the almost apathetic way she received his congratulations on that mag-nificent castle. When lunch was over, he sent her and Job— a great friend of hers—to pack the remnants back into the carriage, then turned to Kate. "Is she just tired?" he asked. "Or is there more to it?"

"More, I'm afraid." How uncomfortably quick he was. "She was nearly run down on the beach by a carriage." This was extraordinarily difficult. And, after an angry exclamation, he was looking at her as if he knew there was more to come. "Mrs. Penrose was in it," she went on painfully, "and a friend of hers, an Englishman, Captain Manningham. A prisoner of war."

"And they nearly ran Sarah down?" She knew that quiet rage of his.

"Of course they had no idea who she was." This must, horribly, be said as soon as possible. "The trouble was—Captain Manningham saw our castle—thought it would be entertaining, I suppose, to drive through it. And Sarah stopped him."

"Stopped him?"

"She stood in front of it. I've never been so frightened in my life. I thought . . . I was too far away to do anything. It was inexcusable of me."

"No—why? A perfectly safe beach." He threw it off carelessly, to return to the main point. "And she stopped him?"

"She just stood there. He came on, expecting her to run; it was—terrifying. She didn't move; just stood and looked at him. At the last moment, he swerved, missed her, missed the castle. Thank God."

"Yes. Do you think she doesn't know how to be afraid?"

"Perhaps. There was that time I found her asleep over the river . . . But—one good thing's come of this—of course she was upset—who wouldn't be? But not, I think—" how impossibly difficult it was . . .

"Not by her mother, you're trying to say?"

"Yes. She hardly seemed to notice her—went straight back to work on the castle. It was only afterward that she seemed . . . well, subdued. And, of course, it's been a tiring day. I expect she will fall fast asleep on the drive home." She was talking on about Sarah because she could not find words for the other thing she had to say.

He laughed, his face nearly normal again. "Well, let us devoutly hope she does, poor lamb. Sometimes, Kate, I despair of her ever speaking. She did not shout, or cry out at the carriage?"

127

"Nothing. Not a word. Just stood there, looking at them come. But—there's something else. Something I ought to tell you. I don't want to."

"Oh?"

"Yes. It's this." She bolted into it. "I knew Captain Manningham, a little, in England. I don't want to talk about it, but—I wonder if he's a safe friend for Mrs. Penrose."

"Safe? For Arabella? My dear Kate, surely you must realize that my wife is very well able to look after herself."

"I'm sorry." Furiously now, she wished she had not spoken. "I thought it my duty to speak. He was a friend of my father's . . . I . . . I don't think he's to be trusted." What could she say to put him on his guard, without saying too much? "I always thought he helped ruin my father—encouraged him to drink more than he should. He was at home, you see, wounded, with nothing to do . . ."

"I'm sorry." He had seen how hard this was for her to say. "And—thank you for the warning." He rose to his feet and held out his hand to help her up. "I'll—look into Captain Manningham." And then, as Sarah and Job came laughing back from the carriage. "All ready? Good then, let's go."

Bending to pick up the carriage rug they had sat on, Kate could only hope that the hot rush of blood to her face was less obvious than it felt. Horrible that his casual touch could do this to her; shaming that he so obviously felt nothing of the kind.

Nonsense, she told herself; that's the only reason you can stay with him.

TEN

THEY MADE GOOD TIME ON THE WAY HOME, returning to
Penrose just as the shadows were lengthening and the day's
sounds dying toward dusk. Sarah had fallen asleep with her
head in Kate's lap, and Jonathan picked her up gently so as
not to wake her. "Put the carriage away, Job," he said, "and
have the boy get out my horse. I'm riding to Boston
tonight."

"Yassuh, Mr. Jonathan, but I'll gladly drive you if you'd
liever."

"No, thanks. The ride will do me good after sitting in the
carriage all day."

"You'll take something to eat before you go?" Kate asked,
and then wished she had not.

"No, thank you. I've no doubt there will be a supper for
me in Boston. Arabella keeps open house these days."

And indeed, when he rode into the Tontine Crescent soon
after eight o'clock, it was to see flares burning at the door of
his house and a carriage in the act of setting down guests.

Arabella greeted him with her usual cool aplomb, almost
as if he had been another guest. "Jonathan! I hardly expected you so late."

"And not dressed for a party either. You must forgive
me."

"Oh, it's nothing; just a few friends and a little music."
But the house was decorated throughout with flowers from
the Botanical Gardens and the "few friends" kept on coming
until there must have been thirty or forty of them in the
two big rooms that could be thrown together on the main
floor.

Downstairs, Jonathan found the usual lavish spread of
buffet food for the gentlemen, and found too an old Har-

vard friend of his already sampling the lobster and pink champagne.

"Josiah, you're the very man I hoped to see." Jonathan refilled his friend's glass and helped himself more modestly to porter.

"Delighted to hear it, Jon. What can I do for you?" He was in that happy state when sobriety is just ebbing away, and nothing else matters.

"You know everyone in town, Josh; tell me about an Englishman—a prisoner of war called Manningham."

"Charles Manningham?" Josiah swept the now crowded room with his wide half-focused stare. "Must be upstairs still—devil of a ladies' man! Handsome, I reckon, if you like them long-haired and stinking of scent. Well—you know the English. Good family, to hear him talk, but short on the dollars—you know the kind of thing—take a lift in your hackney—take just about anything, if you ask me, and not much giving. Not much sign of getting his exchange, either, and going back to the fighting. Well, can't say I blame him for that; nothing elegant about what's going on up there at Niagara; I reckon he's had enough. Besides—he's got . . . interests here. Plenty of them. No need for you to worry, Jon—" This with the formidable frankness of the near-drunk. "It's marriage he's after, and the more dollars the better."

"I see. And will he succeed, do you think?"

"Bound to, if he can just hang on here long enough. Far as I can see, the girls are all mad for him: 'Such an air,' you know, 'such manners.' He kisses their hands." Josiah found this so exquisitely funny that he had to have recourse to his champagne glass to recover himself. "There he is, just come in at the doorway. Pretty, ain't he? Shall I make you known to him?"

"No, thanks, Josiah. I think I'll wait a little." The last thing he wanted was to seem unduly interested in Manningham. "Tell me instead what's new in town?"

"Nothing good, I can tell you. How could there be? What's the use of old Granny Madison taking off his embargo, now the English are blockading us? Mark my words, Jon, there will be bankruptcies by the score if we don't see the end of this war soon. It's all very well for you with your contracts for uniform cloth, but what about the rest of us? I tell you, it breaks my heart to go down State Street and see the ships rotting in the harbour. You'd not think, to see her now, that our poor *Constitution* had ever sunk the *Guerrière*. Or shown the blasted British a clean pair of heels this winter. But look at her now! And where's the end of it? Answer me that. What are they doing, down there in Washington, but talk? A separate peace, that's what we need, and the sooner the better."

"And destroy the Union? Have you thought what that would mean? The blockade's hurting us, it's true, but why? Because it interrupts our trade with the southern states. Well then, break up the Union, and where are you? Where's your trade then?"

"Good God, Jon! Don't tell me you've turned Republican? Why—your old dad would turn in his grave if he could hear you talk like that."

"You forget that my father sacrificed everything he had for the cause of freedom and union."

"Everything your old grandfather hadn't sacrificed for the other side, eh?" But to Jonathan's relief he was losing interest in the subject. As soon fetch water in a sieve as argue politics with a drunken man. Jonathan refilled his champagne glass and left him.

Manningham was at the far end of the long buffet table now, helping himself liberally to smoked oysters. Jonathan debated for a moment whether to go up and speak to him, but decided against it. The sight of him, exquisitely dressed, evidently satisfied with himself, and making the most of a free meal, brought too forcibly to mind what he had nearly done to Sarah that morning. And—one did not make scenes in one's own house. He left the room quietly and went upstairs to find Arabella.

The floor had been cleared for dancing, and the master of ceremonies was summoning the gentlemen to lead the ladies out for a cotillion. To Jonathan's rather savage amusement, the first strains of music brought Manningham hurrying upstairs to claim the hand of a signally plain Miss Betterton whose father owned several successful privateers. Arabella, on the other hand, did not seem to be dancing, and Jonathan crossed the floor to join her. "You do not dance?"

"The floor's quite full enough as it is. Besides, I've had an exhausting day. I want to talk to you, Jonathan."

"Curiously enough, I want to talk to you too. But perhaps we had better delay the pleasure until your guests are gone."

"Our guests, surely?"

"I don't recollect inviting them. I can tell you one, at least, who would not be here if I had had the issuing of the invitations. I don't like to see you connive at fortune-hunting, Arabella."

"What do you mean?" And then, following his glance to where Manningham was leading his plain partner down the set. "Nonsense. Nothing of the kind." She was oddly emphatic about it. "He does it, if you must know, as a favour to me. Since you are never here to help me with my parties, I just have to do the best I can."

"And a very elegant best it seems to be."

If she noticed the irony in his voice, she chose to ignore it. "Thank you, Jonathan. But you have brought up the very thing I wished to discuss with you." She looked around. The dance was set to go on for some time longer and they were, for the moment, as good as alone in the room. "I'd rather get it over with now, if it's all the same to you. It's —painful, Jon, I should warn you."

"If you mean to break it to me that your English friend over there nearly killed our daughter this morning, I know it already."

"Of course. Mrs. Croston would have had to tell you that. I just wonder what else she chose to tell you."

"What else?" He would not get angry. "If you really

132

want to know, Arabella, she told me she thought it very encouraging that Sarah took the whole scene so well."

"Mighty handsome of her, I'm sure." And then, on a totally different note. "Jonathan, don't let us quarrel. I've something I feel it my duty to tell you, and frankly, I don't like doing it. Please help me."

"Of course. I'm sorry, Bella, I don't want to quarrel either." Just for a moment, then, pleading with him, she had been the girl he had married, eager to please, unsure of herself, the young girl who had disappeared somehow into the accomplished woman of the world.

"Thank you." She stopped to look around again, but the dancing was still going full tilt, while men's faces grew red and girls' hair began to tangle becomingly or otherwise on their shoulders. "It's about Mrs. Croston," she said. "Did she tell you that she knew Manningham in England?"

"Yes, she did."

"Poor girl; she'd know she had to." It sounded like genuine sympathy. "But I guess that was all she told you."

"No. She said she thought he had ruined her father."

Now Arabella laughed. "Clever." She said it almost with approval. "Not a bad try. You can't help being sorry for her. To come all this way; to think she had lived it down; and then . . . Almost, Jonathan, I wonder if we should pretend we had never discovered."

"Discovered what?"

"Why—the truth about Mrs. Croston. Had you never wondered—I know I have, many times—how she—a minister's daughter, gently bred, came to be wandering around Canada as the wife of a noncommissioned officer?"

Of course he had. "I look on that as entirely her own affair," he said.

"Very quixotic, I'm sure. And so you gave her the charge of our child—a woman whose misconduct broke her father's heart. I'm sorry, Jon, but you've got to know. To leave her in charge of Sarah . . . it's impossible. She was notorious. Everyone loved her father, Manningham says. They did their best to keep it from him. Why—she made the most

133

shameless advances even to him—to Manningham: that's how, in the end, it happened. Her father was asleep—he was an old man and drank a little more than was good for him. Manningham had gone on visiting him because he could think of no explanation for leaving off. She—no, I can't tell you what she was doing, Jon, when her father woke up. The sight killed him. And do you know what she did? Packed up everything she could lay her hands on and left the house that night; left poor Charles to make the funeral arrangements. How she came to take up with Sergeant Croston, God knows, but I suppose she thought herself lucky to achieve any marriage, however sordid. Of course, she may have had her reasons. So—there's the paragon of virtue you engaged to look after your daughter."

He would not let her see how she had shaken him. "It's merely his word against hers."

"His word, if you like—but backed up by a pretty shady set of circumstances. Of course I may be doing Mrs. Croston an injustice—and you too, for the matter of that. Perhaps, before you took her on to look after Sarah, she did explain to you just how she came to be ragamuffining it about Canada with a parcel of dirty soldiers? Perhaps you did see those papers of hers. Anyway, why should Charles Manningham lie about her? He was most reluctant to say anything at all, but I could see that the sight of her had shaken him. I forced him to speak; after all, I have a responsibility for Sarah, though by the way you treat me you'd never think so. A fine kind of guardian she seems, anyway, letting the child run into all kinds of dangers—the river one day—alone on the beach another. I don't like to have to tell you this, Jon, but she wasn't even in sight when we drove on to the beach. What more likely than that she was keeping some sordid assignation? A woman like her will find men anywhere. Her poor father had to stop keeping a manservant toward the end."

It was horrible, but he was almost convinced. As she said, why should Charles Manningham lie? And, against his will, he remembered something Kate had said about helping her father look after his horse, because they had no groom. But—"I don't believe it." He said it with more certainty than he felt.

Arabella shrugged. "It's your affair. You've taken the charge of Sarah out of my hands. You must make your own decisions about it. But—she's at an age when a child is easily influenced—and—she seems to dote on Mrs. Croston. Who knows what sights she is seeing when you are away at the factory? What ideas she is getting? Mrs. Peters is as stupid as she can hold together; she thinks of nothing but preserves and beeswax. Anything could be happening in that house all day, and you none the wiser. What is happening tonight, do you think? Old Job is black, of course, but judging by what Manningham told me, that might merely be an added attraction."

"Stop it!" He could stand no more. Besides: "It's impossible. In Canada . . . on the journey here . . . I would have seen some sign . . ."

"You, Jon?" Now she was laughing at him. "You! What do you know of women? What would you see, armoured in your New England morality? You don't think she would have been so foolish as to set her cap at you, surely? Why—an expert like her would know your kind at sight. I expect that's why she has felt so safe with you. But—think a little—were there not occasions on the journey when she pleaded fatigue and went to bed early?"

He felt as if the ground was shaking under his feet. But, hedging: "And what, pray, do you mean by 'my kind'?"

She smiled at him and turned away, throwing it back at him over her shoulder. "The cold kind, Jonathan. The frozen New England kind. And now, if you will excuse me, it is time I was looking after my guests."

The cotillion was over. Charles Manningham was approaching from the other side of the room. He ought to stay, to meet him, and decide for himself what his word was worth. But—he could not trust himself to do so. Horrible pictures were flashing through his mind. Kate, always so cool, so elegant—Kate making obscene advances to that

English fop? "I can't tell you what she was doing." No need for Arabella to tell him, when his imagination did so in unspeakable detail.

It was all false as hell. Arabella had lied to him often enough before. Why should he believe her now, or her fortune-hunting Engishman? The answer came horribly pat. He had known, this morning, that Kate was not telling him everything. He knew her so well, knew every inflection of her voice . . . of course he had been aware that there was more to it than she chose to tell. Or—did he know her at all? Would he ever understand about women? Arabella had touched a sore point here. He had been a fool before. How convince himself that he was not again?

The ride out to Penrose seemed to take hours, and yet, in a way, he did not want to get there. And yet again, anything would be better than these nightmare imaginings. Job and the black boy who helped him with the horses had their quarters over the stables. It was perfectly true that, by using the servants' stairs, Kate could visit either of them without any chance of discovery. It was impossible. He would not believe it. He would not even think about it. He could not stop. The pictures would flash into his mind, and, with them, horribly apropos, memory of the time when, as a very young ship's officer, he had agreed to make a night of it with a group of friends. They had gone ashore at Marseilles and his friends had taken him to a street in the Arab quarter . . . a street full of women. No—he surprised his horse with a savage kick—he would not remember the sordid humiliation of that night. Nor would be think of Arabella; so exquisite—a heart's desire before marriage—iceberg disillusion after. He would not think all women were like this, mere masks, hiding hell's fire or, worse, its ice beneath.

He had reached his own carriage road. Now he must decide what to do. Apparently, he had already decided. Dismounting, he led his horse up the grass beside the drive, making as little noise as possible. The house loomed up, silent and dark. That meant nothing. No sign of life in the stable yard either. Why should there be?

It reminded him of his boyhood, to stable his horse thus silently in the darkness. Nothing had changed here since he had ridden home late from a long evening's talk with friends and made not a sound as he hung up saddle and bridle on familiar hooks and bedded his horse down for the night among the well-known shapes and smells of the stable. But in him, what a change! Then, he had made a talkative night of it, perhaps, at Willard's Tavern. Now . . .

Was he really going up the steep stair that was almost a ladder to rouse Job and the boy—and whom else? The very idea of doing so was disgusting. Well then, had he ridden home for nothing? Must he go on enduring this anguish of uncertainty? He stood there, in the dark, arguing with himself. If he roused them, and found nothing, what had he proved? Why—nothing.

Of course it was all nightmare. He was overtired; imagining things. Worse still, he was letting Arabella put ideas into his head. What reason had he to trust her? And, besides—how could he not have thought of this sooner—what a strange light this all cast on her relationship with Manningham. How had he contrived to tell her things that were, apparently, too bad for her to tell her own husband? He should have stayed. He should probably have thrown Manningham into Boston Harbor. Never mind, he could do that tomorrow.

With the chill sensation of sweat on his forehead, he moved very quietly out of the stable into the yard. He had been a little mad since Arabella spoke to him. Now, thank God, he was sane again. He closed the stable door behind him and stood for a moment, enjoying the cool night air and the comfort of recovered reason.

Then, as he stood there, he became aware of a flickering light high up in the bulk of the house that faced him; high up, but coming steadily downward, showing now here, now there, as a candle was carried down the service stair past first one window then another.

He had never been so cold in his life. It was all true. Arabella was right. Manningham was right. The candle was on the first floor now. She must be moving down the long hall that led to the servants' stairway. He must not meet her here in the yard. He had things to say to her that, even in this moment of near madness, he knew must be said in private. Three huge strides across the yard and his key was in the lock of the back door. As he closed it behind him and stood, breathing hard, in the darkness, he heard her step soft on the back stair. A crack of light grew under the door at the bottom. Then it swung open and she was there, candle in hand, her hair falling in random curls around her face, her white nightgown visible under the robe that was merely clutched around her with her other hand. She had not even taken time to fasten it before hurrying to her black assignation.

"Harlot!" His exclamation, coming at her out of the darkness, startled her so that she dropped the candle. But he was already moving forward to where he knew she stood. His hand, stretched out in the darkness, touched something yielding—her breast, clearly defined under the soft stuff of the nightgown. It was the end of reason. He took her by the shoulders and pulled her furiously against him. "Wanton! Jezebel!" She was speechless with shock. "If you must do it, why not with me?" Somewhere outside it all, he could not believe this was happening. "At least, I'll have my share!" And one savage hand turned her face up to his while his lips found hers, crushing, searching, imploring.

Just for a moment, surely, the softness of her, against him, was soft for him, her lips were giving some kind of an unintelligible answer, then, she had pulled clear and her hand found his cheek in a blow that brought tears to his eyes. Then she was across the room from him, breathing hard in the darkness. They stayed like that for a moment, the silence electric.

Then, "You're either drunk, or mad," she said, "or both. But there's no time for it. Sarah's ill. Job must ride at once for the doctor. I'd ask you to go if I thought you capable."

She was moving now, feeling her way to where candles always stood ready on the dresser. She lit one with a hand that was almost steady, then turned her back on him to get a lantern down from its hook and light it. "You may apologize in the morning," she went on. "For the moment, I must fetch Job."

"Oh God, what am I to think?" As he moved forward a little, he saw her instinctive recoil. "Don't worry, I won't touch you. I . . . I don't understand anything. But—Sarah's ill? What's the matter?"

"She had one of her screaming fits earlier on. A bad one. I got her quiet at last and thought it was all over, but just now I heard her call out. She's in a kind of waking nightmare; I can't do anything with her. She needs a sedative I'm sure—anything to quiet her; it cannot but do her harm to be so violent. Mrs. Peters is with her now, but I tell you there's no time . . ."

"Of course not. I'll ride at once for the doctor. Do get back to her." And then, impatiently, seeing her hesitate: "I'm not drunk, though I may be mad. I'll get him all right, and faster than you'll wake Job. But first . . ." What could he say?

"Don't!" Impatiently. "There's no time, I tell you." And she turned, the heavy robe swirling around her, and left him there to his thoughts.

ELEVEN

THE DOCTOR'S VERDICT, when he arrived an hour or so later, was as welcome as it was surprising. "Well, of course," he looked up from the bed where Sarah lay fiery hot, tossing and turning on the pillow, "the child has the measles. They're all over the village."

"What!" Kate could hardly believe her ears. And then, remembering: "Of course, I let Prue take her out the other afternoon . . . I suppose they met some of her brothers and sisters in the woods."

"No doubt." He pulled down the crumpled nightgown to show the rash. "She's probably been sickening for it for days, but after all, she don't talk; how would you have known? A day at the shore will just have put the lid on things. You're going to have trouble with her, I'm afraid, but you'll manage, Mrs. Croston, I know that. No need to look so anxious, Jon. With careful nursing—which I know she'll get—there's no need for there to be any permanent damage." And he proceeded to give Kate detailed instructions for the handling of the case. "Rest's most important of all," he concluded. "You'll need your wits about you, Mrs. Croston, to see she gets that. For tonight, I think some laudanum drops, but we don't want to depend on them too much. I'll come again in the morning and see how she is, but you'd best make up your mind to a hard time of it. Mrs. Croston will need all the help you can give her, Jon. Perhaps Mrs. Penrose . . . ?"

"She's not had the measles," said Jonathan flatly, and rose to see the doctor out.

Returning, he found Kate settled once more in her chair by the bed. The laudanum drops were already taking effect, and Sarah was lying more quietly, her hot face pressed into the pillow. "Well?" she looked up at him, he thought challengingly, but kept her voice low, not to disturb the child.

He seemed to have had time for a thousand years of shame since that disastrous encounter in the dark. "Kate—Mrs. Croston—I don't know what to say."

"Then say nothing. After all, what's the use?" She too had had time—too much time—to think. "You've been talking, of course, to Charles Manningham. No—I don't want to discuss it." It was as final as it was quiet. "For the moment, there's nothing we can do, either of us. Sarah must come first. You know as well as I do that I am the only person who can see her through this. My fitness, or otherwise, has nothing to do with the case. Time enough for you to think about dismissing me when Sarah is better."

She was admitting it. He felt as if the life had been knocked out of him. "Shameless!" But he, too, kept it low, remembering Sarah.

A quick, angry breath and then, still quietly: "I said we'd not discuss it. Good night, Mr. Penrose."

She would not even think about it. And, indeed, she had little enough time to do so while Sarah was ill. Inevitably, Jonathan had to share the burden of the nursing with her, since he and Mrs. Peters were the only other people who could keep Sarah at all quiet in her bed. Even they were not able to do so for long at a time, and Kate was literally too busy and too tired for thought.

She slept and ate in Sarah's room, relieved that by doing so she could avoid meeting Jonathan except when he came to take over so that she could get out briefly into the hot June garden. And even there, sitting in the locust grove by the river, she was too tired to think, too tired to plan. The present was enough. The future would have to take care of itself.

Delirious, Sarah screamed endlessly. This was worse than anything Kate had been through with her. Now, at last, Kate feared for the child's reason. The doctor had insisted that Sarah be kept well covered in bed; a chill, he said, at this point might prove fatal. Kate obeyed him at first but

141

halfway through the second night, when the child came out of a drugged, restless sleep and began at once senselessly, hysterically to scream again, her every instinct rebelled. "It's all right, my poppet, I'm here." She fetched a big knitted shawl from the cupboard, wrapped Sarah up in it, picked her out of bed, and settled on the old sofa, with her in her arms. Now she could rock her, and sing to her, and feel the tension gradually drain out of the small body that weighed so alarmingly little. After that, Sarah would only sleep in her arms.

The doctor was shocked, but had to admit that this natural sleep did her infinitely more good than that induced by laudanum. "If you can do it, Mrs. Croston."

At the end of an exhausting week, he pronounced Sarah over the worst. Kate could have told him that she was. That night she had slept in her bed with Kate merely holding her hand. But her recovery was as slow as her illness had been violent. For another ten days she had to stay in her room with Kate singing to her, feeding her by spoonfuls, like a baby, reading aloud to her endlessly out of her favourite book, *The Pilgrim's Progress*.

All this time, Jonathan had stayed at Penrose, and all this time Kate had managed never to be alone with him except in Sarah's room. The doctor came every night, so as to see Jonathan, who now went to the factory again in the daytime, as well as Kate. On the last day of June, he let Sarah's thin wrist gently down on the shawl she now refused to part with and smiled at Kate: "I congratulate you, Mrs. Croston. I didn't think you'd do it, but you have."

"You mean?"

"It's over. She'll do now. I don't see why she shouldn't get up to morrow."

"Thank goodness for that." As the child grew stronger, Kate had found it more and more difficult to keep her contented in bed. "And go out?"

"In this fine weather? I don't see why not. Not too much sun at first, but the more fresh air she gets, the better, so long as she doesn't get tired. She'll eat better once she's getting out, I expect."

"I hope so," said Kate. Only she knew what a test of her ingenuity it had been to get any food at all into her recalcitrant patient, the rhymes she had made up, the songs she had sung . . .

"Good." He picked up his hat and coat. "I don't think I need call again. Send for me if you're worried, of course, Mrs. Croston, but I'm sure you will manage admirably. I don't know what we'd have done without you, do you, Jon?"

"No." His eyes met Kate's in a look of perplexity that should have been comic. "No, I don't."

"Mrs. Croston certainly has a wonderful way with her," went on the doctor, as he followed Jonathan downstairs. "A mother couldn't have done more for the child. I don't want to raise your hopes, Jonathan, but just the same—if anyone can bring your Sarah about, that girl will. It was a lucky day for you when you found her up there in Canada."

"Yes. You might say so. Yes, thank you. Good-bye, Doctor." He turned abruptly, to stride away across the grass toward the river. The doctor looked after him for a moment, puzzled, then shrugged and mounted his horse. Tired out, poor Jonathan, he thought as he rode away.

Jonathan was relieved to be summoned urgently into Boston for a Federalist meeting that evening. It gave him the excuse he wanted to postpone the inevitable decision about Kate. Saying good-bye to her in Sarah's room, with Mrs. Peters also present, he castigated himself inwardly for a moral coward. But what could he do, so long as Sarah looked so thin and pitiful and depended so entirely on Kate?

Just the same, the problem haunted him all the hot way to Boston. Absurdly, pitifully, he realized at last that he was hoping, deep down below thought, that something would happen to change everything, that Arabella, perhaps, would tell him it had all been a mistake, a misunderstanding . . . But Kate had admitted it. He always came back to that. "Time enough to think of dismissing me," she had said, "when Sarah is better." What could be more conclusive than that?

Impossible, after such an admission, to contemplate leaving her in charge of the child. And yet—how would Sarah bear to part with her? How would he, for the matter of that? Thoughts like this were madness. To remember the softness of her in his arms, that first moment of yielding, was worse. He kicked his horse into a gallop and took the narrow neck road into Boston at such a pace that his friend Josiah, meeting him on the far side, had to shout to him to stop. "What's the matter, Jon? Are the redcoats coming at last?"

"Nothing like that—so far as I know." He pulled his horse to a walk. "What's the news in town?" It was a relief to talk about ordinary things.

"Nothing much. The blockade's tight as ever. I'll bet you a hundred dollars we're out of the Union by Christmas."

"Lunacy—worse! Our job is to stay in the Union and make Madison see sense. It's peace over-all we want, not a private treaty."

"That's all very well, Jon." They were riding side by side along Orange Street. "But what makes you think we are going to get peace? Now France has fallen, it's good-bye to our hopes of a negotiated settlement."

"I hope you're wrong. Of course we've no chance so long as we don't present a united front. With all this talk of secession it's no wonder they think they can do what they like with us."

Josiah whistled. "You've changed your tune, haven't you? I can remember the time when you called this war a folly and agreed that New England would be better out of it."

"Yes." Abruptly. "I have changed."

"Oh well. It's a free country—I hope. And that reminds me—you remember that prisoner of war you were asking me about—Manningham?"

"Yes. What of him?"

Josiah laughed. "He's had his congé from old man Better-ton. You know he was dangling after that plain girl of theirs? I had fifty dollars on it that he'd carry her off, for-tune and all, but old Betterton was too many for him—and for me. Shipped the girl off to Ballston Springs overnight, and I hear he's using his influence to get Manningham sent down to Washington to be exchanged on the southern front."

"And good riddance, I'd say."

"The ladies will miss him." But Jonathan refused to be drawn, merely saying a curt good-bye and turning his horse down Summer Street.

He was less surprised than displeased to learn that Ara-bella was out driving. "With Mr. Manningham." Was there the same sort of gleam of inquisitive sympathy in the ser-vant's eye that had irritated him in Josiah? Or was he imagining things? Probably. In all the years of their mar-riage, Arabella's conduct had been above reproach. Though they had lived so much apart, she had taken good care that no breath of scandal ever touched her. She valued her posi-tion in society too highly to risk it, surely, for a mere adventurer?

But he was late. The Federalist meeting must have begun already. This was no time to be thinking of Arabella. He picked up his hat and hurried along the Crescent to the house where it was being held. Here, too, he rather thought he was greeted with curious glances, but the business of the day was too urgent for him to give them much thought. Josiah had been right. When he arrived, the assembled lead-ers of the Federalist Party had almost made up their minds to summon the other New England states to a convention to be held, perhaps, at Hartford, with the avowed intention of discussing secession from the Union.

Arguing with a passion that surprised even himself, he managed to persuade them to suspend decision. And so the hard-fought meetings continued those breathless July days. The Fourth came and went, with gingerbread stalls on the Common, and little boys throwing illegal firecrackers, and a temporary upsurge of patriotic feeling that helped Jonathan to postpone a decision still further. And every day a brief, stilted note from Kate told of Sarah's continued progress, and Arabella's absence from the house in the Crescent grew longer and less predictable.

Manningham was still in town awaiting his transfer to Washington. Manningham, he knew, was seeing a great deal of Arabella. He ought to do something about this. He ought to come to a decision about Kate. How could he, when all his time and energy were needed for these endless meetings? He was making excuses to himself. He knew it, and went on doing it until one sticky day late in July when everyone wanted to get out of town and the Federalists finally decided to postpone action : "At least till fall."

Returning to his own house, exhausted, but with a sense of achievement, Jonathan was surprised to find Arabella waiting for him in the drawing room. "I began to think you were never coming." She was moving restlessly about the room, stiff satin creaking around her. There was something surely different about her tonight; a sense of violence repressed. Or was it just impatience?

"I'm sorry," he said mildly. "I had no idea you were waiting for me."

"Waiting—" she moved away, picked up a volume of Mr. Channing's sermons and put it down again. "Well, of course." She was at the chimney piece now, running her hand up and down its intricate carving. Then at last she turned, head up, to face him. "Jonathan !"

"Yes?"

She was finding it more difficult than she had expected. "Jon—will you let me go?"

"Let you go? What do you mean?"

Suddenly, she was the young Arabella he had almost forgotten, diffident, pleading. "Jon; I'm in love. I had no idea it could be like this. Jon—I'll do anything . . . only help me."

"Help you? To what? Bella, are you mad?"

"No, Jon; just happy for the first time in my life. Oh— I'm sorry. I understand now what I did to you, marrying

146

you, as I did, without love. But how could I know? Only, that's why—Jonathan, you must understand; this is too strong for me; it's my everything, my future..."

"It's Charles Manningham?"

"Yes. He wants to take me back to England. You can get a divorce there—I don't quite understand it, but through Parliament somehow. And he has—influence. Did you know he is heir to a viscountcy? He says our marriage will be a nine days' wonder: no more. It's constantly done in high society, he says; the Duke of Wellington's own sister—"

"Oh, my poor Bella. And you believed him?"

"Of course I believe him. Why should I not? What has he to gain by lying to me?"

"That, my dear, is just what I am waiting to find out. What is this help you want from me?"

"Oh—that." Here was the centre of her uneasiness. Once again she had to take council with the chimney piece. "I've done my best to be a good wife to you, haven't I?"

"Your best? Yes, Arabella, I think, in your way, you have."

"Well, then. You've always been generous. And—you're a rich man. Richer than ever, they say, because of this war." Again she paused, as if hoping he would take it up, but he remained firmly silent. She moved away to the window, so that her back was turned to him, and spoke over her shoulder. "You told me once, about your will; about what you had left me."

"Yes?" He was ashamed for her, but it must be got through somehow.

"Oh, Jon, if you would only let me have it now! It would be nothing to you, with your fortune. Why—Charles says everything you touch turns to gold. And—you must see how it is. He is here, a prisoner of war, almost penniless. It's not that he wouldn't give his life for me, but what can he do? How can we manage the journey to England? Jon, if you'd only help!"

"Oh, my poor Arabella," he said again. He had not

147

thought he could find himself, in these strange circumstances, so sorry for her. "Don't you know he tried his best to fix his interest with Sophia Betterton?"

"No!" She spat it at him. "It's not true. He told me all about it at the time. It was just for fear that his passion for me would be noticed. If you knew what it cost him to dance attendance on her when I was in the room . . . he was fighting against his feeling for me, don't you understand? He is a man of honour, Jon. He knew I was a married woman with a child. He thought it his duty to conceal what he felt."

"He does not seem to have altogether succeeded."

"It was too strong for him. Too strong for us both. You must understand. You loved me once. I know it is gone long since, but if you ever did, now is your chance to give me happiness."

"Happiness! Poor Bella, if I only could. It's true, of course; I was quite as much to blame as you for our marriage. You told me—no one could have been more honest— you told me you could not care for me, but, poor fool, I thought my love was enough for both. Well, I was wrong, was I not? Miserably wrong."

"Well then," she came toward him eagerly, hands outstretched. "Let me go, Jon!"

"No, puss, I'm sorry." It was years since he had used that pet name for her. "I've loved you too well to let you persuade me into bribing an adventurer to ruin you. That's what it means. Face it, Bella; there's no future in this. Come home to Penrose with me and we'll try to help you forget him. Sarah is better, by the way; much better, Mrs. Croston writes. I had meant to tell you I thought you could come home any time you wished." And was this, after all, a solution? Sarah better . . . Arabella home where she belonged . . . and Kate?

But Arabella had flown into one of her sudden rages. "Sarah! Nothing but Sarah this and Sarah that! What about me, Jonathan! What kind of life am I expected to drag out while you dote on her? Banished from my own home—publicly neglected by my husband—an object of sympathy to my friends! Yes—sympathy. I! Arabella Penrose! And now, of all things, you tell me that Mrs. Croston gives permission for me to come home. Mrs. Croston! The common drab of her father's parish. Are you sharing her now with Job and the boy? I suggest you take a hard look at yourself, Jon, before you play the hypocrite with me." And then, frightened by the anger in his face. "I'm sorry. I shouldn't have said that. But, don't you see, we're no good to each other; we're better parted. Here's our chance; help me take it, for both our sakes. I beg of you, Jon; think again."

"There's nothing to think about." He had had time, as she went on talking, to master the extraordinary wave of rage that had swept through him when she spoke of Kate. "Nor anything to say, either. I think I had best leave you before we say anything else we will regret. But believe me, Bella, you'll be grateful to me one day for saving you from this adventurer."

"Grateful!" She spat it out. "I warn you, Jonathan Penrose, you'll regret this day's work for the rest of your life."

Idle threats, poor Arabella, he told himself as he rode out of Boston. He knew enough, by now, about Manningham to be comfortably certain that there was no chance of his going through with the elopement once he knew there was no money in it. The kindest thing he could do was to allow Arabella at least the dignity of privacy for her disappointment. By what he had learned today, Manningham would be leaving for Washington at once and, he was sure, alone. And he, for his part, would leave Arabella alone to bear the first shock of it without even the suggestion of an "I told you so." She would send for him soon enough, when she felt the need of him.

But these were surface thoughts. All the time, as he turned his horse along the Penrose road, his mind was echoing with what she had said about Kate. "The common drab of her father's parish." And something worse, something he would not remember. It was impossible, all of it. And yet— she had admitted it herself. "You've been talking, of course, to Charles Manningham." He could remember every tone of her voice, all its cold finality. This was something she had been expecting. "Time enough to think about dismissing me when Sarah is better."

Well, Sarah was better. And he was halfway home to Penrose, with no idea of what he was going to do. "Don't play the hypocrite with me." Arabella's voice now. Arabella —Kate. Kate—Arabella. He was not thinking now but feeling, and it hurt. "Don't play the hypocrite with me . . ." Just what game of deception had he been playing with himself? He—Jonathan Penrose, the married man, the father? It was as neither of these that he had been enraged by the story of Kate's past.

So far, he had been pushing his horse unmercifully along the quiet road. Now, hardly noticing, he slackened speed. What was there to go home for but misery? It was all hopeless, horrible, no matter how you looked at it. Except—there was Sarah. Think, he told himself, simply of her; work out what's best for her; forget the rest.

Forget it? Absurd. His hands, still holding the reins, were limp now on his horse's neck. Somewhere, in a remote corner of his mind, he remembered that he had eaten nothing all day. It did not matter, only—he was so tired; tired deep down through mind and bones. It was a relief to give way to exhaustion; to stop thinking, and sit inert, a thing, while the horse plodded along the familiar road to the stable.

It was late when he got to Penrose at last. Old Job, taking the horse, looked at him anxiously but merely said, "Miss Sarah's been in the garden all day, Master Jonathan. She's much better."

"Good." Listlessly. He went in the back way and encountered Mrs. Peters in the kitchen.

"There you are, Mr. Jonathan. I'd quite given you up for tonight. Shall I have Prue get you something to eat?"

"No, thank you." He was beyond food. It would choke him.

She, too, looked concerned. "But you'll take something

after your ride? Some hot punch, perhaps, to warm you? I'll bring it you in the study."

He looked chilled to the bone, she told Prue. "I hope he's not sickening for something." And in her anxiety, she mixed the punch much stronger than usual.

"Here, drink this; it will do you good." She had found him, most unusually, sitting in the half dark of his study, doing nothing. While he took his first warming sips, she bustled about, lighting lamps, drawing curtains, and apologizing the while for not having had things ready. "We never thought you'd come so late, Mrs. Croston and I."

"Where is Mrs. Croston?"

"In her room, I think. It's late, Mr. Jonathan."

"Yes. Yes: I suppose it is. But I must speak to her just the same. Ask her to come down, would you, Mrs. Peters?"

"Of course. But Sarah's wonderfully better. I reckon we can just about quit worrying over her."

"Oh, yes . . . yes, Job told me. But just the same . . ."

"Of course. I'll fetch her right away."

The warm, fierce liquid was having a wonderfully clarifying effect on his mind What had seemed impossible was now, miraculously, quite simple. Everything fitted into place. It was not—of course it was not—at all what he had expected, had intended for himself. But then, neither had Arabella been. Nothing, he told himself gravely, is what you expect; the secret is to compromise. Compromise. That was what he had been saying all day to his Federalist friends. Compromise . . . make the best of things . . . he moved tiredly across the room to the punch bowl and ladled himself another generous helping. Lord, what a long day. And not over yet.

"You wanted me?" She stood in the doorway, quiet as a shadow.

"Yes. Come in. Close the door. We have to talk, you and I." In his exhausted state, words were tricky things, to be summoned with difficulty, pronounced with care.

"Tonight? So late?" But she shut the door behind her and moved forward into the lamplight. There were dark circles under her eyes, and shadows along her cheekbones he had never noticed before. If he was exhausted, she looked it.

But he was on fire now to have it over with, settled. "Yes, tonight. Sarah's much better, they tell me. Well enough to travel?"

"I don't see why not. It might even do her good."

"Admirable." That was a long, hard word. Better keep to short ones. "I've worked it all out, Kate. I know what to do."

"Oh?" Was she looking at him with the same kind of irritating anxiety he had noticed in Job and Mrs. Peters?

"Yes. Now we know where we stand, we can think what to do." But he must go further back; must explain. "Arabella asked me to give her money today," he said. "A great deal of money. So she could run away with your Charles Manningham. Comic, is it not?"

"My?" It was the merest breath and he went on as if he had not heard her.

"Poor Arabella," he said. "No money, no elopement, of course. She'll know in the morning, when he leaves for Washington without her. He's got to go, thank God. So— there it is. She'll want to come here. Away from her kind friends and their sym-sympathy. If I know anything about her. Which I should. And—can't have the two of you under the same roof. Not after what she said today. Not anyway, come to that. Besides, there's Sarah." He took another long drink to clear his head. "I wish you'd sit down."

"No." It was oddly flat.

"I wish you would." But he struggled to his feet, put his glass on the chimney piece, and leaned against it for support. "I've got a house," he said. "A cottage, rather. Out in the hills near Northampton. It's empty, right now. You'll find it snug enough, you and Sarah. And—it's not too far. I'll visit you whenever I can."

"Oh." A long breath of exquisite relief. "Mr. Penrose! Jonathan! You're not going to send me away."

"Send you away? I should rather think not. That's what I'm trying to explain. It's all easy now, don't you see? Now

I know what you are. It solves everything. Arabella can come home. To her empty house. I'll come to Northampton whenever I can. Say that's what you want, Kate. Darling, ex- . . . exquisite Kate, tell me that's what you want." He was all fire now. "Kate!" He let go of the chimney piece and took one long step across the room toward her, only to find that somehow she was not there. "What's the matter?" He turned to face her where she now stood, halfway to the door of the room. "You care for me—I feel it, felt it the other night. No use denying it. Besides; why should you? Only be true to me, Kate, and I'll be as good as a husband to you, I promise it."

"As good?" She stood very still, very straight, her eyes huge in the tired face. "Mr. Penrose, are you by any chance suggesting that I become your mistress?"

"Exactly." He was delighted that she had taken his point so fast. "What a splendid girl you are, Kate, for calling a spade a spade. I think it's what I first began to love about you. You know—" blessed relief to talk to her at last freely, like this. "I didn't understand what was happening to me. Not until Arabella told me about you and Manningham. I just thought—how pleasant the house was these days, how happy to come home to. And then, when she told me, I thought, for a while, I'd go mad. I never want to go through that again. But it made no difference to my loving you. It just made me understand that I did. What you did, years ago, in England, that's all over. You're different now, aren't you, Kate? Your past shall be your own affair. It's you, now, I care about. And now you must be all mine, mine for always. There'll be talk of course, bound to be, but you won't mind that; why should you? What do we care for the Boston gossips, you and I, if we're happy at Northampton?"

"You're serious?" Her face was in shadow, but her tone should have warned him.

"Never more so." He was impervious, just now, to tones of voice. "Oh—I know, it must come strangely from me. I've always had something of a name in Boston for—call it

Puritanism, Well; women! Who's to understand them? Look at Arabella, so mad for that lady's darling that she'd throw away everything she's ever wanted. And I don't mean me, Kate, she never cared for me; I mean my money, that she married me for. That's why, don't you see, I've no debt to her, none I can't pay with money. So, we're free, you and I; the past shall be nothing—forgotten; I promise you I'll never so much as think of it; the future is ours. As for the world, for Boston and my friends there, let them ruin themselves as they please; we'll make our own world, you and I."

"And Sarah?" Once again, the ice in her voice should have warned him.

"Of course. It was for your kindness to her that I first loved you, Kate, loved you before I had any idea, before I understood . . ."

"And what do you understand now? You're offering me"—she boggled briefly for a phrase—"a love nest, a courtesan's paradise! And proposing that I share it with your daughter. It's beyond belief. And you . . . you would visit us, honour us with your company when you could get away from your wife. The world well lost for love. Mr. Penrose, you make me sick."

"But, Kate—" he was shocked almost into sobriety. "I don't understand—"

"You don't, do you? You make a boast of not understanding women. Well, Mr. Penrose, let me tell you this; even if I was for one minute fool enough to consider accepting your insulting proposition, I'd not have it for Sarah. Brought up by your mistress! You must be mad." At all costs she must preserve this warming flame of anger, must not let herself think of the other side of the picture, of all he was ready to sacrifice for her sake. His world, his Boston; she knew what they meant to him. She would not think of that. Instead. "Tell me, Mr. Penrose; I think I have to know. What exactly has Charles Manningham told you about me?"

"What?—But you admitted it!"

"I'm beginning to wonder just what, in fact, I admitted.

I should have known Charles Manningham better. Come, Mr. Penrose, things have gone too far between us now for mincing matters. You must see, you have to tell me."

"Not Manningham," he managed. "Arabella. He told her.".

"Yes, of course. But told her what?"

"Enough. That you were—oh God! Kate! Don't make me say it to you."

"You must."

"Oh, very well." He picked up his punch glass and drained it. "Manningham told Arabella—that you were notorious in your father's parish. That his death, in fact, happened because he found you making"—he stopped for a minute, then took it at a gallop—"scandalous and unwelcome advances to Charles Manningham himself."

She took a long breath. "And you believed that! And, believing it, have left me with your daughter? And now—now you take it further! Now you pay me the compliment of asking me to be your mistress." Her voice told him what kind of a compliment she thought it. "I really believe," she went on, "the kindest thing I can do is to tell you you've had too much to drink. Which is the case. And make my arrangements to leave in the morning. I'm sorry about Sarah."

Too late, he was aware, himself, of his befuddled state. "But Kate—" he had to have it all clear now. "You as good as admitted it."

"I?" And then she remembered. "Yes, I see. You could have thought that." She moved toward the door. "Well, it's all over now. Good night, Mr. Penrose. We will discuss, in the morning, who is to take care of Sarah when I am gone."

"No!" He moved forward to catch her hand and stop her. "We can't leave it like this. You must explain. What then, was there between Manningham and you? What did you mean, when you seemed to admit it all?"

She withdrew her hand with a firmness there was no gainsaying. "He raped me," she said, and left him.

TWELVE

IMPOSSIBLE TO IMAGINE SLEEPING, or even to face the narrow confines of her room. Kate opened the back door to go very quietly, a ghost walking in moonlight, across the lawn and lean her elbows on the wall by the river. Gazing down into the shadowed, hurrying water, she made herself face it all, the bitter past, the intolerable future. What good had ever come of her running away? And yet—must she run away again?

She had been crazy not to realize how Charles Manningham would twist the story to his advantage. After all, she had known Charles Manningham. And yet—hard to remember now—she had been delighted when he first began to visit them. He had come home to their village on leave from his regiment to recover from a wound he had got at Ciudad Rodrigo. Too weak at first to go far for company, he had soon found his way to the vicarage where her father was entering the third lonely year since his wife's death.

Yes. She bit her lower lip angrily. She had been pleased when Manningham took to coming in every evening, had even—she could hardly bear to think of it now—woven a series of daydreams around his handsome figure. But not for long. And yet—should she blame Manningham entirely? After all, her father had been the older man, the clergyman; why could he not have persuaded Manningham to drink less, instead of drinking glass for glass with him?

Their evenings together had grown longer and longer, and her housekeeping money had dwindled as the empty bottles mounted up. And again, in fairness, she had to admit that Manningham was only doing to them what he had already done to himself. Everyone in the village knew how he had run through his own fortune. He had even, in his soberer moments, given her father good advice, had warned him not to leave his tiny remaining nest egg of capital in the local bank.

Father had taken no notice, had been beyond taking much notice. And that had been what began it all. Manningham had been very drunk already when he arrived that disastrous night. Looking back now, with the bitter wisdom of hindsight, Kate thought he had been nerving himself to break the bad news to his friend. And in a way, everything that had followed had been her fault. Seeing him arrive bright-eyed and flushed of cheek, she had made the earliest possible excuse to leave them. Manningham sober, with his roving restless eye, was painful enough contrast by now to the imagined figure of her dreams, but when he was drunk it was his roving hands she had learned to fear.

That was what had started it. Face it, since after so long, she was making herself face, waking, the nightmare that had haunted her. She had brought her disaster on herself. Almost, she had killed her father. If only she had not made Manningham angry . . .

When she rose to leave them he had jumped to his feet and caught her hand to stop her. "Best be good to me, Kate, my dear. Now you're a pauper, I'm about the only friend you have."

"A pauper?" Father had not been too drunk to take that in.

"You've not heard then? This war against the Americans is hitting the banks hard. There have been several failures today. Our local bank among them. I told you, Ffynch, it was rash to put all your eggs in that basket. Now, I'm afraid it's a case of 'all my pretty ones.' We must just hope your devoted parishioners will see fit to increase your stipend— such as it is." His voice was mocking. He knew as well as they how little chance there was of this.

The old man had raised his head to meet that bright and mocking eye. "And you're glad," he said. "Why did I never see it before? You're not my friend. Never have been." He had risen to an odd, heart-catching moment of dignity. "I

157

think you must be the devil himself. Kate!" And, on the appeal to her, he had fallen forward among the glasses and bottles; dead. Kate shivered, there in the balmy moonlight, reliving the scene. It had been too bad to be true. But it had been true. And so had what followed. No nightmare, though she had often enough waked, sweating, from it since. No servant slept in. She had been alone in the house with her father's dead body—and Charles Manningham.

And even then, if she had kept her head, she might have avoided the final disaster. Manningham had been sobered a little by the suddenness of it. "He's dead." He let the thin wrist fall again to the table. "The poor old fool. Believe me, Kate, I never meant—"

But those words of casual contempt had been too much for her. Forgetting everything else, she turned on him, a fury, and told him what she thought of him. Remembering this shamed her now almost as much as what had followed. She had screamed at him there like a fishwife across her father's dead body.

Something she said had got him on the raw. She did not remember—did not want to remember what. In fact, she had shocked him, brought herself down to his level. He had taken her hand, to drag her from the room. "Shame on you! In front of that."

"That! You mean my father. Whom you've killed!" She had tried to pull away from him, but he held her with a grip of iron, his eyes bright, dangerous.

"That's not true. And you know it." He had her by the shoulders now. "Take it back." And then, as he looked down at her, struggling under his hands, she had seen anger give way in his face to something infinitely more frightening. One hand still held her shoulder, the other moved slowly, thoughtfully, down across her breast. "Well, Kate?" The drink had him again now; he had forgotten the body in the next room; forgotten everything but her. "Well, my beautiful Kate?"

She had fought; she had bitten him; she had scratched his face. It had merely enraged him. Perhaps he had meant only—as he said afterward—to snatch a couple of kisses: "To make up for all your past disdain." But when she had fought, he had fought back, not a man, not recognizable any more, but an animal that tore off her clothes and took her savagely, brutally, forced back across the desk where her father used to work.

Afterward, he had cried, and promised to "make it up to her," and fallen asleep. Now, looking back, she blamed herself bitterly for what she had done next. At the time, she had not thought at all. A warm dress. Ironic, surely, to put on a warm dress to kill oneself? And then the half-mile, part running, part walking, sobbing all the way, the pain in her body inextricably confused with that in her heart . . . and, at last, the quarry's edge, dimly seen in the light of a waning moon; the pause to gather strength for the leap; and strong arms around her. "What's all this?" Sergeant Croston had asked.

He and his men had been camped on the downs, on their way to Portsmouth. He had been kind, wonderfully kind, holding her gently, getting the story out of her, little by little, swearing to himself. Friends? No, she had told him, she had no friends. Nor would she go back to that house for anything. Of course, now, looking back with the harsh wisdom of experience on a seventeen-year-old's despair, she knew this for lunacy. She should have gone to her mother's family in Ireland. But at the time, when Sergeant Croston had said, with the dim streaks of dawn like hope on the horizon, "Then marry me, child, and I'll take care of you," it had seemed the answer to everything. Brought up on a mixed diet of hell fire and Mrs. Radcliffe, she had known that marriage or death were her alternatives. Well, she had failed to kill herself, and this man had saved her. He was kind; he was old (thirty-five, she had discovered later); surely he would be gentle. What more could she ask?

When she said yes, he had been taken, suddenly, with a paroxysm of coughing. In a way, it had made the strange moment easier. It was only later that she understood that this spelled for her not only wife- but widowhood. At the time, there was so much to do. His regiment was due to sail for Canada in a week. Somehow, he had managed a special license, found the money for her outfit, got permission for her to accompany him. It had all been such a whirl that she had hardly come to herself till she was married and on board the crowded transport.

It had been a clean break. She did not even know who had buried her father, what Captain Manningham had said or done . . . she did not want to know. That was the past, dead and done with; even the tears were dry now that she had shed, during that nightmare voyage, for her father, for herself. At least her terror, during the first weeks in the unspeakable between decks of the transport, that she might bear Manningham's child, had proved groundless.

Savagely comic, now, to think that her one comfort had been the knowledge that each day was taking her further away from him. In a way, illogical, crazy, she had been running away from him ever since. She remembered how she had begged Jonathan to take her home with him after hearing that Manningham's regiment—the 98th—was on its way to Canada. And yet, now he had caught up with her at last, how strangely different her disaster was from anything she had feared.

Nothing Charles Manningham did could hurt her any more. It was not from him now that she must flee, but from herself and Jonathan. I ought to go now, she told herself; at once, without seeing him again. Not even Sarah could hold her now. Not after what had happened between them tonight. For a moment, she actually thought about rousing Job, making him drive her into Boston . . . But where to?

Besides, she could not leave Sarah like that, without a word, without a good-bye. Sarah was convalescent, beginning to run and laugh again, but tiring still so easily, needing to be coaxed to rest, to eat . . . And, in another sense, Sarah was so much better that any moment she expected words to come tumbling out with her laughter. To disappear without a word might easily destroy everything Kate had done for her.

So this time she would not run away. It would be horribly painful, for both of them, to meet Jonathan in the morning, but it must be done. They must work out between them a way of making the parting less painful for Sarah.

The air was getting cold. It must be very late; too late to decide anything. Morning would be time enough. She turned and moved wearily toward the house, hoping passionately as she went that Jonathan would be safe in bed by now. By peering cautiously in at the study window, she saw him still sitting where she had left him, head in his arms, fast asleep.

Don't think about the exhausting day he must have had. Don't make excuses for him. It's bad enough without that. Very quietly she tiptoed in, turned out the lamp which was flaring dangerously, resisted the temptation to try and settle him more comfortably in his chair—did she want him to wake? And, yes, this was her night for being honest with herself; part of her did; part of her wanted him to wake, to pick up the scene where they had left off, to apologize, to make it all possible somehow.

It was not possible. Very quietly she closed the door behind her, looked in on Sarah, deep in a convalescent's peaceful sleep, and put herself to bed, where, surprisingly, she slept the deep dreamless sleep of total exhaustion.

She was roused by an agitated knocking on her door. It was Prue: "Miss! Miss Kate, is Sarah in with you?"

"Sarah? No. Why—" She was out of bed already, pulling on her dressing gown.

"She's not in her room. Mr. Penrose ain't seen her. And, miss, the clothes she had on yesterday are gone too."

"She must have dressed and run out early to play." Kate knew, as she tried to keep her voice calm, how unlikely this was. All the outside doors of the house were double-locked at night to prevent just this.

But Prue jumped at it. "Yes, that must be it, miss. I'll run down and check the doors."

"I'll be down in a minute." Kate huddled on her clothes, condemning herself, as she did so, for her fright. There would be some simple explanation, of course. Indeed, she had thought of one already. In the state he was in last night, Jonathan might easily have forgotten to lock up. She should have seen to it herself.

Dressed at last, she ran down to Sarah's room. The bed-clothes were thrown back, but otherwise the room was just as she had left it the night before, except that, as Prue had said, Sarah's clothes had disappeared from the chair where she had hung them. But something else was missing too. Where was Sarah's frilly blue nightgown? A quick, desperate search of drawers and cupboards revealed only its pink counterpart, and revealed something else that was equally disconcerting. Sarah's bright red worsted overcoat was missing from its place in her closet. It made an impossible picture. If the child had got up to run out and play, she would have dressed here, and left her nightgown behind. And for no reason in the world would she have taken a coat on this hot July morning.

The window was wide open. Kate took two quick steps across the room to look down and see a trampled path through the plants of the flowerbed below, and the marks, she thought, of where a ladder had stood. She was across the hall in an instant, knocking at Jonathan's door. "Mr. Penrose!" No time now to be thinking of last night. "Are you dressed?"

"Just." He opened the door, cravat in hand. "Have you found her?"

"No. It's worse than I thought. Prue's down checking the doors, but—Jonathan—I'm afraid she's been kidnapped." Hurriedly she explained what she had found in the child's room. "As if they had carried her off in her nightgown," she concluded, "and taken her clothes to dress her at leisure. If they can—" She imagined the battle this would be; little Sarah in the hands of strangers, frightened, angry . . . screaming for help? But no one had heard her. Gagged, perhaps? . . . It did not bear thinking of. "Sarah," she said. "My little Sarah." She followed Jonathan into the child's room and watched him quickly checking on her findings.

"I'm afraid you're right." He too had leaned out the window to see the telltale marks below.

"But who? Why?"

"I think I know." She had never seen him so angry. "At least—after the shock of it—she should not come to any harm. But to do this to her—to Sarah, knowing what she is. My God, I'll make them pay for this."

"Them? But who?"

He was hearing Arabella's voice: "You'll regret this day's work for the rest of your life." They must have had it planned before she made her appeal to him. His refusal had been the signal to put their infamous scheme into operation. By now, they might be well on their way to Washingon. And Sarah—what would it do to her? "I'm afraid it's her mother," he said. "And Charles Manningham. They mean to make me pay to have her back. Yes, Prue?"

The girl came running up the stairs. "The doors was all locked, sir, but Job found this stuck in the front porch." She handed him a letter.

"Exactly. Thank you, Prue!" If it was possible, his face went grayer still as he read the brief message. "Just as I thought." He handed it to Kate.

"A mother has her rights," it ran. "Since you deny me access to my child, I am removing her to my own protection. If you want her back, perhaps you will see your way to being reasonable about what we discussed last night. I will give you time to think it over before I write again." And it was signed, in a bold scrawl, "Arabella Penrose."

"Damnably clever," he said, as Kate returned it to him. "You see, they say nothing about money. No magistrate would act on it. He would say a mother had a right to the custody of her own child. And she doesn't even say when she will write again." He crumpled the letter furiously in his hand, then smoothed it out and reread it. "What will it do to Sarah, Kate?"

"God knows." She would not pretend about it. "And she was so much better." A sob shook her voice. "One thing—"

163

She reached for comfort. "I should think she'll give them enough trouble so they will probably act fast."

"Yes, I expect you're right. At least we should hear soon." He had taken a decision. "I must go into Boston, and arrange to have the money available."

"You'll give it them?" But she had never doubted it.

"Of course. When we have Sarah back will be time to think of punishing them. Mind you," he went on, "the two of them should be punishment enough to each other. But— Sarah . . ."

"I know." Fantastic to remember last night's scene now. He must have thought of it too. "I'll go at once," he said. "Kate, you'll be here? You'll be ready to go to Sarah as soon as we know where she is?"

"Of course."

"Thank you. I knew you would. Kate—try to understand . . . I was mad last night. I . . . there's so much I want to say—"

"And no time." She said it for him. "It's all right, Jon, so long as Sarah needs me, I'll be here."

It was not what he had wanted, but he had to take it. "Thank you. I'll be back as soon as I can. If another message comes, open it."

"Shall I try and stop the messenger?"

"No. What's the use? They've got me, and they know it. I only pray they are not already on their way to Washington. Arabella's from the South, you know. She may well have connections there. With luck, I may be in time to stop them. I'd do anything, pay anything to spare Sarah that journey. But—if the worst comes to the worst, you'll be ready to come after her with me?"

It was all fantastic. "Yes, of course," she said.

Without Sarah, the morning seemed endless. Kate occupied herself for a while in packing a small carpetbag with basic needs for herself and Sarah in case they had to go after her. Incredible, after last night, even to be imagining another journey with Jonathan.

The packing did not take nearly long enough. Downstairs, the household was seething with curiosity. Jonathan had given her no instructions as to what she should say, but the less, surely, the better? To avoid the questions she saw burning in Mrs. Peters' eye, she let herself hurriedly out into the garden. Moving about helped a little, though nothing could banish, for long, the picture of Sarah screaming, furious, afraid . . .

She turned down the drive and walked briskly toward the main road, hardly noticing the hot sun. At least it was a relief to be away from the house, with its exclamations and probing eyes. She was in sight of the Boston road when she saw a horseman turn in off it and was instantly certain that he was the next messenger. He must have just missed Jonathan. Maddening . . . Inevitably, it must mean more delay.

As he approached rapidly up the drive, she felt a shock of surprise and rage. No messenger, but Manningham himself. How dared he?

He pulled his horse to a stop beside her. "The very person," he said: "What a stroke of luck! Mrs. Croston, we need you."

"Need me?" She was almost wordless at the effrontery of it.

"Yes. To quiet that hellcat of yours, that Sarah. Frankly, if I'd had any idea what she was like, I'd have had no part in this scheme, but I'm in for it now, so if you care anything for the little devil, you'd best come along and keep her quiet. Her mother just makes her worse."

"You can't be serious?" A quick glance behind her confirmed that the house was out of sight. How she wished now for the curious eyes she had been resenting.

"Please don't think of screaming." He had interpreted her look. "One squeak from you and I'm away down the road—and with me that child's last chance of keeping her sanity—such as it is. I can't say I care much, myself, but Arabella seemed to think you might. The way things are going now, she'll be a case for a straitjacket long before we get to Washington—if I haven't knocked her silly first. It's all I've been able to do, so far, to keep my hands off her. So, there it is. I've a man and a led horse waiting for you outside the gates. If you care enough for the child, you'll come with me now. On my terms."

"And what are they?" Could this really be happening?

"That you give me your word you won't try to make trouble. Bella said I shouldn't trust you, but I know you better than she does. Besides, if you really care for the child, you'll do as I say. One word from you and we dose her with laudanum and leave you behind. No use thinking, anyway, you'd get anywhere if you did kick up a row. Is it likely, when it's her own mother who's got her? And, if the poor little thing gets an overdose of the laudanum, whose fault will it be, but yours?"

"Oh my God, you couldn't . . ."

"Don't you think so? Just you wait till you hear the rumpus she's making. You've got just five minutes to make up your mind. I can't stay longer; the carriage is waiting. And, besides, how embarrassing it would be if Mr. Penrose should change his mind and come back."

"You saw him go?"

"Of course. Well, it stood to reason he'd head for Boston at once. Only—I'm afraid he won't find us there. I just hope he starts making his arrangements about the money."

"But he's going to. He means to give it you. So where's the need to take Sarah to Washington? I beg of you, Mr. Manningham, just wait a day or two and you will have your money." She did not try to keep the scorn out of her voice.

"But waiting's just what I can't do. Besides, I've got more sense. Wait here in New England where everyone knows Penrose—and Arabella, too, for the matter of that? No, thank you; Washington's where we're going to do our deal. Mr. Penrose will find a message in Boston telling him that, and in the meantime, your five minutes are up. Are you coming or not?"

"But—like this? How can I? If you'll just wait while I run to the house—I've a bag ready packed for Sarah and me . . ."

He laughed at her. "And have you rouse the household? No, thank you." He was turning his horse. "Well, Mrs. Croston?"

If there was only time to think! And yet, what good would thinking do? She had made her decision, or rather it had made itself for her when he spoke of laudanum. "I'm coming," she said.

He laughed again. "Bella said you would. I'm glad she's right sometimes. Well then; your solemn word of honour you won't try to make trouble for us on the journey?"

She looked him in the eye with all the contempt she felt: "You have it."

"Then let's go. As for clothes for the journey; you'll just have to borrow Arabella's. And a proper dust-up she'll make about it too. Well—serve her right; a fine mother who can't control her own child." He had dismounted as he spoke and now set a brisk pace toward the road.

Walking beside him, and amazed all over again to find herself doing so, Kate considered his last speech. There had been nothing loverlike about his reference to Arabella. Could they be quarrelling already? She remembered what Jonathan had said; they would be punishment enough, he thought, for each other. If they really fell out, might there not be a gleam of hope in it for Sarah? The idea confirmed her in the decision she had taken, and she walked steadily beside him, resolutely putting out of her mind the question of what Jonathan would think when he found her gone.

To her surprise, they turned away from Boston when they reached the main road. Once again, Manningham picked up her thought. "No, my dear, not Boston," he said. "That would be a little too easy, would it not? Washington may not be Rome, but there are more roads than the direct one will take us there. And less trouble on the way, I wager. And here's your mount; isn't it fortunate I know you for an intrepid horsewoman?"

This light-hearted reference to the intolerable past made her so angry that she mounted in silence. Was she mad to have come?

A brisk ride, spurred on, in Kate's case, by tearing anxiety over Sarah, brought them, early in the afternoon, to a neat, white-painted village inn. "Here we are." Manningham jumped down from his horse and held hers for her to dismount. "At least I can't hear the brat screaming. Now, remember"—he turned to lead the way indoors—"one word out of turn and the child pays for it."

"I'll remember." Retribution would come later, Jonathan had said. Jonathan! Where was he now? Had he got home yet, and found her gone? Impossible not to feel a little stab of bitter pleasure as she thought of it.

They found Arabella sitting alone, angrily rocking, on the inn's small screened porch. Seeing them, she rose with such sudden violence that the rocking chair skittered away across the porch. "At last!" This for Manningham. And, "So you came," to Kate.

"Yes, I came. How is Sarah?" She had already decided to say as little as possible.

"Asleep. Thank God. Yes, go to her if you wish. She may wake up more quietly for finding you with her. Much more noise out of her, and we'll be asked to leave. The landlady as good as told me so."

"We'll be leaving directly anyway." This was Manningham.

"What? But I've given orders for dinner!"

"That's too bad." He did not sound as if he cared. "Time enough to think of eating when we have put a few more miles between us and Boston. Your husband's no fool, you know. When he finds no evidence that we've hired a coach there, he'll think of other possibilities. I bribed a man I hired from in Worcester as heavily as I could afford, but—" he shrugged. "Mrs. Croston, you'll find the child upstairs in the ladies' bedroom. Wake her, if you please, and have her ready to travel as soon as I've had the horses put to."

"Has she had anything to eat?"

"To eat!" Arabella was on the verge of one of her rages. "What do you think! We're to pay for the damage in the dining parlour, Charles." But he had turned to leave the room and took no notice. "Well!" For a moment, Kate thought she would let rage conquer discretion, but, recollecting herself, "Best lose no time, Mrs. Croston," she said, "if we are really to start at once."

Grateful for her experience in just such little country inns when travelling with Jonathan, Kate began by finding her way to the big, hot kitchen at the back of the house. As she expected, the landlady and two of her daughters were hard at work there preparing the dinner Arabella had ordered. It was none of her business to warn them their labour was to be wasted. "How do you do," she had learned from watching Jonathan, that the owners of an inn must be treated as rather better than equals. "Forgive my intruding when I can see how busy you are, but I'm Sarah's nurse. I came to apologize for all the trouble she's caused you. Poor child, travelling always upsets her."

"Upsets!" The red-faced landlady handed her wooden spoon to the taller of her two girls. "I'm upset too, I can tell you, by the mess she's made in my dining room. They'll find it on their bill, and so I warned Mrs. Manningham."

Mrs. Manningham? But—of course. "I am so sorry." Kate really meant it. "There's nothing worse than a panicky child, is there? It's almost an illness with Sarah. I can see you've had no trouble of that kind." Here a glance for the two stout, red-faced girls who so unfortunately favoured their mother.

"No, ma'am; never a day's trouble with mine." The landlady was thawing. " 'Make them mind you,' that's what I say. First and last, that's the secret of child-rearing. But that Mrs. Manningham—why, you'd think she'd never had the care of the child before. In fact, we had begun to wonder, my good man and I, just what was going on?" Her curiosity was almost palpable in the room.

For a moment, Kate was horribly tempted. If she told this good-natured, inquisitive woman what was, in fact, going on, surely she would fetch help? But—what help, in a village this size? Charles Manningham would carry it, she was sure, with a high hand. The only result would be that she was left behind, and Sarah taken on, helpless, drugged with laudanum. And what effect that might have on the child's already disordered nervous system . . .

It did not bear thinking of. "You might well wonder," she said as cheerfully as she could. "The trouble is, Mrs. Manningham's not had much to do with the child. She's—well, you know what Boston society is like?"

"One of those is she? Just what I thought. I've read of their doings, the painted Jezebels; balls and parties, picnics on Sundays; and even going to the theatre." She made it sound like the uttermost depth of debauchery. "Yes, I reckoned that was what it was, miss, but glad to have you confirm it, and will set my husband's fears at rest. We're a respectable house, mind, and a God-fearing one, and no wish to get mixed up in anything underhand."

"Of course not." It was frightening to have succeeded so easily. "I can see you're a good woman, ma'am, and not one to stand by and let a child suffer. And it makes me bolder to ask a favour of you."

"A favour?" She was all bristling suspicion at once.

"Oh, nothing much. It's just—could I possibly, do you think, have a glass of milk and a bit of cake for the child? I know it's asking a lot, when it's not your regular dinner hour, but by all accounts she's had nothing to eat all day, naughty little thing; and you know, don't you, ma'am, how badly growing children need their food? I'm sure your handsome daughters had plenty of midday snacks from you when they were growing."

"That they did." The woman moved across the room to pour a mugful of milk from a big stone crock. "No child shall starve in my house, that's one thing certain. As for some folks that want their dinners to suit themselves, not me, that's something else again." She cut off a lavish slice of fruitcake as she spoke, and Kate was able to thank her and retreat with it before she had drawn breath for a new volley of questions.

The ladies' bedroom was on the shady side of the house, and the air struck pleasantly cool when Kate entered it. At first sight, the room seemed empty, then she saw the small figure, curled in a tight knot on the farthest bed. Sarah was fast asleep, her arms clutching the pillow among a welter of disordered bedding. She was still wearing the nightgown in which she had been carried off, and Kate had a horrified vision of her mother trying—and failing—to get her dressed.

She had lost weight while confined with the measles, and her face, relaxed in sleep, looked alarmingly thin, pale and dark-shadowed. At the sight, Kate abandoned any thought of trying to rouse the landlady on their side. It must inevitably mean a scene—another scene for the poor child to endure. No, for the moment, she must co-operate with Manningham and Arabella, simply to protect Sarah from the kind of inquisition to which she would be subjected if the question of her parentage should be raised. Imagine some bungling country lawyer trying to find out from speechless Sarah whether Arabella was indeed her mother. Of course—she sat down quietly by the bed—this was the strength of Manningham's position. What did it matter that Arabella was travelling under an assumed name, when her daughter could not speak to accuse her—and Kate would not?

The sound of horses being got ready in the yard below reminded her of her mission. Reluctantly, she put a hand to Sarah's cheek in the gentle gesture she had found efficacious in waking her. The child reacted like a wild animal, awake in an instant, trembling all over, curled even more tightly in on herself, hands over her eyes, as if what she did not see, could not hurt her.

"It's all right, Sarah pet." It was an effort to keep the anger out of her voice. "It's me; Kate."

The hands came down at once. Two huge eyes stared at Kate as if they did not believe what they saw, and then, astonishingly, her lips moved: "Kate," she whispered, and for the first time since Kate had known her, big tears began to fill her eyes.

"It's all right, my poppet, it's all right my honey." Kate had her in her arms now, rocking her like a baby. "I'm here now; I won't leave you for anything." And Jonathan Penrose will just have to arrange his life around that, she told herself. But harness was jingling in the yard below. "Sarah, honey, we're going on a long journey, you and I. You'll like that, won't you, now I'm here? We'll ride in the coach all day and see all kinds of new things and people—and I'll be beside you all the time. But first we must get you dressed, mustn't we? Just look at you sitting there in your nightgown in the middle of the day. I don't know what your father would say. No." The big eyes had asked a question. "He's not coming too, but I hope we'll see him when we get there. We're going to Washington, Sarah, where the President lives in his palace. Won't that be a treat! I'll take you to see all the sights when we get there." No use worrying now as to whether she would be able to keep the promise. At any rate, while she talked, she had been expertly helping Sarah out of her nightgown and into pantalettes, petticoat, and frilled muslin dress. "And now, before we go down and say hello to our horses, something to eat, don't you think? I'm famished, aren't you?" She broke off a piece of the cake and fed it to Sarah, whose mouth opened willingly, like a small bird's.

By eating a few crumbs herself, she managed to keep up the fiction of a shared meal, which had always been the best way to get Sarah to eat. "And now, your hair, Sarah! You never saw such a bird's nest. And we've no brush either, so be patient with me, love; we don't want to shame our travelling companions do we?" She was busy with her pocket comb as she spoke, teasing out the tangles in Sarah's hair. Usually, this would have been apt to provoke rebellion or even a screaming fit, but today Sarah just leaned confidingly against her, the big tears still pouring down her cheeks.

"It's all right, honey." Unbearably touched, she bent

172

down to kiss her. "It's all right now, I promise you." How she hoped it was true.

Downstairs, there was, inevitably, a row going on between the landlady and Manningham about the uneaten dinner. Kate shepherded Sarah quickly through the contending parties and got her out into the village street, where the coach Manningham had hired stood ready. The coachman, a gloomy-looking man with a squint, was standing by his horses, ostentatiously consulting a huge pocket watch.

Kate smiled at him. "They'll be out directly—I hope." And then, remembering the lessons in friendliness she had learned from Jonathan. "I'm Mrs. Croston—you've met Sarah, but not at her best, I'm afraid. May she say how-do-you-do to your horses?"

"Surely." He spat out his quid of tobacco neatly at her feet. "I reckon she looks a sight better than she did this morning. Feeling better now, hey?" This to Sarah, who hung back, clinging to Kate's hand.

"Much better, thank you," Kate answered for her. "She does not speak, you know." The memory of that whispered, "Kate," was warm in her heart. "But she loves horses, don't you, pet?" And she lifted Sarah up to make much of one sleek brown nose after another.

When Manningham and Arabella emerged, still angry, from the inn a few minutes later, the coachman was Sarah's established friend, busy trying to make the rear seat of his clumsy vehicle comfortable for someone with such short legs. He was called about his business sharply by Manningham. "Must we wait for you all day, my man?"

"Just fancy." He emerged, broadly grinning, from the back of the coach. "And there was I thinking I was waiting for you."

Watching Manningham swallow the familiarity, Kate smiled to herself. She might be able to get Sarah through this journey after all. Arabella, brought up in the South, had never understood the democratic, anti-slave Northerners, and Manningham would not learn in time how to treat these independent upstanding Yankees who actually thought themselves as good as he was. It was almost a pity, in a way, that she had abandoned the idea of trying for help, but— no—the feeling of Sarah, already nodding off to sleep against her, enjoying security again, was an antidote to this. Time enough to think of escape when they got to Washington.

THIRTEEN

SARAH BORE THE JOURNEY much better than Kate had feared. The coachman, Silas, her firm friend, managed in all kinds of small ways to make it pleasant for her. If these attentions also succeeded in irritating Manningham and Arabella, why, so much the better. He had fixed his price for the trip. Take it or leave it, was his attitude, and like it or not, they had to take it.

Inevitably, taking this western route which was to avoid all the major cities along the coast, they spent their days on bad roads and their nights at one small village inn after another. Kate watched almost with awe as, night after night, Arabella and Manningham contrived to irritate their hosts, she by her complaints and he by his hauteur. When she could, she managed, by explaining Sarah's condition, to achieve, at best, an early meal for the two of them, at worst a position at the big, communal table as far as possible from the other two. Thus, she was able to follow, with a kind of sympathetic horror, the worsening of their relations. For Arabella, everything was Manningham's fault, while all the things that infuriated him about Americans in general, were, inevitably, part of Arabella. Watching their tiffs become quarrels, Kate began to wonder whether this ill-starred venture might not be abandoned before ever they reached Washington.

The best thing, so far as she was concerned, was that Sarah appeared miraculously immune to their behaviour. The days when her mother's mere presence might bring on one of her screaming fits seemed to be gone forever. So long as she had Kate always with her, nothing seemed to trouble her. They did everything together, and Kate, watching Sarah's cheerful acceptance of one strange meal and bed after another, even found herself wondering if this fantastic journey might not be, in some incomprehensible way, just the thing she needed. Had she been, at Penrose, too engrained in the habits of a difficult case? If only it ended right, this ruthless uprooting might even prove good for her.

If only it ended right . . . There was the crux of the matter. That was what she tried not to think about, because Sarah always grew restless when she did. So Kate thought determinedly about nothing but the farms, fields and orchards they passed, the excitement of crossing a horse ferry, or the pleasure of getting out to walk beside the coach as the horses laboured up a long hill (Arabella never did so) and the reward, at the top, of a whole new prospect of smiling America.

"Lord, it's a vast country." Manningham, to do him justice, always got out and walked with them, when the horses were hard-pressed.

"Yes. Doesn't it make you understand, travelling like this, day after day, how Napoleon must have felt when he took his great army into Russia and found nothing but fields, and forest, and burning villages?" How odd it was, she thought, turning to help Sarah over a rough bit of the hill road, to be talking thus to Manningham, of all people, Manningham, who had . . . She checked herself; these thoughts were best left deep in the well of the mind. There would be a time for them, later. Or—would there? Wounds heal, she thought. If you survive, that is . . . Now she did not even hate Charles Manningham, she just despised him.

But Sarah was pulling impatiently at her hand. "Tired, honey?" She swung her up into her arms. "Not far now to the top of the hill. Or would you like to ride with Silas?"

The head that leaned against her shoulder shook itself vigorously, and she sighed. That one miraculous word she had spoken, that whispered, "Kate," did not seem, after all her hopes, to have been the beginning of anything.

"Let me take her; she's far too heavy for you." Manningham had misinterpreted the sigh and tried to disentangle Sarah from her perch on Kate's hip.

In an instant, she was a wild thing, clinging frantically to Kate, and at the same moment Arabella leaned out of the open side of the coach. "Charles! Must I be shouting for you forever? I'm suffocating in here!"

A rueful, almost conspiratorial smile for Kate, and he had moved forward to offer his sympathies and suggest that Arabella might enjoy a stroll in the cool of the evening.

"The horses might profit, too, I reckon," put in Silas, who was walking at their heads, encouraging them up the steep slope.

Regrettably, Arabella swore at him with a freedom that cast an odd light on the education of a southern young lady. For a moment, Kate thought that he was going to refuse to go any further, but all he did was laugh. "I reckon you'll owe me danger money when we get to Washington," he told Manningham. "The things I have to put up with. If it weren't for the young ladies . . ." He left it at that, but Manningham did not. Kate, a reluctant eavesdropper from the ladies' bedroom above the porch of the inn that night, heard his voice and Arabella's furiously raised and could only congratulate herself as she drifted off to sleep that except for the odd hysterical phrase on Arabella's part, she could hear only the angry tone, not the words.

Arabella was visibly subdued in the morning, and the journey went more easily after that, but they were all deeply travel-weary and proportionately relieved when Silas waved his whip in an easterly direction one heavy August evening and said, "Baltimore's over there, I reckon. Two days now should see us home, I guess, if all goes well and we don't run into your friends."

This was directed at Manningham. "My friends?" he asked. "What do you mean?"

"Why, that tarnation British squadron that's been raising Cain down here on the Chesapeake for the last year. The word is, they're to be reinforced, now the war's over in Europe. Well, I reckon that stands to reason, don't it? Anyways, don't expect to find yourself just the most popular man in Washington, speaking the way you do. If you run into any kin of the womenfolk who were attacked at Hampton last summer, I'd cut and run, if I were you. Those Virginians are mightily touchy where their honour is concerned, and I don't guess you're much of a duelling man."

"Insolent!" But Manningham said it under his breath. Already the journey had taken longer than he had expected. "We can't afford to quarrel with the man—" he explained to Arabella that evening. "We must get there as fast as possible—and if he were to leave us in the lurch here . . . Suppose we were to find your husband there before us!"

"Suppose what you like!" Arabella no longer even pretended to keep her temper with him. "I can think of nothing more likely. Jonathan won't have wasted his time running over every side road and patronizing every filthy, bug-infested inn he can find. He'll have gone the direct way, never fear, and be waiting for us."

"Yes, maybe, but he won't find us. You did say, did you not, that he knew nothing about your cousin's house?"

"Of course I did. He's never even heard of her. And as to the house, it's not in Washington at all, but a couple of miles out on the brow of a gorge called Rock Creek. Once we get there, he'll never find us, but just be so good as to explain to me how we are to get there. You know as well as I do that Kate Croston means to make trouble the moment we reach town, and that oaf of a driver will side with her; and Sarah will have one of her screaming fits and draw people in from miles around—and then what will become of us?"

He laughed. "Give me credit for having thought of these hazards too, my love. And admit that we could not have made the journey without Mrs. Croston." Now that they were approaching Washington he was making a determined effort to improve the strained relations between them. He had not gone to all this trouble merely to lose the money he meant to have with her because of a little quarrelling on the way. Sometimes, it was true, when she was at her most captious, he found himself wondering whether it was all worth it, but then, despite what he had told her, the chances of his ever having to marry her—or even being able to do so, were slight enough to be negligible. And money he must have before he returned to England to face his creditors.

So he put out a tentative hand to play with the hair that grew in stiff golden curls about her temples, and wondered, as he felt her instant response to the touch, whether he had made a mistake in his handling of her. Her response, in Boston, to his first cautious approaches to love-making had been so instant and so violent that he had lost interest at once. She was his for the taking when he decided to have her. For the moment, he had convinced himself, it would be best to leave her on the alert for his least caress. Only—it did not seem to have worked out like that. She had said nothing when he acquiesced, night after night, in the arrangements of small inns that found it easiest to sleep their male and female guests in separate dormitories. Only, each morning her temper had been worse than the last. And now they were near to Washington and the moment of crisis. And—he was not sure he could count on her.

He looked around. It was almost dark now, and they were alone on the inn porch. His hand was still mechanically playing among the crisp curls at the back of her neck and he could feel her body respond to each tiny movement. Kate's hair, he thought, with an irrelevance that disconcerted him, would not be tough like this; it would be soft, yielding to the touch; he would want to pull it, to make her cry for mercy . . .

This was madness. He moved his hand down to a smooth, cool shoulder, and noticed belatedly that Arabella had changed into an unusually elegant gown. Oh well . . . that settled it. "You're very splendid tonight, my love." He murmured it into her ear, and was aware, as he did so, of the heavy, cloying odour of the make-up she wore, and of the fine lines that showed beneath it. Kate would not smell like that, nor look so. Kate's skin was firm and brown, ripened by the sun. Suddenly he was back in her father's house; the

179

body slumped once more across the table, the candles guttering, and Kate—Kate fighting for dear life in his arms, biting, scratching, altogether delicious . . . Oh, why in the name of God had she not been there next day when he woke resolved to marry her at once?

Arabella was not fighting. She was leaning close against him now, the crisp curls tickling his chin. "I thought I'd never be alone with you again," she said.

"And I, too. These dreadful country inns. If you knew the nights I've lain awake, dreaming of you . . . But it will be all over soon, my love, and we'll be together for always."

"Oh, Charles, you really mean it. I've been a fool. I—I began to wonder whether you really cared; whether it was not all a mistake; all for nothing."

"Care!" This was danger indeed. "Arabella, my love, look at me." With a hand that was not quite as gentle as he had intended, he forced her chin up so that he could gaze down into her eyes with what he hoped would pass for passion. "Do you not realize what anguish this journey has meant for me? What longing? What torments? But how should you know of the nights I've lain awake, tossing on my bed (and that was true enough, he thought, on these devilish American feather beds) thinking only of you," he finished, pleased with himself.

"Oh, Charles. Have I just been imagining things? Sometimes, I've seen you looking at Kate Croston—"

"As if I could kill her," he finished quickly. "I'm sure you have, love, and do you wonder? If we had not had her along as the unwelcome third, do you not think I would have found my way long since to your 'ladies' room'? You'd not have slept so sound these nights, I can tell you, if she'd not been there as a dragon in the next bed. But I have to think of your reputation, my queen; of the harm she could do you." And that's true enough, he thought, like it or not.

"Oh, Charles—was that all?" She was soft as a cat against his hands.

"Of course it was all! What in the world have you been imagining, my foolish love?"

"Oh: everything—nothing. Charles!"

"Yes?" Her tone alarmed him, but he made his hands more urgent than ever. He was pushing the muslin now, down from her breast, and felt it stiffen to greet his hand.

"You're alone tonight, are you not? We're the only people in this wretched inn. Silas sleeps above the horses— and the right place for him. I am chaperoned by Sarah and your Mrs. Croston. But—Charles—I cannot bear to see you suffer; to think of you sleepless for my sake. Charles! I will come to you!"

His brain was racing, considering pros and cons. But there was only one thing to say. "My darling! But is it safe for you? I'd rather suffer anything than injure you."

She smiled up at him, pressing closer to his hand. "Dear, scrupulous Charles. But we are passing for a married couple, remember? If I need my husband's comfort in the night, who is to say me nay?"

He was in for it now. "My darling," he said. "What can I say but, thank you?"

She left him soon afterward, and he moved at once into the little room that served both as parlour and bar and ordered himself a stiff dram of the fierce, sweet drink the Americans called whiskey. He flattered himself that he had always been a man for civilized drinking, for his bottle of wine over dinner and his port afterward, but this was an occasion that called for strong measures.

If only he could stop thinking about Kate. Getting himself ready, at last, for bed, he could not shake his mind from the memory of the feel of her, furious, fighting, conquered at last. He must think about Arabella and all that money. He looked about the bleak men's dormitory. All the beds were equally narrow and equally horrible with feathers. Not much chance of pleasure here, he told himself gloomily, and then put his mind forcibly to work on the money.

Just the same, he was almost asleep when the door opened at last very softly. It had been a long day, and that American whiskey was stronger than he had thought. He pulled himself together to receive her. "Arabella! It's too good to be true!" When the door shut gently behind her, it was quite dark in the room. He moved forward to where she had stood outlined against the light in the hall. "Where are you, my love?"

"Here!" Suddenly she was pressed against him, the soft velvet of her negligee hardly masking her need of him. "Here I am, Charles."

His hands were gentle, too gentle, on her shoulders as he led her back to the narrow bed. Why would she not fight, like Kate?

FOURTEEN

WAKING TO FIND, WITH SOME RELIEF, that he was alone,
Manningham turned from the problem of Arabella to that
of Kate. In the course of the journey, he had made, and dismissed, one plan after another for dealing with her when
it became necessary. His idea when he first decided to bring
her had been to leave her behind on the last morning of the
journey. A dose of laudanum should ensure that she slept
through their departure. And then, even if she should
manage to follow them to Washington, she would never
find the secluded house where they would be staying.

But the alliance she had struck up with their driver,
Silas, cast doubt on this plan. He was not at all sure that
Silas would agree to start without her. Besides—he did not
want to leave her behind. For one thing, there was the problem of Sarah, who would doubtless become a screaming
maniac again if she were returned to her mother's care. No
—he must think of something else. Indeed, he had already
made a plan, which impressed even himself by its audacity.
His easy success with Arabella added to his confidence . . .
All he needed was a chance alone with Kate.

This came that afternoon when they reached a steep hill.
Sarah was fast asleep, spread out along the back seat of the
coach. Arabella never walked if she could help it, but the
horses were suffering under the August sun. Inevitably, he
and Kate found themselves climbing the hill together. The
very fact that she did not object to his company encouraged him, and he made a little business of being stiff from
sitting so as to give the coach a start on them. "We'll catch
them up soon enough when I've got rid of this wretched
cramp." He made, he flattered himself, a very convincing
job of his limp.

"Yes." Kate was doing her best to force the pace. "I don't want to be too far behind in case Sarah wakes up."

"Alone with her mother! Poor little thing. If I'd only known, I would never have let myself be persuaded to this mad venture."

"Oh?"

Something a little daunting about her tone, but he went boldly on. "Yes—I had no idea. Well; you expect a mother to be able to manage her own child, don't you? I hope to God we do find that Jonathan Penrose has reached Washington before us and is ready to come to terms. I can't say I fancy the idea of crossing the Atlantic with that child."

"You'd never take her?"

"Why not?" It seemed to him entirely reasonable. "What else could I do? I'm committed, aren't I? If Jonathan Penrose doesn't see reason here—why, he'll just have to come to England, and pay up there. More trouble for all of us. But—that's not what I wanted to talk about. Kate—I wanted to talk about us."

"Us?"

"Yes. I was beginning to be afraid I would never get the chance. Kate; I've never forgiven myself. When I woke up, that day last year, and saw your poor father's body, and remembered, I could have killed myself. You must understand, Kate. It was your fault, really; there's something about you that rouses the devil in a man. That's why I can't forget you. Don't want to. I looked everywhere for you that day. I'd have married you on the spot."

"Oh?" Stark unbelief in her tone. She looked ahead to where the coach had vanished around a turn of the road and quickened her pace.

"Yes. Truly I would." Did he dare to suggest that he had come to America merely to look for her? No, that kind of lie might work with Arabella, never with Kate. "But there was no trace of you," he went on. "I confess, in the end, I gave up. What else could I do? But I've never forgotten you. And now, finding you again like this; it must mean something."

"Mean something?"

He was beginning to find her cool repeated questions irritating. "Yes—that I should have an opportunity—a chance to atone for what I did."

She stopped and faced him squarely in the dusty road. "Mr. Manningham, what in the world are you saying?"

He was in for it now. "Why—that you're the only woman for me. No, let me go on. This journey has been torment to me. To see the contrast between you and Arabella . . . to remember what you and I have been to each other—"

"Mr. Manningham," she broke in. "You and I have never been anything to each other and never will. I find what you are saying infamous."

"No! Don't say that. What could I do, when that poor woman set her cap at me? She'd have run away anyway, I can tell you that. At least she's had me to protect her. I'll do what I can for her, but of course she is deluding herself when she thinks we will be able to marry. No sense troubling her now with painful truths. Time enough, if we get to England, for her to discover that divorce is not so easy there as she has convinced herself. And then, don't you see, that's where we come in."

"We?"

"Yes. You and I. You can't wish to stay in this barbarous country. It's impossible. This journey should have convinced you, if nothing else has. Filth, discomfort, insolence . . . Oh, I know you've borne it like the angel you are, but you're not one who won't notice . . . Besides what is there here for you? A stranger alone in an enemy country. Don't delude yourself Jonathan Penrose is going to have much to say to you, however we come out of this. You left without a word. What must he think? I don't know, of course, what terms you and he were on, but he's not exactly likely to welcome you back with open arms, is he? I know the child's devoted to you, but—I ask you—a child's devotion . . . No, Kate, trust mine. I'll see you through somehow. Did you know, I'm the heir to a title?"

Her thoughts had been racing while he talked. Madness to let herself show how angry he had made her. This might be her chance—hers and Sarah's. For inevitably she too had been wondering what would happen at the end of the journey; whether, in fact, he would let her reach Washington. It did not matter whether he meant what he said; the important thing was to make him think she believed him. That way, she would seem no threat to him. She had been silent too long; he was looking at her doubtfully. She made herself slow her step just a little, lean toward him. "Yes—I know. But—why should I believe you?" Her tone begged to be persuaded.

At last. He had really begun to think he had failed with her. "Why believe me? Look in your glass tonight, and then look at Arabella, at what this journey's done to her. Oh, she's a beauty of course, has been—and all a beauty's foibles. And now she's a woman for the lamplight, for the ballroom. But you, Kate, you're all fire and air—you're real, a creature of out-of-doors, someone a man could live for." And the worst of it was, he thought, he meant it. Surely there must be some way of getting Jonathan's money—and Kate. If he could, he told himself, he would. In the meantime, it was easy enough to put conviction into his voice. "You're not a woman a man can forget. You're in my blood, you haunt me . . . have, ever since . . ." Best stop there.

She did almost believe him and was filled with fury and disgust and an astonishing wave of pity for Arabella. She bent to hide her face and tie her shoe. She had been awake last night when Arabella tiptoed from the room, awake, too, when she returned much later. And now, this. Oh, poor Arabella. But it was Sarah she must think of. She made her voice a masterpiece of near-conviction. "You think I should trust you?"

He looked ahead. The coach was out of sight. Dared he risk it? He thought he must. There was, after all, only one sure way to convince a woman. "Of course you must." His hand found hers to pull her toward him. "My first and only love."

"No!" It came out oddly violent. Then he saw that like him she was looking anxiously ahead. "Suppose she should come back?" she said.

He let her go. "You're a woman in a million. We'll defer it, then, till happier times. In the meanwhile—you'll bear with me, Kate, if I keep up the pretence. Anything for a quiet life."

"Of course." This was going to be even more unpleasant than she had thought. "What will you tell her—about me? I imagine you had planned to leave me behind at the inn tonight."

"You're no fool, are you? That's just what I intended. Now—I'll tell her that I've fooled you properly by threats against Sarah; you've promised not to make trouble. Right?"

"Yes, of course." Who was fooling whom? It was a risk she had to take. She managed a melting look. "I'll do whatever you say."

"Admirable girl. Then—just go on behaving as you have done; treat me with that little scornful air of yours. I shall enjoy it—and wait for my reward. With money behind us, Kate, we'll make a partnership to beat the world."

Jonathan's money. Or Arabella's, look at it how you would. And—how difficult it was not to grit her teeth when he called her Kate. But here, thank goodness, was a turn of the road and, predictably, the coach waiting for them beyond it. A pity, of course, that she had not had time to find out more about his plans, but—how much longer could she have successfully kept up the pretense?

"What in the world happened to you?" Arabella leaned angrily out of the coach window.

"Mr. Manningham had the cramp." Kate let all her dislike into her voice as she climbed back into the seat by Sarah, who was beginning to stir restlessly in her sleep.

They stopped early that night, since the distance to Washington was just too great to be completed in a day. "We'll be there bright and early tomorrow," said Manningham, leading the way into the little inn. But he emerged from the bar a few minutes later, looking badly shaken. "Arabella, my love, you had best speak to the man." She had dropped into an upright chair on the inn porch, complaining, as usual, of the heat.

"I? Why in the world?"

"He seems to think me a spy! The English have landed at Benedict. The whole country's in an uproar; no one knows where they are headed, and the landlord here seems to think I have something to do with the business."

"Well now," the landlord himself emerged from the bar at this point, "I calculate I've got grounds enough. News of the redcoats landing this morning, and you turning up tonight, with your mealymouthed way of speech. What have you to say for yourself, ma'am?"

"To say? I? What should I say?" But she made a practical suggestion just the same. "Ask our driver if we have not come straight from Boston. How can we have any connection with the English landing?" And then, on a note of panic that was more convincing than anything: "There's no chance they'll get here tonight?"

The man laughed. "I guess they'll have better things to do than trouble themselves with a one-horse place like this. Washington or Baltimore's their goal, I reckon, or Commodore Barney's fleet of gunboats up river. With eight thousand men—and every one of them Peninsula veterans—I reckon they can have the lot, if they want, before Jemmy Madison so much as gets around to saying boo to them. Hang on there, ma'am—"Arabella's panic and her southern accent had had a mollifying effect, "and I'll jist have a word with your driver." Returning, he declared himself satisfied and shouted for his wife to "take the ladies upstairs, do."

They were the only guests in the inn that night, and Kate was glad of the company of the landlord and his family, who ate with them according to the gregarious American custom. Anything was preferable to being on their own.

Arabella was full of anxious questions. Had there been any more news? Which way did the landlord think the

English would turn? And what should they do? Turn back? Go on? Stay where they were?

"We go on, of course," Manningham interrupted her at this point. "If they only landed this morning, it's impossible—even if they are going there—that they should reach Washington for several days. If we stay here, we may fall into their hands; if we turn back, we may encounter them between this and Baltimore, which I think their most likely target. Think of the damage the privateers out of there have done to English shipping. Besides, if they do march on Washington, it stands to reason it will be hotly defended. Think of a march through this thick forest, in enemy country, with every man's hand against you. And I have always understood"—this to the landlord—"that your people were admirable marksmen. I wouldn't want to be part of an army that had to march, blind, through country like this, with your riflemen everywhere among the trees."

"You might be right at that." The man was mollified by the tribute to American skill. "And as to getting to Washington; I reckon you're right there, too. Stands to reason, if the redcoats do turn that way, they won't get there without a fight. And, meanwhile, you can slip in by the back door, as it were. Didn't you say you were heading for a house to the north of the city? Take the old road, and you've no need to go through the centre of town. I guess you've no cause for alarm, ma'am." He cut himself a huge slice of blueberry pie. "You'll be making an early start tomorrow?" to Manningham. "You'd best, if you want breakfast. I'm off first thing to join the militia, and Mrs. Jenks and the girls won't stay here alone. Not with your men about," this, again, directly for Manningham. "Not after what happened at Hampton last year."

"But that was French volunteers."

"That's what they *said*, but I'm not leaving Mrs. J. and the girls here to chance it, so if you want breakfast in the morning, be up early, that's all."

Arabella grumbled a good deal, but they were up early just the same, and drove off at the same time as the landlord and his family, who were going straight to Washington. "You're not afraid of running into the British?" asked Manningham.

"Course I am, but I reckon we've just got to chance it. By all reports, they are still at Benedict—God knows why! —With a bit of git-up-and-go they might have been at Washington by now, and not a soul to hinder them, save Jemmy Madison, and Armstrong and Monroe—" he used a couple of extremely picturesque native adjectives to describe the Secretaries of War and State. "I reckon you British jist can't stand our weather," he decided as he helped his wife and daughters mount their old-fashioned wagon. "Mebbe if our soldiers ain't got the spunk to beat 'em, our heat will. Let's hope so, anyways. I calculate it's just about all the hope we've got. So—good luck to you." And he whipped up his ancient horse and moved off down the Washington road.

Silas, too, urged on his horses and turned them along the little-used country lane that would take them directly to the Rock Creek house.

"How long should it take us?" Arabella leaned forward to ask it eagerly.

"Not too long." Silas was never one to commit himself. "With a bit of luck, I reckon you'll be at your friends' for dinner. I certainly mean to have my horses safe stabled by tonight."

"Safe?"

"Yes, ma'am. Didn't you hear landlord say the redcoats had no cavalry? Well, stands to reason they wouldn't have; coming by sea like that. So—horses is going to be a mighty vallyable commodity round here, I reckon; and I'm taking no chances with mine. No, ma'am," and then, for emphasis, to Manningham, "No, sir." And he turned his attention to his horses.

They saw a few families that day, obviously in flight, with all their possessions heaped, as the Jenkses', had been, in a covered wagon, but those they stopped knew no more than they did themselves. Some were convinced that the redcoats had turned away toward Baltimore, others were equally sure that it was Commodore Barney and his flotilla of gunboats that they were after, but a depressing majority seemed certain that Washington was their target. "Well," drawled a harassed-looking man whose shabby blacks indicated that he belonged to one of the professions, "stands to reason, don't it? We burnt that Canadian capital of theirs — York. They'll burn Washington, and serve us right, say I. But I won't be there to see. It's me for Tenallytown before night." And he whipped up his horse and hurried past Silas, who refused to push his horses for anything or anyone.

But he was as good as his word, just the same, and it was still early afternoon when he pulled up his horses and pointed with his whip at a narrow track that led steeply up from the road. "I reckon that's your turning, ma'am, by the directions you gave me."

"Do you think so?" Arabella leaned forward to look out through the open sides of the coach. "It doesn't look very well used, does it?"

He shrugged. "We can but go and see. One thing's sartin; there ain't so much as a chipmunk about we can ask." And without more ado he turned the coach down the narrow track, which wound upward through thick woods for three quarters of a mile or so.

Kate, on the back seat as usual, with Sarah, was absorbing two shocks at once. She had not realized before that even Arabella had never visited these cousins of whom she spoke so confidently. And—she had taken it for granted that a house on the outskirts of Washington—the capital city of America—would be—she looked about her—well, not in the deep forest. What hopes of help had she here among the trees?

But it was no good indulging in second thoughts now. Perhaps she should have asked the Jenkses for help before they parted. Perhaps not. At all events, here she was. And, at this moment, in fact, the coach pulled up a last steep slope and emerged from the trees to the sight of a house perched above them still, in a large clearing among fields that Kate had learned to recognize in the last few days as growing tobacco. It was a big gray stone house, well positioned on the brow of the hill, its pillared portico facing them as they pulled up the last weary incline of their journey.

"That's better," said Arabella with satisfaction. "You see"—to Manningham—"I told you it was an old estate. My grandfather built here long before the town of Washington was so much as thought of."

"Yes," said Manningham, "but where is everyone?"

It had struck Kate, too, that the scene was oddly lifeless. She had got used by now to the sight of southern plantations with their abundance of black labour—whole families working in the tobacco fields together, and laughing black children who came running from all directions at the sound of a coach. But here was not a soul in sight. The house faced them, as Silas turned his horses into the carriage sweep, blank and silent, its windows shuttered against the afternoon sun.

The big front door, too, that should have stood hospitably open, was tight shut. Silas looked at it. "I suppose," he said to Arabella, "your cousins are expecting you?"

"Well, not precisely. There was no time. Charles—"

"You mean you never wrote them?"

"Well, what was the use, since we would be here as soon as the letter?" She meant to sound reasonable, but merely sounded pleading.

"Idiotic!" He turned away from her to beat a resounding tattoo with the door knocker. Nothing happened. They had all known that nothing would. "Your cousins are doubtless safe in Virginia by now." Manningham's tone was withering. "But I confess I am surprised that they left the house empty. It's asking to have it sacked."

"I guess they didn't," put in Silas. "I guess they left the slaves to run the place. Only I calculate them slaves had a better idea. Have you heard tell of the redcoats' black regiments? That's where they'll be, by now, and giving information about this place here, nineteen to the dozen."

"I expect you're right." Manningham turned angrily away from the door to look about him. "So—what's to do?" Kate had emerged from the coach now, and he spoke as much to her as to Arabella.

"What can we do?" asked Arabella. "But go on to Washington? We can't possibly stay here, with no servants. It won't take long, will it, Silas?"

"Depends on the roads—and what you find. You're going nearer to the enemy, every step you take; that's one thing certain."

"Oh." In her preoccupation with immediate discomfort, she had forgotten the greater threat. "What shall we *do*, Charles?"

"Stay here of course. As the man says, who knows what we might not find in Washington?" His tone underlined the words. "No. We're all tired out. We'll manage here somehow for tonight; then tomorrow Silas can drive me into town to see what goes on."

"Not me," said Silas cheerfully. "I contracted to bring you here. Right? Well, I've brought you. If you'll put me up for the night, I'll say thank you kindly, but tomorrow I start for home. By the back roads like we came. I'm not losing my good horses to the redcoats. Nor having them commandeered by the militia down there," he gestured with his whip in the direction where Washington must lie. "No sir." He finished. "No, ma'am." And meant it. Manningham argued and Arabella tried to cajole in vain. He ended the affair by stumping off to see if the stables were "fit for my horses to spend the night."

Arabella turned on Manningham: "Well, of all the ill-managed—"

"You're a fine one to talk." He was as angry as she. "Who didn't trouble, if you please, to write and say we were coming. I suppose you were ashamed—" They were at it hammer and tongs, all the irritations of the journey bubbling to the surface. Kate looked into the coach. Blessedly, Sarah was fast asleep. She moved away along the front of the house, looking for a means of entry.

She found it around at the back, where the stable yard was bounded by the miserable hovels that constituted the slaves' quarters. Someone, it appeared, had been before her. A window at the back of the house had been smashed and now hung drunkenly open on its hinges. Peering in out of the bright sunshine, she could see a large, untidy kitchen showing all the signs of having been hastily left. There was even half a loaf of bread and what might be a pitcher of milk on the table. She hurried back around the house and found the other two arguing more bitterly than ever. "We can get in at the back," she interrupted them unceremoniously. "If we are to spend the night here, had we not better get to work?"

"You're right, of course." Manningham turned to her with obvious relief. "How do we get in?"

"I'll show you, if Mrs. Penrose will stay with Sarah. I don't want her to wake up all alone."

"I?" Arabella bridled at the suggestion. "I thank you, no. I'll not be landed with one of her tantrums."

Kate shrugged. "You're probably right. Anyway"—to Manningham—"you'll have no trouble in finding your way. There's a broken window around in the stable yard, leading straight into the kitchen. By the look of things, we're lucky. I don't know what happened, but I don't think there's been much looting. Oh!" Sarah had waked. She climbed back into the coach as Manningham and Arabella disappeared around the side of the house, still arguing.

Silas returned just as she had got Sarah settled in a cool patch of shadow on the front porch. "I've got the horses fixed up," he announced, "and found myself quarters in the coachman's house. Plenty to eat and a good bed. Tell Captain Manningham I'll see him in the morning, before I go."

"Of course, Silas." At least it avoided the scene Arabella would inevitably have made if she found she had to eat with Silas. But—he was her friend, she thought, and certainly

Sarah's. Should she let him go like this? And yet, what could he do for them? Nothing. She held out her hand. "Good-bye, Silas. And thanks for everything."

"You'll be all right? You and the child?" What must he think about their strange party?

"I think so." After all, Jonathan would certainly be in Washington by now with the money.

"Good. I'll say good-bye then." He turned away, all too evidently relieved to have made his offer of help and been let off.

So much for that. The big door swung open behind her, revealing Manningham. "Welcome to Liberty Hall," he said.

The house was smaller than its imposing façade had led Kate to expect. Arabella had already found the best bedroom and had shut herself in there. "A crisis of the nerves, she says." Manningham led Kate and Sarah down the corridor that ran from front to back of the house on the second story. "I thought you and the child could sleep in here."

"Admirable." It was obviously a room belonging to two little girls, with narrow beds side by side and everywhere the signs of rapid packing. "We shall do splendidly here, shan't we, Sarah? But right now, I think food, don't you? I'm ravenous, and I'm sure Sarah is, too."

"Yes." He turned to lead the way downstairs again. "I shall be in there," he pointed to the second bedroom at the front of the house. "If you should need me."

"I shan't." It came out more firmly than she had intended, and she hastened to qualify it. "Give us a proper bed, and we're set to sleep for fourteen hours, aren't we, Sarah?"

On closer examination, the kitchen showed signs of rapid, disorganized looting. "Something must have panicked them, I think," Kate decided after her rapid, competent inspection. "Lucky for us. There's plenty of everything we shall need for a day or so." She was busy tidying up as she spoke. "I wonder about livestock." The milk in the pitcher was sour. "Surely they must have their own. Would the slaves have taken them?"

195

"I'll go and look." Manningham returned in a few moments to report that he had found hens and a cow in a shed at the far end of the stables. "The cow's in a bad way. Do you think she needs milking?"

"I'm sure she does." Kate laughed and sighed and rolled up her sleeves. "Pass me that bucket, would you?"

FIFTEEN

SARAH THOUGHT IT A GREAT GAME to help look for eggs in the poultry yard, and Kate smiled and followed her and thought once again how wonderfully better she was. Had she really left her tantrums and her terror of Arabella behind at Penrose?

It seemed almost a miracle, she thought later, slicing ham from the cold underground larder and expertly frying eggs on the fire she had contrived to kindle in the huge kitchen range. Under these strange conditions, Sarah was being good as gold, trotting to and fro setting places at the big kitchen table. "You are a help to me, honey." Kate bent impulsively to kiss her and heard, for the second time, a tiny threadlike whisper: "Kate."

Her eyes were suddenly painful with tears. Whatever happened, she vowed to herself, breaking another egg, Sarah was not going to be hurt. She would do anything, risk anything to protect her, to safeguard this extraordinary improvement. Anything? Her mind flashed back to Manningham upstairs: "I shall be in there . . . if you need me." Yes, if necessary, anything.

As a great concession, Silas agreed to drive Manningham part of the way to Washington next morning: "I'm turning back before we enter the town itself—such as it is," he stipulated. "I'm not taking any chances with my horses. But no doubt you'll be able to get a hackney carriage once you're nearer in. If things aren't too bad." They had seen no one since they arrived at the house and felt as isolated as if they were on the moon.

"But we would have heard the sounds of a battle," said Manningham. "I expect no difficulty. I'm sure I will find that the English are safe back on their ships by now—or, at the very worst, turned towards Baltimore. What in the world would they want with a ghost town like Washington?"

"I hope you're right." Kate was delighted to see him go. Arabella had stayed in bed this morning, complaining of palpitations, so she and Sarah had the house to themselves. It was a happy day. They began by tidying and cleaning the big kitchen, and then, "Washday now," said Kate. After a brief moral struggle she had appropriated clean clothes for herself and Sarah from the bedroom closets, and now they set to sociably to heat up water in the big copper and wash out everything they had worn on the journey. Insensibly, with occupation, some of the burden of anxiety that had weighed on her ever since the beginning of this strange venture eased away, and she found herself singing as she worked. Surely Manningham would find a letter from Jonathan waiting for him at the address he had given in Washington? He would return to say the nightmare was over. Perhaps by this evening she and Sarah would be safe with Jonathan in a Washington hotel. Safe—with Jonathan? What would that mean? What would he and she have to say to each other after all that had happened? The question caught like a sob in her throat, and Sarah, who had been singing and scrubbing beside her looked up anxiously. How terrifyingly quick the child was to catch one's every mood. "It's all right, poppet," she smiled reassuringly. "I was just thinking . . ." Tone was always more effective with Sarah than words. "Now I'll show you how the wringer works." Sarah was quick to learn, and they were soon out in the sun-drenched garden, hanging their washing on the line that stood ready among neglected corn in the vegetable patch.

When they had finished, Kate turned to look at the straggling plants of corn. "Look, Sarah, here's an ear that's ready, and here's another. Let's shuck them out here, shall we, and I'll cook them for our dinner. There's plenty of butter in the larder, and ham to go with them." Her hands were busy as she spoke, peeling the green outer leaves away from the golden spike of corn, and Sarah picked up another ear to imitate her. Was it really as simple as this, Kate wondered? Was all that Sarah needed real things to do?

She sat back on her heels, idle for a moment, watching Sarah's little hands working absorbedly at their task, and made herself face the future. So far, on this fantastic journey, the present had been problem enough. But now, with every chance that they might see Jonathan tonight, she must make herself look ahead, must face the fact that after what had happened between them she could not, for any consideration—no, not even for Sarah—live at Penrose with him again.

She caught Sarah's anxiously questioning eye and picked up a new ear of corn while she faced another fact. Sarah needed her. No getting away from that. It was her own presence, always there, always loving, always the same, that had brought the child through the stresses and strains of the journey. Occupation might be important, but her own constant presence was equally so. Sarah adored Jonathan, but—the journey had proved it—she could do without him. So—there it was. Kate smiled wryly to herself, remembering the incredible proposition he had made that night—it seemed a lifetime ago. But though so much had happened, nothing, in fact, had changed. His suggestion of a ménage à trois with Sarah for the third member could never be anything but outrageous. She must hold fast to that; never give way to the little devil inside her that asked: what difference did it make? What reputation had she to lose? Because that was not the point: she had Jonathan to think of, and, still more, Sarah.

The ear of corn broke in her hands, and Sarah dropped her own to look at her in anxious surprise.

"Goodness, look how clumsy I am! I shall let you finish, honey, while I watch." She had come to her decision as her hands, betrayed her. She and Sarah would go and live in Jonathan's remote cottage, but he would never visit them.

Never? It was a hard word. Something in her rebelled against it. It was all so unfair. Arabella had left her husband. What did she deserve? She picked up a long green corn leaf and began systematically stripping it into sections. That was not the point. Jonathan was married to Arabella. She remembered—now, of all times must she remember?—her father's voice, discussing an aristocratic divorce, pushed through the House of Lords. "Whom God hath joined," he had quoted, "let no man put asunder."

It was all absurd anyway. Massachusetts was Jonathan's life, and—divorce in Massachusetts? But Sarah had finished. She picked up the shining, sweating ears. "Splendid. Now let's go indoors and see how your mother is."

Wonderful how Sarah had lost her terror of her mother. Kate would never understand how it had happened, but it was the crowning mercy of the journey. When she told Jonathan—she pulled herself up short. She was going to tell Jonathan Penrose as little as possible. Perhaps, even, the question would never arise. At the time, she had discounted Manningham's suggestion that Jonathan would have been enraged by her unexplained disappearance. She had taken it, she supposed, for granted that he would understand what had happened, would realize that inevitably she would put Sarah first. But—he had surprised her painfully enough before. Suppose he failed, too, in this. Suppose she were to find herself dismissed at once without discussion.

No good pretending it was not possible. She understood Jonathan well enough now to recognize that his instinctive distrust of women (and could you blame him for it?) left him all too ready to believe the worst, even of her. Odd, but not entirely so, to find herself thinking about Othello. Had *he* had a mother, ever, or sisters? He had certainly, like Jonathan in his seafaring days, lived a life mainly free from female contact. A cold shiver ran down her spine. What was Jonathan thinking now? But at least—she was making now a conscious effort to pull herself together—I'm no Desdemona. If he tries to dismiss me, I'll make him see that Sarah has to come first. And she needs me.

Kate made, as best she could, a game of the rest of the morning. They cooked their corn early, and took up a tray to Arabella, who still proclaimed herself very ill indeed. Then, the kitchen tidied, Kate said, "Shall we rest outdoors, love?" And out they went to a patch of shade under a huge butternut tree, where she could lie and dream her unhappy dreams while Sarah "rested" by chasing the multi-coloured butterflies that played like wind-borne jewels in the sunshine.

Their halcyon time was not disturbed till the shadows of the trees were lengthening and a cool breeze had blown up from the crevasse by which the house stood. The evening birds were beginning to sing and the crickets were in full chorus. Kate felt a batswing of anxiety brush her consciousness. What was keeping Manningham so long?

She rose. "Time to go in, love, and think what it's to be for supper. Ham and eggs, do you think? Or, maybe, eggs and ham?" Of course, Sarah never reacted to this kind of simple verbal joke in words, but, as always, a delighted smile showed that she had taken it. Really, speech was not all that important.

Arabella was up at last. "Where in the world have you been?" And then, seeing their arms full of clean linen: "You might have told me you were washing!"

"I'm sorry." Kate made herself take it coolly.

"And my bed needs making."

This was too much. Kate turned to look at her. "Does it?" she said.

It was lucky that Manningham came in, just then, from the stable yard, but evident at once that he, too, was in the worst of tempers. "Of all the slugs, that horse is the worst." He threw hat and riding gloves on the kitchen table. "And the only carriage I could get liable to fall to bits any moment. I thought I'd never get here. And then—to have to stable the brute myself. And, my God, the heat: it's insupportable."

"But what's the news?" Arabella wasted no time on sympathy.

"Bad. The town's in a panic. At last reports, the English were at Nottingham—it's barely thirty miles from Washington. There are all kinds of rumours, of course, and not much organization that I can see . . . General Ross might have a walkover if he quit fooling around and attacked."

"A walkover!" Arabella shuddered. "But what about us? Did you get the letter?"

"Of course I did." A furious glance reminded her of Kate's presence. "I'll tell you about it after supper. Thank God for the sight of food."

Kate, who had had everything ready, had been busy frying eggs as he talked, and now put lavish helpings onto four plates. They ate for the most part in silence, and then Arabella and Manningham withdrew to the front of the house, leaving Kate and Sarah to wash the dishes. Kate could hear their voices raised in furious argument. Whatever the letter Manningham had received might be, it had not been good news. What then? It must have been from Jonathan. Could he have refused to ransom Sarah? It seemed impossible. And yet, what else could those furious unintelligible voices mean?

Idiot that she was; she had been so sure Jonathan would pay up, that Manningham's return tonight would mean the end of the affair. She had let herself spend the day in dangerous relaxation, enjoying the improvement in Sarah, when she should have been planning ahead for just such a crisis as this.

Quick, as always, to sense her mood, Sarah was looking at her anxiously. She put away the last plate. "Come, love, it's not quite bedtime yet. Let's go out into the garden. I've thought of a new game." Not a very nice one. But if they went quietly out the back way, and crept around to the front of the house, they had a fair chance of overhearing what Manningham and Arabella were saying so angrily, in the big front drawing room.

She had her hand on the latch of the back door when Manningham's voice stopped her. "No, Mrs. Croston." His tone was regretful. His hand held a pistol. "This is the end of the road, I'm afraid. No—don't move. Remember: if I am compelled to kill you, I shall have to get rid of the witness." A tiny jerk of the head indicated Sarah, who had got down from her chair and was watching, wide-eyed. Mercifully, Kate thought, the pistol itself almost certainly meant nothing to her.

"That's right." He recognized her silence as that of defeat. "I don't at all like violence," he went on. "You can rely on me to avoid it at all costs—or almost. So—do as you are told and no harm will come to you. Or to the child. Sit down, Kate, and put your hands on the table. I have to talk to you."

"Talk!" But she kept her voice as calm as possible, for fear of alarming Sarah, and sat down obediently with her hands where he could see them on the table.

"We don't want trouble, you see." He actually sounded apologetic. "Well, I don't, anyway. I suppose you heard us arguing in there. Arabella wants an accident . . ." Fantastically, he was explaining to her. "Well—figure it for yourself—it could happen so easily in a strange house. The well . . . that steep flight of stairs . . . anything. But I won't have that. Of course I won't." Was he trying to convince himself, or her? "I still hope it will all work out for the best. I'll try to come back for you. When it's all settled. I promise I will. I'll do everything I can. Only, you see, I've got to have the money. I can't go back to England otherwise. You've got to see; right now, it's hopeless. It's all Penrose's fault, God damn him!"

"Quietly!" She made herself say it coolly, for Sarah's sake. The child had settled herself on a chair by the table and was sitting there, listening to everything he said, her hands busy with that old, strange habit of arranging a line of spoons and forks across the table. It was a bad sign. She had not done it since she had been ill. "Don't forget the child."

"I'm not. I'm not forgetting anything, Kate. But what can

I do? I must have money." For him, it explained and excused everything.

"Yes." The longer he talks, she thought, the longer I have to plan. "I see," she said, while her brain raced, searching for a thread of hope. She was consumed with rage—at herself. To have been caught like this . . . But she must keep him talking. "Do I gather," she made it light, "that Mr. Penrose has not come through with the money?"

"No, damn it." Rage outran discretion. "Writes me as cool as you please, that we shall have it when Sarah is safe back with him. A likely story!"

"He gave you his word?" Why had she never thought of this?

"Naturally. And what's that worth? The word of a Yankee? That's what I've been trying to explain to that obstinate woman in there. Give him Sarah, and it's good-bye to everything. No, no; I'm too old a bird to be caught with that kind of chaff."

It was absurd: it was disaster. If Arabella could not convince him that Jonathan's word was sound as the Bank of England, what hope had she? But she must try just the same. "You're crazy," she said. "You don't understand . . ."

"These cursed Americans? Thank you, Kate, I think I understand them a little too well. Fight us with one hand and feed us with the other! Float loans against us and then buy our own bills at discount as investments? What kind of honourable thinking is that? And then you expect me to trust the word of a twisting New Englander! You know as well as I do that the Yankees are famous for sharp practice, even here where the most flagrant cheat's called the best bargain."

"But Jonathan's not like that! You must believe me." In her eagerness to convince him she hardly noticed that he was moving slowly nearer. "I promise you, if you have it in his writing, you might as well have the Bank of England notes in your pocket."

"Thank you," dryly. "But that's what I'd rather have."

And then, on a different note, "What's that confounded child doing now?"

Kate turned in a flash, to see Sarah still apparently absorbed in laying lines of forks across the table. "It's too bad," she heard, then the pistol crashed against her temple and she fell oceans down into blackness.

SIXTEEN

HER HEAD WAS SPLITTING. Where was she? Worse still, why could she not move? Hot sunshine on her face told her that dangerously much time must have passed since she plunged into unconsciousness. Calm now; don't panic. She could move her head. She was lying flat on her back, hands and feet tied to a narrow bed. Yes, one of the beds in the room she had shared with Sarah.

Sarah! Where was she now? The scurrying thoughts exacerbated the pain in her head as she worked frantically against the bonds that held her. But they were like iron against her wrists and ankles. She only hurt herself. An accident! She remembered Manningham's apparent rejection of the idea. Idiot, ever to have believed a word he said. Instead of killing her outright, he had left her to a lingering, helpless death in this deserted house.

Deserted? Why was she so horribly sure of this? Well, of course it stood to reason. They must have left as soon as they had tied her up. They would be safely settled in some Washington hideaway by now. Doubtless that was really what the argument had been about last night. Arabella would not have been pleased with the idea of moving nearer to the invading British Army. But Manningham! Was this his plan of escape? Perhaps he had already taken Arabella and Sarah across the lines. She could hear her own breathing, harsh and desperate in the stillness of the house, and made a conscious effort to calm it.

This was no time for panic thinking. Manningham could not join the British Army until his exchange came through. So—if she could get to Washington, there was still a chance. For Sarah's sake as much as her own, she must manage to get free. She made herself lie quiet for a few endless moments, resting, clearing her mind of everything but the immediate problem. Her hands were by her sides, tied to the frame of the cot bed. Her feet were tied together to its foot. Concentrate, then, on her hands. Put all the pressure she could bear first on one, then on the other. It hurt horribly. But slow death by starvation would not be pleasant either. And then there was Sarah.

What kind of rope would they have found in this house? Nothing very splendid from what she had seen of the other household equipment. She strained harder and more painfully than ever, but still with no effect. She was sobbing now, at once with pain and with rage at herself. She had thought she was fooling Manningham so finely by pretending to fall in with his blandishments—and all the time he had been one jump ahead of her. To have spent yesterday so light-heartedly in the garden with Sarah . . . folly ! They should have escaped : might have been safe by now. But Jonathan had told her he intended to pay the ransom : how could she have foreseen the absurd, the tragi-comic misunderstanding between him and Manningham.

But she should have. She should have realized that neither would trust the other. If she died here alone, it would be entirely her own fault. And—Sarah? Her fault too : all her fault. She who had been so grandiloquently ready to sacrifice everything for Sarah ! Hot colour flooded her cheeks as she remembered just what she had meant by that "everything." Oh, he had fooled her finely, had Charles Manningham. Her hands fought furiously against the rope that held them. No use : only intolerable pain that was somehow comforting. She bit her lip and tried still harder. And—that letter from Jonathan. Did it mean that he was in Washington? Surely it must. So—if she could only get loose, get there, find him. Absurd to plan like this, as she lay here helplessly fighting despair and pain.

But better to plan than to despair. Besides, it took her mind off the agony of her hands. Five miles to Washington, Silas had said. She had worked out a rhythm now. Push, strain against the rope, count five as the pain got worse, count ten if she could make herself, then relax for the same count. And think of the clothesline where Sarah had helped her hang their washing. Old, surely, and frayed?

But perhaps there had been a new one stored somewhere in the kitchen. Don't think like that. Defeatist thinking. Five miles to Washington—and no money. Throughout the journey, this had been one of the difficulties of her position. When Manningham had fetched her, so unexpectedly, from the garden at Penrose, she had had none on her. But this was defeatism too. There must surely be money somewhere in this big house. Yes, wryly, she found herself smiling: and here you lie helpless, thinking about looking for it.

It made her angry, and anger made her bear the pain to the count of fifteen, and then on up to twenty, and at twenty it happened. A tiny rending noise, the barest perceptible giving of the rope around her right hand. She gritted her teeth and went on pushing. It was easier to bear the pain now, with hope for company, but it took her an agonized half-hour or so of pushing and resting before she had her right hand free. And then it was so numb with pain and constriction that it was some time before she could use it to work fumblingly at freeing her other hand. After that, it was easy. Untying the rope that had bound her feet, she saw that it was in fact a brand-new piece and shivered at her good fortune that they had used the older bit on her hands.

Her feet, too, were numb, but she must lose no time. She managed to crawl to the two little chests of drawers that stood side by side under the window and sat by them as she went methodically through their contents. She disliked herself as she did it, but found, at last, a purse with two dollars in it. It might not be wealth, but it was a great deal better than nothing.

She could stand now and walk, limping. The five miles to Washington were going to be a long way. She took time, just the same, to make herself eat some ham and stale bread and drink a mugful of yesterday's sour milk. The poor cow . . . she could only hope that some neighbour would think of it today.

Her watch had stopped, but when she got outside she

thought by the position of the sun that it must be pretty close to midday. The food had helped to ease her headache, but she was shivering all over and grateful for the heat of the sun. She shut the big front door carefully behind her and started to hobble down the driveway.

The pain in her feet eased gradually with walking and she pushed herself forward steadily, trying to map out a plan of campaign as she went. The first thing, of course, was to find Jonathan. Surely he must be in Washington, and so new a town should not have too many hotels. Or—would it? Here an alarming memory assailed her. Someone, surely, had told her that many congressmen found it too expensive to bring their families to Washington with them, preferring to live in one of its many boardinghouses. Well, nothing for it but to make the round of them.

The sun was very hot. She had stopped shivering and was sweating instead. Dust rose from the road and choked her. If she could only lie down in that patch of shade over there and rest, and rest, and rest . . . She pushed on and heard, as she did so, the sound of a carriage behind her. She turned, a dishevelled enough figure, she knew, to hold out a pleading hand.

It was a small, shabby, one-horse chaise driven by an elderly man. For a moment she thought he was going right by, then, miraculously, he spoke to the horse and pulled it to a halt a little way past her.

"Going into town?" he asked, as she limped up to him. "You don't look just in the shape for walking."

"I'm not." Now she had time to worry about her accent. "If you would be so good—"

"Of course. Couldn't leave a dog to walk in this heat, and with the damned redcoats about too. Up you get, ma'am," he reached a bony hand down to help her up beside him. "You're not from these parts, I reckon?" The question was both inevitable and, luckily, expected.

She had her answer ready. "No, I'm from Boston."

"Ho! I thought as much. One of them tarnation Feds are you?" But his tone was as friendly as ever, merely more inquisitive. "Well now, ma'am, do you reckon those New England states of yours are really going about to secede from the Union?"

"I hope not." Odd to realize that she really meant it. "But what's the news today, sir? I've heard nothing."

"I thought not, or you'd not have been walking the country roads alone. By all I hear the redcoats will be here any time now. Did you hear the explosions yesterday? That was Commodore Barney blowing up his flotilla of gunboats so they wouldn't be captured. Gunboats!" He spat expressively. "Where are our frigates, that's what I want to know? What's Jemmy Madison been doing all this time? Barney's a fine man—everyone knows that—but what use are a pack of gunboats against the British Navy? Well—we've seen. And now, what's left but Washington? It stands to reason. By all reports they camped night before last at Nottingham —well now, I reckon that's not more than thirty miles from the village."

"Village?" she was puzzled.

"Washington. Of course, you're a stranger: a village in a swamp, they call it, and just about right too. Look!" He slowed his horse as the road emerged from trees on the crest of the ridge they had been following. "There!" He pointed with his whip. "There's the mighty capital of these United States. I don't reckon it looks much like Boston, does it?"

It was hardly the moment to tell him she had never actually been into Boston. Besides, she was absorbed in the view of winding river with blue hills beyond and, this side, a scattering of houses here and there among the trees. "That must be the Capitol?" She pointed to the largest building she could see, far off to the left, white and conspicuous on its hill.

"Yes—and not finished either! And if you look this way" —he gestured with his whip—"you might get a glimpse of the President's palace through the trees. Palace they call it, but I reckon Mrs. Adams—or Dolly Madison come to that —ain't found it any bed of roses. I guess Congress was plumb crazy when it voted to move down here. You can call that half-done building the Capitol—and Goose Creek the Tiber, too—but it don't make the place anything better than a village in a swamp, and like to remain so. Who in their senses would live here if they could help?" And with this rhetorical question he whipped up his horse and started down a long slope among trees through which Kate could now see, here and there, an isolated house.

"Oh yes," he replied when she commented on this. "There are houses all over among the woods. Lonesomer, I reckon, than living on the frontier. Well," he explained, "you expect to be lonesome there. But tell me, ma'am, where am I to set you down?"

"Oh!" She should have been ready for this. "Wherever suits you. I'm most grateful . . ."

"No, no." They had emerged from the trees on to a much broader street crowded with every possible kind of vehicle. "Just what I expected." He sounded almost pleased. "The place is in a panic. I'll not leave a Boston young lady to walk a step she don't have to in a crowd like this. So, where will suit you, ma'am?"

"You're very good. Well then, if it's not too much trouble, could you take me to the principal hotel?" On their journey, Jonathan had always stayed at the best hotel in town.

"The chief one?" His answer was discouraging. "Well, you see, ma'am, there's so many, Washington being the kind of place it is. There's Long's, and Tomlinson's—would it be either of those?" And then, as she shook her head doubtfully. "Well, I reckon the best thing I can do is set you down at Flood's on Pennsylvania Avenue. I'm for the Navy Yard myself, so it won't be taking me out of the way."

"Oh, thank you!" They were moving much more slowly now, weaving their way through the throng of miscellaneous vehicles, all piled high with boxes and bundles.

"It don't look much as if there's been good news, I calculate." He slowed his horse on a wide, poplar-lined avenue. "There you are, Flood's Hotel, ma'am, and good luck to you."

She jumped down, thanked him warmly, and then, feeling an odd little qualm as he turned away into the throng of vehicles, squared her shoulders and went into the hotel. It was a big place, its downstairs rooms so full of vociferous people that it took her some time to attract the barkeeper's attention, and she was grateful, as she waited, for the experience she had had of American hotels, and the confidence it gave her that she would be courteously treated.

Imagine arriving alone at a similar hotel in London! There, she would have been the object of scornful looks and *sotto voce* comment; here, men automatically moved aside for her and even seemed to be trying not to spit on the skirts of her gown.

How odd to realize now, at this moment of crisis, public as well as private, that she liked it here. And horrible to think that the confusion around her, the panic-stricken families in the streets, were all because of her own people, the invading English.

But here was her chance at the barkeeper. She swallowed a lump in her throat and asked him if Mr. Penrose was staying in the hotel.

"Penrose? No, ma'am, I guess we ain't got no one by that name here."

Absurd to have been so hopeful. She asked the man to direct her to Washington's next largest hotel. "I know this is supposed to be the best."

"Well, ma'am, the place is full of them," but at least the compliment had caught his sympathy, and he reeled off an alarmingly long list of names and addresses. She thought, at the last moment, of asking whether Mr. and Mrs. Manningham and their daughter were staying here, but again he shook his head. That, too, would have been too easy. Anyway, she told herself, back in the hot and crowded road, it it was not much use finding Sarah until she had Jonathan's support. But, oh, Sarah, what is happening to you?

The sun blazed down; the air was heavy with the threat of thunder; the streets were more crowded than ever. The bag that had seemed so tiny when she packed it this morning now dragged on her arm. If only she had dared ask for a room at Flood's Hotel . . . but with merely two dollars . . . She must find Jonathan before anything else.

She had heard about the long distances between houses in Washington and was now to prove it the most painful way. The heat of the dusty streets burned up through her thin shoes. Most of the roads were unpaved and rough; houses tended to stand well back so that even when she thought she had reached them, there was a rough carriage way to be plodded over. Her head ached unmercifully. She visited four more hotels and two boardinghouses, and received the same answer at each. "Mr. Penrose of Boston? Sorry, ma'am." But each one had a further suggestion, a boardinghouse, perhaps, run by a friend.

All the time, as she trudged from house to house, her sense of urgency was mounting, exacerbated by the panic around her. After the eighth blank, she sat down, a little giddy from heat and headache, and made herself think. There must be some other way. Delving deep back in memory, she tried to remember everything Jonathan had said about Washington. Surely, at some point, he must have mentioned where he had stayed? Suppose it had been with friends. What hope was there then of finding him, what hope for Sarah? She could see now that it would be useless to appeal for help to the forces of law and order. At the best of times, she had heard, Washington had a curious police system all its own. Today the very idea was lunacy. To be talking of one kidnapped child, when the whole place was simmering with panic . . . No, whatever she did, would have to be on her own.

She had rested enough. The pain in her head was a little easier, but she made herself take a piece of stale bread out of her bag and eat it. There had been no inspiration, no memory of a friend, or an address; she would just have to go on, doggedly, as she had been doing.

At the fifth place she tried, the barkeeper was unusually helpful. "There is a little place on F Street," he said, "where

213

a lot of the Boston Feds often go . . . Quiet, you know—you might try there."

It was a long walk back to F Street, but at least the heat was going from the sun now, and the crowds were less. Many people had already left Washington; others, no doubt, were indoors packing up. The slackening of the panic seemed to suggest than an attack on the city was not imminent. She had heard all kinds of rumours, as she waited for attention in one inn after another. The English had turned back to Baltimore after all; they were still at Marlborough; they had turned off the Washington road and were on their way to Alexandria . . . Nobody really knew anything; not even, with any certainty, where the American forces under Winder had got to. "At least, there's been no battle," she heard one man say. "They're so near, we'd have heard it." And, "Trust Winder to avoid a fight if he can," said another.

She had been searching now for nearly five hours. Soon, mere exhaustion would compel her to give up for the night. Would her two dollars buy her supper and a bed at Washington prices? They probably would, she thought, unless the panic had inflated things beyond reason. Tomorrow would have to take care of itself.

The hotel on F Street was set far back in a wood lot, so that she passed it once without realizing it was there. As she struggled wearily up the carriage way and saw the pleasant white frame house with its big screened porch, she thought that it did, in fact, look the kind of place where Jonathan might stay.

Indoors, too, it was quieter than most of the places she had visited. The bartender was at her disposal at once. "Mr. Penrose, ma'am? Mr. Penrose from Boston?" Her heart gave a great leap; he spoke as if the name was at least familiar. "Why, yes, ma'am, he was here all right, but he left us Saturday morning. Went out to Bladensburg to dig fortifications with the rest of them—and about time too! And I reckon he must have meant to spend the night there. Hey! What's the matter?" He caught her as she swayed, and helped her into a chair. "Here"—he poured from bottle to glass—"drink that. You won't like it, but it'll do you good."

It was pure fire, and she gulped and shuddered and felt almost instantly better. "That's the dandy," he took the glass from her shaking hand. "I reckon you never tasted straight Kentucky bourbon before. Now: Mr. Penrose. He was here, sure enough, but when he'll be back, with things as they are, God knows. Wait a minute, though. I guess there was something . . . a message, surely . . . Now where would I have put that?" He rummaged on a shelf behind the bar and finally came up with a piece of paper. "That's it." He was pleased with himself. "Never forget a face and never lose a message, that's me. He said, if anyone should come looking for him, they were to get in touch with his lawyer: Mr. Hillingford—lives quite a ways up 16th Street. I doubt you've strength to walk there tonight, ma'am, and hackney carriages aren't to be had today, not for love or money. You'd best spend the night here, I reckon. We'll contrive to fit you in somehow. There are enough rats have run already to leave room for a friend of Mr. Penrose's.'

"It's very good of you"—when she remembered her forlorn appearance, she thought it quite extraordinary—"but I must find Mr. Hillingford as soon as possible. I feel wonderfully better for that fire-water of yours. So if you'll just set me on my way . . ."

"Not before you've had something to eat. You can spare the time for that surely. No need to wait for tea: my wife will rustle up something for you right away, if your errand's so urgent."

So it was fortified by a scratch meal of fried ham and hominy grits that she started back on the long walk along F Street and up 16th. The landlord had advised against trying to short-cut across lots. "You'll lose yourself, sure as shooting," he said, "and this is no night for a young lady to be wandering about alone. The looters will be out among the empty houses. I don't like the feel of things in town tonight, and that's for sure. So whatever you do, ma'am, keep to the streets and keep going."

It was good advice. Night fell faster down here in Washington than she had been used to at Penrose. The shadows were long already, and the air pleasantly cool at last. She felt the bourbon, for which the landlord had refused to take payment, still burning through her as she walked as fast as her sore feet would let her along the rough pavement of F Street. It was much less crowded now, but when she got to the President's house, she found it still surrounded by a loosely moving throng, mostly of young beaus in new-fangled long pantaloons and high, light-coloured hats. Among them moved brightly clad women, in daring décolleté. There was loud talk, and laughter, and she could see, here and there, bottles being passed from hand to hand. As she threaded her way as inconspicuously as possible through the fringe of the crowd, she heard an odd phrase here and there: "Eat, drink, and be merry," said one. "Let Jemmy fight his own wars," said another, and then moved aside as a sweating horseman pushed his way through the crowd. "Did you see who that was? Monroe himself: they say he's been out scouting the enemy." The girl with him laughed. "He's welcome," Kate heard her say as she hurried past into the comparative quiet of 16th Street.

Lights showing here and there made it seem darker than it was. But she quickened her pace just the same. The landlord had been right; this was no time to be benighted. A little shiver of pure panic ran through her at the thought that Mr. Hillingford, like so many others, might have run for it. But, no, she would not let herself think that. At last, this should be the house. And—there were lights in the downstairs windows. With a sigh of relief, she turned wearily in at the entrance and began to think what she should say.

She had to lean for a moment against the doorway to steady herself before she lifted the big brass door knocker and let it fall with a disappointingly feeble effect. Nobody came. No sound of life or movement inside the house. Could it be abandoned after all, the lights left burning to discourage possible looters? No: absurd. She had not knocked loud enough: that was all. She tried again, achieving this time a tattoo that would wake the dead—and shivered un-controllably at the thought.

And still no sound, no movement inside. With darkness, a little wind had sprung up: she could not stop shivering, with cold, with fatigue, with everything . . . How long was it since she had knocked for the second time? Too long, that was certain. It was not her own plight that gave her this feeling of urgency; it was the knowledge that Manningham and Arabella had had almost twenty-four hours' start now. And she had no idea what they would be doing. Suppose they had already succeeded in joining the English forces? It did not bear thinking of. Knocking again, louder than ever, she reminded herself of two sources of hope. One was Arabella: would she venture into the no-man's-land be-tween the two armies? Surely not if she could help it. And the other was Manningham's own position: so far as she knew, his exchange had not yet come through. To rejoin the English without it would be to mark himself for all time as dishonoured. And yet, odd things had happened, she knew, about exchanges in this war.

It was no use standing here dreaming. No one was going to answer the door. She moved stiffly along the front of the house to peer in at a lighted window. A dining room, with the remains of a meal still set out on a polished mahogany table. And nobody in sight. Well then . . . back to the other side of the front door, where another lighted window showed her a room full of books; a desk; and, near the window, a high wing chair with its back to her. And some-one sitting in it. A pair of feet were stretched out onto a convenient footstool. Jonathan? Absurd: the legs wore old-fashioned black knee-breeches and buckled shoes. Mr. Hillingford surely. Enjoying an after-dinner nap? Why frighten herself with other possibilities? A band of looters . . . a scuffle and a blow . . . She would be hysterical in a minute. She rapped on the window as sharply as she dared, and was rewarded by the slightest possible stirring of the feet on the stool. Mr. Hillingford was asleep. She rapped again. No use. Mr. Hillingford was dead to the world. What next? The window was securely locked. So was the one in the dining room. Around at the back, the house was in darkness and more difficult to explore. Mr. Hillingford's servants must have left after serving dinner. How long before he woke up?

She remembered how the Rock Creek house had been broken into. Break the window with a stone; a hand in to turn the catch; child's play. Child's play? Oh—Sarah! It would be safer at the back, where it was dark, but much easier at the front, with the light to help her. She picked up a stone and went to the front gate to look up and down the dark street. Not a soul stirring.

It took a surprising amount of force to break the dining room window, but she managed it at the third, trembling try, wrapped her hand in her shawl, and reached in through the jagged edges to turn the lock. After that, it was comparatively easy. The whole bottom half of the window ran up smoothly; she dropped her bag inside and climbed in after it.

As she did so, the door of the room swung open. "Hands up, or I fire." Mr. Hillingford had waked at last. He was holding an immense, old-fashioned blunderbuss in shaking hands, and peering at her myopically over it. He was a very old man, she saw, disappointment mastering every other emotion. What help could he be?

"Don't fire." The blunderbuss was shaking alarmingly, and she hurriedly raised her hands in the air. "I'm not a burglar."

"A lady housebreaker!" But he lowered the blunderbuss slightly. "I thought I'd seen everything. Invasion and a lady housebreaker. Well, well, well . . . and on a night like this, too. What in the world am I to do with you, ma'am?"

"Just listen to me, please." She stood very still, watching the gun in those alarming uncertain hands. "I'm not a housebreaker. I'm a friend of Jonathan Penrose." As she said it she thought with something like horror, that, after all, this might be the wrong house. Suppose the bartender

218

had misdirected her; suppose this old man had never heard of Jonathan.

He lowered the gun to point it shakily at the floor. "A burglar friend of Jon Penrose? Just fancy that. Poor Jon, he never did have much sense about women." He tried to bow to her, found the gun in his way, looked at it, puzzled, as if he could not imagine what he was doing with it, propped it in a corner, and finished the bow. "Delighted to make the acquaintance of any friend of my friend Jonathan's, ma'am. Pray, do come in—oh, you already have." He looked baffled all over again at sight of the window behind her. "Take a glass of something with me, and tell me how I can serve you. But first, if you will not think me unpardonably inquisitive, do you always enter your friends' houses by the window?"

"Of course not. I am so very sorry about yours. But you see, sir, I could not wake you."

"Of course not. It has taken me years to achieve it, but now, I flatter myself, I can sleep through anything. Except, it seems," he looked behind her, "the clatter of breaking glass. No, no, don't apologize. It can be fixed easily enough in the morning—unless the English come, in which case we shall have worse things to worry us." And then, apparently forgetting all about the broken window, he moved a chair forward for her, and turned to the sideboard to pour a glass of wine. "But, I'm forgetting. Have you dined, ma'am?"

"Yes, yes." The sense of urgency was driving her again. She took the glass because it seemed easier than to refuse. "Thank you, sir, but I must find Jonathan—Mr. Penrose— at once. I was told you knew where he was."

"Of course." And then, on a new note. "But you're English! Can it be—are you by some miracle Mrs. Croston?"

"Yes. Why do you say a miracle?"

"It seems like it." He drank with a shaking hand. "And yet, I thought it might not be true: tried to persuade Jonathan not to despair. But there was something about the very casualness of it that made it convincing."

"Mr. Hillingford, what are you talking about?"

"I'm sorry, my dear, I'm an old man and it's been a terrible day. Poor Jonathan. It was bad enough before. Of course he was desperately anxious about that poor child. And then the letter came saying that they were gone and you were dead—'a most unfortunate accident,' was the phrase, as I recall. Do you know, I was frightened for Jonathan then. He had said all along that while you were with the child we need not be too anxious." Was he trying to convince himself that this was the only cause for Jonathan's despair? "And then, to hear, so casually that you were dead, and the child probably with the British Army already. It was too much for him. There was nothing I could say . . . He's gone back to the army—to Bladensburg. I don't think he wants to live. Have you ever seen anyone lose hope? But —forgive me." He had seen how it hit her. "I should not be saying this. It's very likely just an old man's imagination. He always had a lot of sense, Jonathan. Except where women were concerned." And then, as if aware that this, too, was not the happiest of topics. "But what can I do for you, Mrs. Croston?"

"Help me find Jonathan—Mr. Penrose. I must tell him—" She stopped. What must she tell him? There was a more urgent question. "The letter: it said they were with the British Army? Mr. Hillingford, when did it come?"

"This morning. Jonathan came in specially. He thought there might be an answer; hoped, I think, that you might bring it. That's what he asked, you know, in his; that you should be trusted with the money, with Sarah. Where is she, Mrs. Croston? What happened?"

"Manningham hit me last night—stunned me—I didn't come round till this morning, and then I was tied up. It might easily have been true, about my being dead, but I was lucky. I've been looking for Mr. Penrose all day. Where is he, Mr. Hillingford? If they really mean to cross the lines, there's not a moment to be lost. But, surely"—she remembered one of her crumbs of comfort—"Manningham's exchange?"

"Came through yesterday."

"Oh, my God! Then indeed there's no time to be lost. Mr. Hillingford, we must get Jonathan and find them, at once. If they're not already gone."

He looked at her with compassion. "But they are, Mrs. Croston. That's what the letter said. I wish I had it here, but Jonathan took it with him. It was clear enough; written just before they left. 'You'll have to pay more, to fetch her from England.' That's what Manningham said."

"But why should we believe him? It's a bluff, Mr. Hillingford, to keep us from looking for them here in Washington. I suppose presently there will be another offer—as if from the English camp. I tell you, we must lose no time . . ."

"I wish I could agree with you." He was humouring her now. "But it all seems logical enough."

"No!" Explosively. "You say the letter came this morning? It's just not possible. Think a little, Mr. Hillingford. Charles Manningham came back from here last night. We were in a house up Rock Creek—it was deserted; not a soul for miles. There was nothing I could do. Or so I thought. I've blamed myself since; but what's the use of that? Anyway, he went into Washington yesterday and came back last night, furious. He had had a letter from Jonathan—from Mr. Penrose—saying he would pay up, when Sarah was safe back. I didn't know what it said about me. Of course Manningham didn't tell me that. He'd never have trusted me. He didn't trust Mr. Penrose either. He said he was a Yankee; they were notorious . . . he and Arabella argued— I heard them; they were furious." She looked at him pitifully. "I'd been such a fool, Mr. Hillingford. I took it for granted Jonathan would pay up on the spot. That as soon as Manningham got in touch with him, Sarah and I would be able to go back. When I realized . . . when I began to think about getting away, it was too late. I was just at the door . . . he caught me . . . he had a pistol. Oh God, I've been such a fool. But you see," she made herself come back to the important point, "they had expected him to pay up too. They had no plans made, up to last night, for joining the enemy." How odd to be calling the English that. "And out there we did not even know where the armies were. Can they have managed it so soon? Must it not have been a bluff? Besides, I can't imagine Arabella taking the risk of crossing the lines. I expect that is what they were arguing about."

"That's just what I said." At last he seemed to be coming round. "Not Arabella; not a chance like that. But Jonathan was beyond reason, beyond discussion. He was exhausted, of course. He'd been out at Bladensburg since Saturday, helping with the works there—not enough sleep; not enough to eat. And that's a terrible business, too, he says. Do you know that when the militia were called out Saturday morning, half of them had neither uniform nor weapons? Some even had no shoes! And no order, no sense of discipline . . . Jonathan only came away because of the letter."

"With all those lies. And he believed them?"

"I'm afraid so. I'm very much afraid he's gone back to get killed, Mrs. Croston."

She was on her feet. "We must find him. At once."

"Not tonight, I'm afraid. No, listen! It's just not possible. Not in the dark. But it's not so bad as you think. I made him promise he'd send word in the morning where he would be, just in case there was another message from Manningham. The last one came here, you see, by Jonathan's instructions. You didn't know that?"

"No. They told me nothing. That's why it took me so long to find you. It was the purest luck . . . Oh God! if I had only got here earlier! But, Mr. Hillingford, if we can't get in touch with Jonathan tonight, at least we can make a start at looking for Sarah. They must be staying in town: I'm more and more sure of it."

"You may well be right. But that too will have to wait till morning. A moment's thought, and you'll agree with me. We haven't the strength, either of us, for anything more tonight; but even if we had, what could we do? Wake up a lot of hotel keepers, with the town in the kind of panic it is, and try and take a child away from her own mother? Just think about it, Mrs. Croston."

"You're right, of course." She sank wearily back into her chair. "I kept thinking, today, that even if I should find them, there'd be nothing I could do. Not without Jon— Mr. Penrose. But at least I know a lot of places where they're not."

"Yes. I'm afraid, for tonight, that must be our comfort. And now, it's late and you're exhausted. Let me show you to your room. It's not luxurious, I'm afraid, but at least you will be safe. I hope."

SEVENTEEN

KATE WOKE TO THE SOUND OF BUGLES alarmingly near. Fantastic to have slept. She was out of bed in a bound. Cold water; shaking hands; it seemed hours before she was dressed; in fact it was only minutes. Downstairs, she found Mr. Hillingford in the dining room, a cup of tea untasted on the table. He looked older than ever this morning, fragile, paper-white, a straw in a gale. And all the hope she had.

"Good morning, Mrs. Croston." He rose shakily and managed a travesty of a smile. "I'd have had you called before now, but Jonathan's message has only just come. It's not good news, I'm afraid." He pulled out a chair for her. "No," he forestalled her protest. "We'll do nothing till you've had your breakfast. You'll be no use to yourself, or anyone else, if you collapse for lack of food."

There was such obvious sense in this that she submitted with as good a grace as possible as he rang and gave his orders. "But the message?" she asked at last.

"Merely that he'd still be at Bladensburg this morning. I think he expects a battle. At all events, he says if I need to, I should be able to get in touch with him through General Stansbury of the Maryland Militia."

"Oh, thank God! I was afraid you did not know where he was." Her first bite of food made her realize that she was famished, and she fell to with a will on hot bread and scrapple.

"We know where he is." His cup rattled in the saucer as he put it down. "But what's the use of that? I've no one to send, Mrs. Croston. My man's out with the Militia. I had meant to ride out myself, but this morning I know I'm not up to it."

"Of course not." It was obviously true. "But"—here, at

last, was a ray of hope—"you mean you have a horse? That I can ride?"

"You?"

"Why not? There's nothing else to be done. I confess I had not looked forward to having to walk it: four miles is it not? And in these panic conditions. But on horseback I shall do admirably. Have you, by any miracle, a sidesaddle?"

"Oh yes. There's an old one of my wife's somewhere in the stable. But, Mrs. Croston, I can't let you—"

"You must. Consider, Mr. Hillingford, even if we should find Sarah, we can do nothing without her father. Besides— I must see him. If there's really going to be a battle. You said—he wanted to be killed. I have to see him. To tell him—" She stopped. Tell him what?

Hillingford's faded old eyes missed nothing, but they were wonderfully kind. "Do you think it's wise, Mrs. Croston?"

"I must," she said. "You're a good friend of Jonathan's I can tell." She had given up trying to call him Mr. Penrose. "Don't worry. I know it's impossible . . . hopeless . . . I've made up my mind. I'm going to ask him to let me take Sarah away, look after her. I won't see him again; not after today. But today I must." Tears choked her. "If I can only find him in time. Tell him there's hope."

"Hope?" There was something ruthless about the dry, lawyer's question, and yet she was sure he meant it kindly.

"For Sarah," she explained. "If he knew we were together, were happy." She managed a travesty of a smile. "Thought we were happy. I'd do my best."

"I'm sure you would." His voice was friendly now. "But —just the same—I don't see how I can allow you to take the risk of riding to Bladensburg today."

"Oh, risk!" Impatiently. "Surely you must see I'm beyond caring about that?"

In the end, inevitably, Hillingford agreed that she should ride out to fetch Jonathan while he set his housekeeper to work making inquiries for Manningham's party at the hotels Kate had not visited the day before. Even the housekeeper, unwilling enough at first to venture out into the streets—"they were bad enough when I came this morning, and that's the truth"—yielded at last to Kate's persuasions. "Well"—she was tying the strings of a formidable black poke bonnet under her chin—"I reckon we can't stand by and let a child suffer." She picked up a huge umbrella fit for use either as weapon or parasol. "And if I meet that Mr. Manningham I promise you I'll give him a piece of my mind. But I want a promise from you, sir," she turned on Mr. Hillingford, "that you won't budge from this house all day. You look like death this morning, and I'd be no friend not to tell you so."

He smiled his shaky smile. "I promise. Besides, it makes sense. I must stay here to co-ordinate your movements."

"My oh my." She pulled on black mittens. "You make us sound just like an army."

"I wish we were one," said Kate.

Half an hour later she was riding across lots on a narrow path, which, Mr. Hillingford had told her, would bring her out on the Bladensburg road well beyond the Capitol. "At least that way you will not have to ride through the village," he had said, "but I wish I was sure I do right in letting you go. Supposing there really is a battle? I'll never forgive myself if any harm comes to you."

"And I'd never forgive myself if I didn't go." Safe in the saddle, Kate had smiled at him reassuringly. "I promise you, we'll do splendidly, Sampson and I."

Luckily Sampson was elderly like his master and of a placid disposition, so that even after being shut up in his stable for the duration of the panic he started out soberly enough under the unfamiliar sidesaddle. "Don't hurry him," Mr. Hillingford had said, "and he'll go all day."

Much though she wanted to, she did not dare hurry. There was no knowing what she might have to ask of Sampson before the day was over. She must favour him now. So they went demurely across lots, with time for Kate to notice, here and there, a flash of scarlet in the undergrowth that spoke of autumn on the way. She passed several houses with closed shutters, and one where the people were busy loading their possessions into a small wagon. "Hey!" shouted the father. "You're going the wrong way."

"I know." She pulled up Sampson for a moment. "What's the news this morning?"

"Terrible. The redcoats were camped at Woodyard last night. Only eight miles from Bladensburg! And all Winder does is retreat to the Navy Yard—and talk! But there'll be a battle today just the same, and if you keep going that-a-way, you'll likely be mixed up in it."

"I can't help that. I've an errand. To Bladensburg."

He shrugged. "You're crazy." And went on piling bundles in the wagon.

But at least she had confirmed that she was on the right road. She pushed on, ignoring heat and flies, and was soon rewarded by a view of the Capitol, now well behind her as she turned onto the main road. Little more than a country lane, it was crowded with militiamen in various stages of uniform, all making their disorganized way toward Bladensburg. From time to time a family wagon piled high with furniture, carpetbags, and children came pushing through in the other direction, but most of the houses she passed seemed to be already deserted.

Coming out, at last, on the bare green hill above Bladensburg, she saw the village silent and empty on the far side of the river, while on the slope below her everything was bustle and confusion. Men were still working on the new entrenchments that scarred the meadows; here and there a gun was in position already, with its complement of weary looking militiamen around it. She stopped beside a group who were boiling a kettle on a small fire and noticed with amazement that they were wearing winter uniform and sweating miserably in the hot sun. "General Stansbury?" One of them looked up in response to her question. "God knows. Over there somewheres last time I seed him." And then, taking her in. "What the hell are you doing here, ma'am? Don't you know there's going to be a battle?"

"But not yet, surely?" The confusion all around her lent point to her remark.

"I hope to God not."

He looked deathly ill, she thought, and she leaned down to ask, "What's the matter? You don't look well."

"Well!" He laughed hysterically. "We're all sick as dogs, —spoiled rations for three days, and a false alarm last night kept us at arms till daybreak. We're sick all right. Not but what we'll give the redcoats a warm welcome when they show up, but if I were you, I'd be on my way, and quick."

"I will, when I've found General Stansbury."

"Well, it's your funeral. Try over there, ma'am; by that barn."

It was noon now; the sun blazed down; Sampson's coat was dark with sweat. No wonder if the toiling soldiers looked exhausted. More men were arriving all the time, and being directed here and there by officers on horseback. One of these rode up to her. "You'd best be going, ma'am. Any minute now, the British will come into sight over there"— he pointed beyond the village, with its white-painted church and deceptive Sabbath air of calm. "And half our army still on its way from Washington! God, what a mismanaged business," he was talking to himself. Then he remembered her. "What are you doing here, anyway?"

"Looking for General Stansbury."

"He's over there, but—"

She did not wait for more, but rode quickly toward the group of officers he had indicated, noticing as she passed five militiamen working desperately at a gun emplacement, one of them in militia blue, two in black jackets, one in a cotton tunic and one, fantastically, in a dress shirt and black patent leather pumps. Mr. Madison's "citizens' army," lived up to its name.

General Stansbury was in a fury. "Colonel Monroe indeed!" she heard him exclaim as she rode up. "Change all my arrangements, will he? And who does he think he is, pray, the Commander in Chief?" He saw her. "And now what?" Rage sizzled in the hot air around him.

No time for explanations. He was near explosion point. "I'm looking for Jonathan Penrose," she said.

228

"Penrose?" At least he was beyond surprise. "I sent him back to the Navy Yard, first thing, to see what the hell was keeping Winder. You should find him there, ma'am, and a much better place for a lady than the battlefield. Yes?" He turned away from her to a young officer.

"Mr. Madison's just coming, sir," said the youth, who could hardly, Kate thought, have been more than seventeen.

"Madison! That's all I need!" He had forgotten about Kate already as he turned away to look across the valley. Despite the heat, the day was extraordinarily clear. "Look!" he said suddenly. "Here they come."

Straining her eyes, Kate followed the direction of his pointing hand, and saw, two miles or so beyond Bladensburg, the thin red column appear around a plantation of trees. Englishmen! Trained soldiers; marching, she could see even from here, in impeccable quickstep. A horrible muddle of feelings convulsed her, so that for a moment the bright light turned black around her. These were professionals, cold-blooded soldiers marching over the hill, men like Fred Croston and his friends. And here, waiting for them, was a rabble of amateurs, a citizens' army, men who took time to worry about a lonely girl on a horse. Passionately, incredibly, she wanted them to win, and knew all the time how hopeless it was.

"The Moore Quickstep," said General Stansbury. "I've always wanted to see that. As for you, ma'am, you'd best be getting back to town. There'll be a battle here before the hour is out. If you're lucky, you should meet Penrose on the way. He reckoned to join Commodore Barney and his sailors if he could."

"Thank you, sir. And—God bless you." Tears blinded her eyes as she wheeled Sampson away toward the Washington road. They might have been for disappointment at this failure to find Jonathan, but were not. They were for the man in the black jacket, the man in the dancing pumps, these men, these individuals, standing here in the hot sunshine, waiting for juggernaut.

Tears heavy in her eyes, she hardly noticed the dusty,

229

gray-faced little man with the huge pair of duelling pistols belted around him who rode past her in the opposite direction. President Madison had come to cheer on his army.

Most of Winder's force must have arrived from Washington at last, Kate thought, finding the road almost deserted now. She stopped a straggler, who carried an immense blunderbuss.

"Commodore Barney!" He surprised her by bursting into a delighted guffaw of laughter. "I should just about think I do know where he is. He's right on the road behind me. Law, I laughed so much, I thought I'd die. I just wish you could have heered him."

"Why? What happened?"

He laughed some more before he could manage to tell her. "Old Winder forgot all about him. Well, you can understand that, with the panic that was on, and Jemmy Madison there at the Navy Yard, and Armstrong, and I don't know who else, all together there talking fit to bust. Council of war, they calls it! In the end they all decides to come here to Bladensburg, seeing as how even a child could a' told 'em this was where the battle would have to be, and why we weren't ready here last night the dear only knows. So Winder starts off at last, and our Jemmy says he'll follow — spunky little cuss is Jemmy, mind you, when all's said and done. I was looking after his horse, see, or I'd a' been here sooner. Battle's not started, has it, ma'am? I wouldn't want to miss my first battle."

"No, no," she reassured him. "The redcoats have only just come in sight. They must be a couple of miles from the village still." Calling her countrymen redcoats? What in the world had happened to her?

"That's all right then." He had time to enjoy his story. "Out comes Jemmy to his horse, and up comes old Josh Barney, red as my aunt's petticoat and swearing like my uncle, and asks what the hell he's to do: old Winder's forgotten all about him. And a proper turnout that was: I wish you could a' heard his language. To the President of these United States! I tell you, ma'am, it's a pleasure I'll remember to my dying day. 'Stay and guard the Navy Yard, will I?' says Barney. 'I'll be . . .' excuse me, ma'am. 'I'll be jiggered,' he said, 'if I do.' So in the end Jemmy gives in and makes Secretary of the Navy Jones say Barney can come here and fight, and they're on their way right now, back along the road a piece, with the guns they saved from their gunboats. And won't that jist be a surprise for the redcoats? What's that? Gunfire, ma'am! They've started! You'll excuse me. I can't miss my first battle." And he left her at a sweating trot, the blunderbuss clutched lovingly to his chest.

She was over the brow of the hill now and into the woods. And no time to turn back and see what was happening. Anyway, she was afraid she knew. What chance had these amateurs against men trained under Wellington? No, she must ride on, find Jonathan, get him back to Washington with her. What business had he here, a Federalist, a man of peace, Jonathan . . .

At all costs she must find him before the battle. Before? What hope of that? Over the hill, the deadly thunder continued, bringing with it a horrible picture of the two American guns she had seen covering the main street of Bladensburg from the hill. The English would not get to the bridge that the Americans had so strangely left standing, let alone across it, without suffering appalling losses. Terrible to think of, worse still to be grateful for the time it gave her.

But there—thank God—were Commodore Barney's men in their smoke-grimed naval uniform, unmistakable both for this and for their look of order and discipline. Busy manhandling their big guns along the rough road, they took no notice of her as she rode slowly down their line, looking with a kind of desperate hope for Jonathan.

She saw him at last, and swallowed hard as tears—of joy?—of pity?—started to her eyes. He was walking with a party of sailors who had apparently just ended their turn of duty on the rearmost gun. His gray face, aged surely by years since she had last seen him, and his automaton's pace

231

contrasted heartrendingly with the swinging march and bronzed health of his companions.

She pulled up her horse beside them, and called, as loud as she could make herself. "Mr. Penrose! Jonathan!"

He did not hear her, but the man nearest her did, looked at her with amazement, and passed the word along. Jonathan looked up; their eyes met; his whole face changed. Now he was working his way across the line to join her. She had just time to see how ghastly he looked, as if he had neither slept nor eaten for several days, before he was beside her. "Kate!" His hand, warm on hers where they held the reins. "You're alive!"

"Of course. You always did believe the worst too easily, dear Jonathan." Surely, in this moment, she could allow herself that "dear"?

"Dear Kate!" His hand gripped hers harder still. "But," a glance over his shoulder, "there's no time. Only to say, 'Thank God,' and, Kate, where's Sarah?"

"Jon! I don't know. They knocked me out: took her away: wrote you a lying letter. Mr. Hillingford told me. But they're in Washington somewhere. I'm sure of that. I hunted all day yesterday—for you, for her. In the end— thank God—I found Mr. Hillingford."

"In Washington?" He was watching the column draw away from them. "Oh God, there's no time." He turned her horse's head, so that the two of them could follow behind the guns. "No time for anything—maybe it's as well. Kate! When I thought you were dead!"

She smiled down at him lovingly. "Well, I very nearly was." No time for that either. "Jonathan, Mr. Hillingford's housekeeper is searching the hotels for them. Only—when we find them, we'll need you. Who else can claim Sarah?" She made as if to turn Sampson's head back toward Washington.

"No." His hand was heavy on hers. "I can't, Kate. You must see that. Not even for Sarah. Not even for you. Don't you see, if they're not stopped, they'll be in Washington tonight. And Windsor—our army—you never saw any-

232

thing like it. Barney needs every man he can get. He's my old friend—not that that makes any difference. I couldn't leave him now, were he ten times my enemy. But you'll manage, Kate, you and Hillingford. You'll find her. You'll save her for me. And as for me—don't look like that! I'll fight to live, now I know there's something to live for. And if—if I should be killed, forgive me, Kate, for everything. But I won't, not now. I'll see you in Washington tonight." And then: "My God, what's that?"

She had never heard anything like the horrible, high-pitched scream that rose above the clamour of the guns. "I don't know. Some new weapon? Jon, you can't, it's horrible—"

"It's no place for you. Get back to Washington, Kate, and find Sarah for me. I know you will. I trust you. I love you. Let me say it, this once. And—I'll come to Hillingford's as soon as I can."

"But, Jonathan—"tears fought with speech.

"No." His eyes held hers for a timeless moment before he pressed her hand once, hard, then turned away to take his place in the line.

She sat for a few moments quite still, watching the little band of sailors pull away, Jonathan's figure gradually becoming indistinguishable from the rest as they moved steadily, relentlessly toward the battle on the other side of the hill. Tears streamed down her face. See him tonight? She would never see him again. But that did not absolve her from doing what he had asked. She turned Sampson once more and set out toward Washington.

The old horse was tiring now, and she had not the heart to press him. It was still intolerably hot, and a grisly picture flashed through her mind of the Baltimore militia sweating it out in their winter uniforms. A little party of horsemen caught up and passed her at an uneasy trot, and this time she recognized the man in the black suit. Jemmy Madison had left the field of battle.

She tried to tell herself that this need not be so sinister as it seemed. Very likely he had merely been there to encourage the men before the fighting started. After all, he was known for a man of peace.

Yes—a man of peace, like Jonathan. War did strange things to people, she thought, and came to the top of a hill to see the Capitol standing before her and realize that she had missed the turn-off that would have taken her across country to Hillingford's house. Nothing for it now but to take the road through town, and, perhaps, pick up some news on the way.

Outside the Capitol, sweating clerks were loading papers into wagons. She saw Madison's party stop to speak to them and paused after them to ask, "What's the news?"

"Terrible. The battle's lost, he says. They're in full flight on the Georgetown road. And look! this way too."

Turning in the saddle, she saw the first wave of fugitives coming in sight along the road and heard at the same moment the sound of gunfire from a new direction. Barney must have set up his guns at last, but surely too late for anything but a doomed rearguard action?

"I'm sorry. What did you say?" The clerk was looking at her curiously.

"That you'd best get going, ma'am, before they blow up the bridges. The redcoats will be here any time now, from what he says." He did not dignify the President of the United States with any fuller description.

Full panic in Pennsylvania Avenue now, and when she got to the President's house it was to see wagons drawn up there, too, and a hostile-looking crowd surrounding them. No time to hope that the President's wife, Dolly, was safely out of town. She must get quickly to Hillingford's house and warn him of approaching disaster.

But when she got there she found that he had already heard the news from a party of stragglers who had paused to ask for water in their flight. "A shambles," he said, "a disgrace. The English had some newfangled weapon, it seems, a rocket or something—a red glare and a great deal of noise, and no damage whatsoever, from what they say, but it panicked our men just the same. And now the Capitol's wide open. We'll never live this down. Never."

"Not quite wide open." Breathlessly, she told him about Commodore Barney and Jonathan. "But they can't hold them long; a handful of men like that. I tried to get him to come away, Mr. Hillingford, but it was useless."

"Of course. He and Barney are old friends, from his sea captain days. Comfort yourself that Jon was right, my dear. He couldn't have come away."

"I know." It was cold comfort. She slid down from Sampson's hot back. "Mr. Hillingford, what about Sarah?"

"No news I'm afraid. Mrs. Ellicott came back half an hour ago. Not a trace of them. Of course, in the general confusion—and, suppose they've used other names. An elementary precaution."

"Yes." She had thought of that too. So—what hope was there? But she had promised Jonathan. Very likely her last promise. A sudden vision of him, shirt sleeves rolled up, marching alongside Barney's sailors, filled her eyes with tears. "Mr. Hillingford, we must find Sarah tonight. Don't you see, if the English take the city—and there's nothing but Commodore Barney to stop them—Manningham will be able to join them without the slightest difficulty. It's tonight or never."

"Yes," said Hillingford, "and—the guns have stopped." He regretted it when he saw her blanched face. "Don't worry too much, my dear. Barney's a man of sense as well as courage. He won't throw his men's lives away. Wait; hope; Jonathan may be here any time. In the meanwhile, you must have something to eat. When he gets here will be time enough to think about Sarah." He would not tell her now, while she looked so near to collapse, how little hope he really had of their finding the child. Instead, he made her sit down, eat some cold meat, and drink a glass of wine.

They tasted of dust and despair but did her good. "You think he'll be able to get here?"

"Of course. The army's retreating to Georgetown—even

beyond, some of the stragglers say, but Jonathan won't go. Well, there's no need. He's a civilian, a Federalist. Naturally, he'll come here."

"But Mr. Hillingford." Here was the secret core of her terror. "If he's taken prisoner, may they not shoot him as a spy?"

"Nonsense!" He was roundly comforting. "You've seen our soldiers! If they shoot everyone without uniform—why they'll be busy with firing parties all week. Don't worry so much, my dear. He'll come back, I promise you. He was always lucky, Jonathan. Did he ever tell you about the time he fought the Barbary pirate? No? I thought not: he's a great one for not talking about himself. Let me pour you another glass of wine, and I'll tell you . . ."

"No! No, thank you. We ought to be doing something."

"What?" he asked reasonably. "Think a little, Mrs. Croston. The confusion is at its very worst now. Soldiers everywhere, civilian refugees still making their escape—I hear Dolly Madison left it pretty late, among others. It would be courting trouble to go out now—and, besides, we'd miss Jonathan. Just wait an hour or so: all the rats will have left; the streets will be empty—or at least emptier. Then, I promise you, if Jonathan has not arrived, I'll come with you in one last round of the hotels. After all, there is one thing on our side. No need for Manningham to flee—or to hide, once he knows the English are here. He'll be convinced everything is going his way."

"And so it will be." What comfort was there in this?

"Yes, but don't you see, the last thing Manningham must actually want is to be saddled with Sarah. Trust me; he's been bluffing it so far; there will be another message from him. That's what I've been counting on."

"I see. Yes. You might be right at that. But, Mr. Hillingford, you ought not to stay here. Suppose the English sack the town."

"I'll suppose nothing of the kind. They're not barbarians, after all. Oh—we may have trouble, just as we might from our own stragglers, but that's a chance I'm prepared to take,

236

and so is Mrs. Ellicott. We talked it over this morning. We're too old, both of us, to be wandering round the country in an open wagon. And we've taken our precautions."

"Precautions?"

He laughed his dusty lawyer's laugh. "I'm afraid you will think them very mundane, Mrs. Croston. But you must have noticed that all the fugitives who have knocked at the back door while we have been talking have gone away quite soon and quite cheerfully."

"Yes, it's true, I had thought it surprising."

"Not surprising, Mrs. Croston; strategy. I always believe in expecting the worst: it's part of a lawyer's training. As soon as I heard the English had landed at Benedict I began making my preparations—or, to be precise, Mrs. Ellicott did. She has enough beer and meat pasties out back to feed a small army. And that's what she's doing. She gives them a drink—not too little, not too much—presses a pasty into their hand, and urges them to lose no time in getting to safety. They're panicked already: it works like a charm. When the English come, it will be the same thing (I do hope she will not have run out of pasties) only, of course, she will marvel at their daring to stray so far from their camp— wherever it is. She's a fine woman, my Mrs. Ellicott. I'm not sure I won't marry her, when this is all over."

"Mr. Hillingford," she heard her own words with a kind of horrified surprise. "If Mrs. Penrose really goes to England with Charles Manningham, will . . . will Jonathan be able to divorce her?"

"No, my dear." The dry voice was extraordinarily kind. "I would not be your friend if I let you indulge in hopes of that sort. And Jonathan—well, you know him; I don't have to spell it out for you."

"Thank you. No, you don't. I—would you excuse me for a moment?"

"Cry here." His voice was gentle now. "Just let yourself cry here, Mrs. Croston. I won't interrupt."

EIGHTEEN

THIS WAS NO TIME FOR TEARS. Kate took the silk pocket handkerchief Hillingford handed her and dabbed angrily at her eyes. She had known perfectly well, all along, that there was no hope for her and Jonathan, that Arabella's flight with Manningham changed nothing. It was better to have faced and admitted it. Besides, it was monstrous—superstitiously, it even seemed dangerous—to be thinking of marriage, even as an impossibility, when already Jonathan might be lying out there cold on the green hillside.

That was the way back down into despair, and, whatever she might feel for herself, she had a first duty to Jonathan, to Sarah. "Mr. Hillingford," she stood up. "You said we'd wait an hour."

"Or so," he amended. "We'll give him ten minutes more. In the meantime, I must have a word with Mrs. Ellicott. I can't say I altogether like to leave her alone in the house."

"Oh Lord ! How selfish I am. I ought not to ask it of you, but—could I go alone?"

"No. Jonathan would never forgive me if I let you. Nor I myself, for the matter of that. What a pity it is—"

"Yes, is it not?" In the curiously strong friendship that had sprung up so fast between them, she felt no need to pretend not to understand him. "Only—if he'd not married Arabella, there'd be no Sarah." Tears caught at her throat again.

"And you would think that so unfortunate?"

"Oh, yes ! You've not met her, have you? I know she's a difficult child, but it's—" how to explain? "It's because she has so much, I think. She's—she's extraordinary, Mr. Hillingford. No; whatever happens, I'll never be sorry about Sarah." And then. "I hope."

"Very well." He answered the appeal in the last two words. "We leave in ten minutes. I'll tell Mrs. Ellicott."

Kate was alone in the dining room when the quiet knock came at the front door. Her hand shook so much as she lighted herself into the hall that the flame of the lamp wavered dangerously. She put it down and struggled with trembling fingers to shoot back the big bolt. Suppose it was not . . .

She swung the door open. "Jonathan!" She went into his arms as if it was the most natural, the most inevitable thing in the world.

He held her there for a long, breathless minute, his lips in her hair. "Kate!" But now he had remembered, now he was pulling her gently over the threshold, closing the door behind him, trying for a light note. "I told you there was no need to worry. See; not a scratch on me." Just for a moment, his hand still held hers, telling her all the things he would not; then, gently, reluctantly, he let her go. There was nothing, after all, to say.

"And Barney?" she asked.

"Wounded." It hurt him to say it. "Not seriously, please God. He made us leave him; said the English would look after him and the other wounded. We had our duty still to do. Duty! A duty to flee, to run away! I tell you, I'm ashamed. They're not even making a stand at the Capitol. They could have held out there for hours; but it's all of a piece. Do you know what Winder said to Stansbury's artillery this morning? 'When you retreat,' he said, 'take notice that you retreat by the Georgetown Road.' When you retreat! With a commander like that, small wonder that nothing was done as it should be. Think of leaving the bridge at Bladensburg for the enemy to cross. They might as well have put up notices saying, 'Welcome to Washington.' They'll be here any minute; here, in the capital of the United States. Kate, it's more than I can bear.'

"I know. I feel it myself." It was true. "But, Jonathan, all the more reason why we should go at once to look for Sarah. Mrs. Ellicott's had no luck today, but I'm sure they must be somewhere in town. If we don't find them to-night—"

"I'll go to General Ross in the morning."

"Ross?"

"The English general. He's one of Wellington's men; a gentleman, not a blackguard like Admiral Cockburn. His soldiers have been meticulous, I'm told, about private property; none of the wanton damage Cockburn's sailors have done. He'll not connive at kidnapping and adultery."

"I'm relieved to hear it." This, dryly, from Hillingford who had just come through from the servants' quarters. "Jonathan I'm delighted to see you safe." He handed him a note. "This has just come for you. Mrs Ellicott could not make the messenger stay, but he came from Carter's Hotel. I told you there would be another message." This to Kate, as Jonathan rapidly read the brief note.

"You were right, Kate." Jonathan crumpled the paper in his hand. "They're still in town. At Carter's Hotel. Have been since yesterday. Damn him! He knows there's nothing legally I can do tonight with the town in this chaos. He gives me 'one last chance.' A straight exchange. Tonight at the hotel. The money they asked for—at least they've not put up their price—for Sarah. You've got it for me, Hillingford?"

"Of course. It's come high, to get it in cash, with things as they are, but I managed on Monday, just before the Banks sent away their specie. But can you trust them?"

"Trust them! Of course not." He was marshalling his plans. A quick, considering glance for Hillingford, who looked frailer than ever today, and he turned to Kate. "I shouldn't ask this, but I must. Will you come with me and wait outside with the money, until I'm sure they do not plan any kind of trick? My days of trusting those two are gone forever."

"You're right, of course," said Hillingford. "But let me come, Jonathan."

"No." Jonathan and Kate said it simultaneously, but she went on. "You must let me, Mr. Hillingford. I love Sarah.

240

I feel . . . I've felt all day that she needs me. I must go. After all, Jonathan will be there to protect me."

"Not when you are waiting outside. Suppose the English should come then?"

"I'm English myself, remember." How long had she been modulating into American without even realizing she was doing so?

"Of course. So you are. But, wait a minute." He dived back through the servants' door and returned with a small pistol. "Mrs. Ellicott's been carrying this but I think you should have it tonight. It might give you time to convince an English soldier that you *are* English. Do you know how to use it?"

"My husband taught me." She shivered. Oh, Jonathan: my dead husband; your living wife.

"Mrs. Ellicott carried it in this." Hillingford handed her a big embroidered handbag. "She said it made her feel much safer. It's loaded, of course."

"But for God's sake don't use it," said Jonathan. "Let's go, Kate. With luck, we may have Sarah back here before the English take over the town. Even unopposed, it will take them some time. Are you ready?"

"Of course."

"Good." He turned back to Hillingford. "Whereabouts is Carter's?"

"On 18th Street. Not far from the Octagon House. Jon; do you think it's safe?"

He shrugged. "God knows. Kate and I don't much care, do we, Kate?" He held out his hand to her.

"Not much." She smiled and took it. Just for tonight, its pressure told her, they would pretend, in the face of danger, that there was a future for them. Tomorrow would be time enough to face the truth.

Hillingford had disappeared into his study to return with a green lawyer's bag. "There's the money, Jon. All of it. Don't give it to them if you don't have to."

"I won't." Jonathan swung open the big front door. "Look! The English are here."

"Oh, no!" From where she was standing, Kate, too, could see the red glow that lit the sky in the direction of the Capitol. "Jon! The Capitol? They can't have?"

"No? Remember York. Remember what we did there."

The "we," the assumption that she was an American like the rest of them, brought a mist of tears to her eyes. "When will it end?" she asked.

"God knows."

The streets were quieter. "Our soldiers must be safe in Georgetown by now." Jonathan was still somehow holding her hand, and there was extraordinary comfort in his touch. "At least there should be no brawls, no skirmishes. If we are stopped by the English, I've been with you all day, Kate. I had nothing to do with the fighting. I'm just a simple New England businessman." Indescribable bitterness in his tone. "They'll pass me as that. After all, we have as good as been their allies."

"Don't mind it so much." They were hurrying down 16th Street hand in hand. "After all, how were you to know?"

"You did. You've been telling me all the time. Quietly, without making a fuss over it, you've been telling me."

"What?"

"That war is everybody's business. That one can't choose to stay on the sidelines when one's country is at stake. Why do you think I have been working so hard to oppose this mad idea of a New England secession from the Union but because of you, of what you taught me! Kate, whatever happens, you will remember, won't you, that you've changed me, changed everything for me?"

"Thank you. I'll remember." She was glad that it was dark and he could not see the tears that streamed down her face. But there was something she needed to know. "Jonathan, when you got back to Penrose and found me gone, what did you think?"

"Think? Why, that you'd gone after Sarah, of course, somehow, and had no chance to leave a message. It gave me hope, a little, though I was afraid for you. Why? What should I have thought?"

She gave a shaky laugh. "Why, just that. Only I was afraid—"

It was his turn to laugh. "That I'd jump to the wrong conclusion as usual? Oh, Kate, I don't blame you, but never again, not where you are concerned. I feel so ashamed . . . I should have known . . . If you'll only forgive me—"

"Of course." But what was the use? Any minute now they would reach Carter's Hotel, and Arabella. "Jon, what are you going to do when we get there?"

"Do?"

"About Arabella."

He turned to her in the darkness. His hand was warm on hers. "Make her come home with me. I have to. You know that, don't you?"

"Yes, Jon, I know." Now was the moment to tell him of her plan for herself and Sarah. But they had just come in sight of the President's house. She caught her breath. "Look!" A dark crowd surged around it. As they watched, a single tongue of flame lit up one of the downstairs windows. Then came another, and another, throwing up the shape of the house against the sky. And a hoarse, horrible roar of pleasure from the crowd.

"Jon! It's monstrous. Mr. Madison's house. How could they?"

"War is monstrous," he said. "I've learned my lesson. All my lessons, God help me." They had reached I Street now. "We'd better cut over to 18th Street here," he said. "Keep close to me, Kate, whatever happens."

Hurrying along I Street, they could still hear shouting, and the harsh crackle of fire from the direction of the President's house. "I always thought it comic, somehow, when people called it the palace," said Kate. "It doesn't seem so funny now. Jon, do you think they'll have got to Carter's?"

"I don't see why they should have. Anyway, Ross will spare private property, I'm sure."

"Even with Cockburn there to egg him on? Jon! What's that?" Her voice had been drowned for a moment by a violent series of explosions from somewhere toward the river.

"I expect they're blowing up the powder magazines at the Navy Yard. Well, you can't blame them for that: it's a military installation. But, look, all the government buildings are burning." And indeed as she looked back, the red glow of many fires lit up her face. "Think of the records, the books that will be destroyed tonight," he went on. "There was an admirable library at the Capitol: I've used it myself. We're losing our history tonight."

"Or finding it?"

"Perhaps. Ah—this must be 18th Street. Oh, my God!" The exclamation was forced from him by the sight of the crowd around a building a little way down the other side of the street. Here, too, flames were just beginning to appear in the ground floor windows, and by their light they could see people milling around below; others leaning out of up-stairs windows, throwing things down. He began to run.

"Jonathan!" It was hard to keep up with him. "It's not Carter's?"

"I'm afraid so."

"But why?"

"Not the English. Looters, I expect." One end of the ground floor was burning furiously now. "It must have started there, on the porch." He stopped for a moment, panting, on the outskirts of the crowd. "There must be stairs at the other end." Still holding her hand, he began to work his way forward.

"You're not going in? They've probably escaped already." The words came out staccato, in breathless gasps.

"Suppose they left Sarah behind? They're capable of anything. I must make sure." Reaching the front of the crowd, he paused to look down at her, his face illuminated by the flames so that she could see every feature. "Hold this." He handed her the bag of money. "And wait for me here. And, Kate, whatever happens, remember I loved you."

"Jonathan!" She could feel the heat of the fire on her face. How could she let him go in there? Instinctively, she

244

put out a hand to hold him back, then paused, head up, listening. "Kate!" She had heard the voice only twice before, but recognized it instantly. "Kate!" it came again.

"Sarah!" They both looked up to see a small dark figure leaning out of an upstairs window at the end of the house away from the fire.

It changed everything. "Go, Jon. Hurry! I'll stay here. And—God speed you." And then, as loud as she could against the noise of crowd and flames. "Wait there, Sarah, your father's coming."

The crowd was thinning. Standing there, with unnoticed tears streaming down her cheeks, Kate watched Jonathan's tall figure disappear into the blazing building. She was praying and did not know it. Looking up, she could still see Sarah's small figure at her window, but looking inward now, as if expectantly. Then she vanished. Could Jonathan have reached her so soon? Please God he had. Already fire showed at the windows below. It would be a near thing.

"What a pleasant surprise." The voice, Manningham's voice, close behind her made her start and turn away from the burning building. "Do you know," he went on, "I'm delighted to see you, Mrs. Croston. I was really afraid for you, though I made the knots as loose as I dared. But poor Arabella was a bad woman to cross, as I'm sure you know as well as I do."

"Was? What do you mean?"

He shrugged. "It's a pretty safe assumption. I've never been so surprised. Arabella, of all people."

"What do you mean? What happened?"

"She took the bit between her teeth; that's what happened. We only had to come downstairs and out when the fire started, but would she? Not Arabella. Of course it was a pity I'd locked the little hellcat in, but what else could I do, with her carrying on so? Her room was at the other end. There wasn't a chance. The corridor was full of smoke, but Arabella would go."

"And you let her?"

"What else could I do? No time for arguing. One minute

245

she was there, shouting something about 'not again,' the next she was gone, right into the smoke. Well, there it is. Poor Arabella . . ." He was silent for a minute while she took it in. "I wonder—is it any good to try to persuade you? No," with his charming laugh, "I can see it isn't. Well, I don't blame you, Kate, though it's a pity: we'd make a fine pair, you and I. Never mind, here's my consolation." His hand shot out and tore the lawyer's bag from under her arm. "Obliging of Mr. Penrose. I really hope he gets to that mad child of his in time. But just in case he does—and gets her out, which seems even less likely, I'll take my leave of you, Mrs. Croston, for good."

"No !" While he was talking she had had time to feel in her bag for Hillingford's gun and bring it out, cocked and ready. "Don't move, Mr. Manningham. It would give me pleasure, right now, to shoot you where you stand." So far, what had passed between them had gone unnoticed by the people around, whose attention was fixed on the blazing building. Now she raised her voice. "Help !" she cried. "That man has robbed me. Stop him !" Her first shout, pitched still too low, was lost in the roar of the fire, but a few heads turned inquiringly, as if they had half heard something. She shouted again louder, and this time a couple of burly men turned, saw the tableau she and Manningham made in the light of the fire, and came to her help. One of them caught Manningham by the arm that held the bag.

"Robbed you has he? Of this? Money, I reckon." He weighed the bag thoughtfully in his hand before giving it back to her. "You're in luck tonight, ma'am. But what shall we do with him? There's no law and order in Washington right now, unless you call what the English are doing law." He spat expressively. "But, things being as they are, shall I just let him go and be done with it?"

She had been half turned away to gaze anxiously at the hotel. Flames showed everywhere on the ground floor now. If Jonathan did not come soon . . . What did she care for the money? "Oh yes, by all means let him go," she began to say, but her voice was drowned by Manningham's.

"You'd best let me go," he said, "and look sharp about it. And give me back my money too which that hussy pretends is hers. Don't you see she's no better than she should be? What other kind of woman would be out tonight?"

"He might have something there, I reckon." This was the second man, who had remained in the background so far. "The lady's mighty anxious about something, sure enough. But what? Maybe we've been just a mite hasty."

"Of course you have." Manningham pressed home his advantage. "Take me to the English general, if you like. I know him. He'll vouch for me."

"Will he now?" The first man took a firmer grip on his arm. "I calculated you spoke pretty funny, mister, and now I know what it is. You're a dadblasted murdering blackguard of an Englishman, and I'll see you damned before I let you cheat this lady out of what I have no doubt is hers."

He raised his voice on the word Englishman, and at the same time a lull in the roaring of the fire let it carry clearly among the crowd. Other voices picked it up. "An Englishman! An Englishman!" A growl at first, it swelled to a threatening roar. "Look what they've done to us!" The crowd pressed closely round them. "Look at the President's palace burning, and the Capitol, and, here, Carter's Hotel that never did worse than overcharge a bit for their drinks. What do you say, boys, what shall we do with this Englishman?"

"Tar him and feather him." A voice from the back of the crowd.

"I reckon that would take too long." The two men now each held an arm of Manningham's and turned him so that he was facing the burning building. "Let him have a taste of his own medicine, I say. Throw him in the fire."

"No, no! I tell you, it's all a mistake!" Manningham writhed in their grasp, his face ghastly in the reflected glow of the fire. "Kate! Mrs. Croston! Tell them I'm innocent: I've done nothing."

Nothing! The thought flashed through her mind. Nothing but leave her and, it seemed, Arabella too, for dead?

And—Sarah? But just the same, she could not stand by and watch this. "It's true what he says," she moved forward to stand between the struggling trio and the fire. "He's a prisoner of war: he's only just been exchanged. He can have had nothing to do with what's happened today."

They paused for a minute, but, "A prisoner of war," said the second of Manningham's captors. "And where was he taken, I'd like to know? This ain't the only outrage we've suffered. Suppose he was at Hampton last summer, or at Niagara this winter, where they left our women and children to choose between death of cold and death from the Indians. No, no: out of the way, ma'am. This is men's work."

"Men? Cowards!" She staggered back as he pushed her aside and the two of them began to drag Manningham, frantically struggling, toward the blazing building. The rest of the crowd moved forward with them, growling approval. "Don't! Don't let them!" Kate's appeals were ignored as the whole crowd surged forward. She turned from them, sickened, and saw the door by which Jonathan had entered swing open and a curiously elongated figure appear, silhouetted against the fire. The crowd forgot its blood lust for a moment and gave a roar of approval. It was too good to be true. It was true, though. She pushed her way forward through the crowd. "Jon! Jonathan! You're safe. And Sarah?"

"Kate!" said the black-faced little figure on his shoulder, and held out her arms.

"Take her. Quickly." Jonathan smelled of smoke. "I have to go back for Arabella. She's hurt."

"No!" But of course he must. "Be careful, Jon." He had turned away already to plunge back into the burning building. Fire showed at every window now. It was madness. He had to do it. She held Sarah close. "Are you hurt, honey?" What hope of an answer?

But in fact the child in her arms shook her head, and snuggled closer into her arms, shifting the bag of money as she did so. For the first time, Kate remembered Manningham and looked around for him. But he had seized his chance to escape when the crowd's attention was centered on Jonathan. So much the better, she thought, and forgot all about him as she turned once more to gaze fearfully at the burning building. No one had come out from either end since Jonathan had brought out Sarah. What hope had he?

Sarah was whimpering against her shoulder. "It's all right, my precious; it's all right, my honey." If only it was true.

"Why doesn't he come?" Sarah's voice, at once strange and heart-stirringly recognizable.

She bent impulsively to kiss the child. "He'll come, honey." Please God, let it be true. "He had to go back for your mother." Madness to have said that.

But Sarah merely stirred a little in her arms. "Poor Mother," she said. "She came for me."

Was this Arabella's epitaph? And Jonathan's? Tears filled Kate's eyes as she strained them, in vain, for any sign of life in the fiercely burning building. Then, as she watched, there was a roar of flame, and a crash, and a great sigh from the crowd. "I reckon the staircase has gone, this end," said one of the men who had helped her with Manningham. "I'm sorry, ma'am. He shouldn't have tried."

She shook her head mutely, holding onto Sarah as if for dear life.

"You'd best be getting home, ma'am, you and your little girl." He meant it kindly. "This is no night for a lady to be out on her own."

Still she could not speak for tears, but stood there, helplessly shaking her head, holding Sarah in a grip that hurt.

"Don't, Kate." Once again, astonishing, it was Sarah's voice. "Don't cry. He'll come. He always comes."

And miraculously, with the words, came a sort of groan from the crowd. Kate, blinded by tears, could see nothing, but: "Well, I'll be jiggered," said the man beside her. "He got clear through and out the other end."

And, "There he is," said Sarah. "There's Father." And was down from Kate's arms, holding her hand, pulling her through the crowd toward the far end of the building, where a dark figure had staggered from the house and reeled forward, blinded by the smoke, with something in his arms.

Something? Someone. Arabella, but Arabella almost unrecognizable, horribly burned, and writhing with pain.

"This way, sir," a man pushed forward through the crowd. "Bring her this way. I'm a doctor. My house is right here, on K Street."

"Thank you." The crowd fell back respectfully as Jonathan turned to follow the strange doctor. "Kate! You've got Sarah?"

"Yes, we're here." Kate picked up Sarah again and felt her shiver uncontrollably in her arms. "But, Jon, you're not hurt?"

"Nothing to signify. But Arabella . . . I don't know. She'd fainted—the smoke, I suppose. She saved Sarah, Kate. If she'd not unlocked that door, I'd never have got to her. If I could only have brought them both at once—"

"This way." The doctor opened the door of his house. "Lay her down there." Pointing to a sofa in the front room. "Gently, now." He bent over her.

Arabella moaned. Then: "No use." She spoke with difficulty, in a hoarse whisper. "And I'm glad. What's left . . .? But—Sarah. Where is she?"

"She's safe." Jonathan was on the other side of the sofa. "Quite safe. You saved her, Bella, God bless you." Across her body, his eye caught the doctor's, to ask a silent question. Almost imperceptibly, the doctor shook his head; his lips formed the words, "Nothing I can do."

"I know." Arabella had understood. "I'm dying. I don't even care. Not now. Only—first—Jonathan, I must tell you. It was all my fault." The words came in painful gasps. "Sarah. That day at Saratoga. I was meeting"—she fought for breath—"Josiah." A travesty of a smile distorted her ravaged face. "I didn't love him. I didn't know, then . . . anything . . . But it was so dull, Jon, with you away. Only —that day . . . Sarah followed us . . . through the woods . . . down the long, straight path . . . to the hut. She caught us. She didn't mean to." Her strength was failing. "I was angry . . . I shut her in. Then—the search was out—I couldn't get back. I'm . . . sorry, Jon." She tried to raise her head. "Charles! Where's Charles?" And then, remembering. "He left me, of course. He never cared . . . for me. What a fool—" Her head fell back.

"She's gone, I'm afraid," said the doctor. "Poor creature."

"She didn't want to be saved," said Jonathan. "Not after Manningham left her like that. She told me so. But she saved Sarah. She'd got her out of that room. She could have gone with Manningham, but she didn't." He was talking across the doctor, to Kate, who had stayed at the door of the room, holding Sarah so she could not see.

But, "Poor Mother," said Sarah. "She's hurt."

Jonathan was across the room in one stride. "Sarah! You're talking!"

"Talking?" Sarah sounded puzzled.

This was no time for discussion or exclamation. "Jonathan," Kate put in quickly. "Do you think we could take Sarah home? It's way past her bedtime." She was afraid it sounded heartless, but there was no help for it. Sarah had had all she could stand.

"Yes," said the doctor. "You're quite right, ma'am." And then, to Jonathan: "I'll take care of everything, sir." He bent to lay a knitted shawl gently over Arabella's body. "Your nursemaid, I take it? Went back for the child? Gallant of her. And of you. Poor thing; she did her best. And so did you. Remember that. And now, you must think of the living. Best get your wife and child home, sir. Call on me tomorrow, if you will."

"My—? Oh, thank you. Yes, I'll do that. Tomorrow." He was beyond thought, beyond feeling. For a moment, he just stood there, gazing down at the brightly coloured shawl.

"Father!" Sarah's voice again. "Can't we go home. Home to Penrose?"

He roused, shook himself. "Not tonight, honey. It's too far."

"Tomorrow then?" Her voice shook. "I want to go home."

"And so you shall," said Kate. "Just as soon as we can. Home to Penrose."

Now that Jonathan had roused himself, their sad arrangements were soon made, their thanks and farewells said. The doctor went on speaking as if Jonathan and Kate were man and wife, and after one brief, expressive exchange of glances they let him do so.

At last, they were outside, walking up 18th Street, with Sarah between them and the fires behind.

"She's talking. I can't believe it." Jonathan looked across the child to Kate.

"Don't—" The less they commented on it, the better.

"No." He understood at once. "Arabella saved her." It was still strange to him. "Poor Arabella. She wouldn't try to save herself. There was nothing I could do."

"I know," said Kate. "You did everything you could."

"Now, yes," said Jonathan. "But not before. It was my fault, all of it. I brought her away from Richmond, where she was happy. She was gay, Kate, she loved to laugh, and dance, and flirt. I left her alone in Penrose. It was my fault."

"Don't think about it. It's no use." What was there she could say?

But now another voice broke in. Sarah's. "Kate! What did the man mean? Whose wife and child?"

"He was in a muddle, honey."

"Muddle?" Here was a word that was strange to her. "I like his muddle, Kate." Only she pronounced it muggle.

Kate looked up to meet Jonathan's eyes across hers. "Do you honey?" The glow of firelight was less intense now, as

252

they walked steadily away up 18th Street, but they could still see each other, strangely illuminated.

The child gave a little skip, supporting herself on both their hands. "Yes, I do."

"So do I," said Jonathan.

MARY STEWART

"Mary Stewart is magic." *New York Times*

Mary Stewart "is one of the most stupendously successful authors ever". *Sunday Express*

"I can't think of anyone who tells such stories quite so well as Mary Stewart". *New York Times*

All Mary Stewart's books are in print with Hodder Paperbacks

MADAM, WILL YOU TALK?
THE MOONSPINNERS
THE IVY TREE
MY BROTHER MICHAEL
THIS ROUGH MAGIC
THUNDER ON THE RIGHT
NINE COACHES WAITING
AIRS ABOVE THE GROUND
WILDFIRE AT MIDNIGHT
THE GABRIEL HOUNDS

"Dorothy Eden is a mistress of the Macabre". *The Guardian*

This is an author whose popularity increases at every turn and whose books are reaching an ever-larger following

THE MARRIAGE CHEST

BELLA

NEVER CALL IT LOVING

NIGHT OF THE LETTER

WINTERWOOD

SLEEP IN THE WOODS

WHISTLE FOR THE CROWS

THE BIRD IN THE CHIMNEY

SAMANTHA

SIEGE IN THE SUN

THE DEADLY TRAVELLERS

"No one can suggest an eerie atmosphere and the sinister trifle better than Dorothy Eden". *The Guardian*

JANE AIKEN HODGE

THE ADVENTURERS   5/–

As Napoleon's army retreats through Germany, a group of stragglers plunders the von Hugel estate, leaving Sonia von Hugel apparently alone in the castle. Her father has been killed, her governess wounded, all seems lost. But then there appears a mysterious stranger, called Charles Vincent, who leads Sonia and her wounded friend into safety, and from there into further adventure.

"Most romantic historical novels are marred by two things: inaccuracy and psychological vulgarity. *The Adventurers* is a triumphant exception ... an unputdownable thriller" *The Scotsman*

"A romantic, thrilling and diverting historical novel" *Liverpool Daily Post*

"A mixture of high adventure and romance which makes a most readable story" *British Books*